RETURN OF THE GIANTS

"Chris!" Hunt exclaimed. "That long gray panel with the switches on . . . I've seen those same markings before! They were on . . ."

He stopped speaking abruptly as the camera swung sharply upward and focused on a large display-screen that was set immediately in front of the ship's two empty seats. Something was happening on it. A second later they were staring speechless at the image of three alien beings. Every pair of eyes on the Bridge of Jupiter Five opened wide in stunned, shocked, mind-numbing disbelief.

There was not a man present who had not seen that form before—the long, protruding lower-face . . . the massive torso and incredible six-fingered hand with two thumbs. Danchekker himself had constructed the first eight-foot-tall, full-scale model of that same form.

He had done a fine job . . . as everybody could now see.

The aliens, as impossible as it seemed, were Ganymeans . . .

Also by James P. Hogan
Published by Ballantine Books:

INHERIT THE STARS
THE GENESIS MACHINE

The
Gentle Giants
of Ganymede

James P. Hogan

A Del Rey Book

BALLANTINE BOOKS • NEW YORK

To my wife, Lyn, who showed me that greener grass can always be made to grow on whatever side of the field one happens to be.

The
Gentle Giants
of Ganymede

prologue

Leyel Torres, commander of the scientific observation base near the equator on Iscaris III, closed the final page of the report that he had been reading and stretched back in his chair with a grateful sigh. He sat for a while, enjoying the feeling of relaxation as the seat adjusted itself to accommodate his new posture, and then rose to pour himself a drink from one of the flasks on a tray on the small table behind his desk. The drink was cool and refreshing, and quickly dispelled the fatigue that had begun to build up inside him after more than two hours of unbroken concentration. Not much longer now, he thought. Two months more and they should be saying good-bye to this barren ball of parched rock forever and returning to the clean, fresh, infinite star-speckled blackness that lay between here and home.

He cast his eye around the inside of the study of his private quarters in the conglomeration of domes, observatory buildings and communications antennas that had been home for the last two years. He was tired of the same, endless month-in, month-out routine. The project was exciting and stimulating it was true, but enough was enough; going home, as far as he was concerned, couldn't come a day too soon.

He walked slowly over to the side of the room and stared for a second or two at the blank wall in front of him. Without turning his head he said aloud: "View panel. See-through mode."

The wall immediately became one-way transparent, presenting him with a clear view out over the surface of Iscaris III. From the edge of the jumble of constructions and machinery that made up the base, the dry, uniform reddish-brown crags and boulders stretched all the way to the distinctly curved skyline where they abruptly came to an end beneath a curtain of black velvet embroidered with stars. High above, the fiery orb of Iscaris blazed mercilessly, its reflected rays filling the room with a warm glow of orange and red. As he looked out across the wilderness, a sudden longing welled up inside him for the simple pleasure of walking under a blue sky and breathing in the forgotten exhilaration of a wind blowing free. Yes, indeed—departure couldn't come a day too soon.

A voice that seemed to issue from nowhere in particular in the room interrupted his musings.

"Marvyl Chariso is requesting to be put through, Commander. He says it's extremely urgent."

"Accept," Torres replied. He turned about to face the large view screen that occupied much of the opposite wall. The screen came alive at once to reveal the features of Chariso, a senior physicist, speaking from an instrumentation laboratory in the observatory. His face registered alarm.

"Leyel," Chariso began without preamble. "Can you get down here right away. We've got trouble—real trouble." His tone of voice said the rest. Anything that could arouse Chariso to such a state had to be bad.

"I'm on my way," he said, already moving toward the door.

Five minutes later Torres arrived in the lab and was greeted by the physicist, who by this time was looking more worried than ever. Chariso led him to a monitor before a bank of electronic equipment where Galdern Brenzor, another of the scientists, was staring grim-faced at the curves and data analyses on the computer output screens. Brenzor looked up as they approached and nodded gravely.

"Strong emission lines in the photosphere," he said. "Absorption lines are shifting rapidly toward the violet. There's no doubt about it; a major instability is breaking out in the core and it's running away."

Torres looked over at Chariso.

"Iscaris is going nova," Chariso explained. "Something's gone wrong with the project and the whole star's started to blow up. The photosphere is exploding out into space and preliminary calculations indicate we'll be engulfed here in less than twenty hours. We have to evacuate."

Torres stared at him in stunned disbelief. "That's impossible."

The scientist spread his arms wide. "Maybe so, but it's fact. Later we can take as long as you like to figure out where we went wrong, but right now we've got to get out of here . . . *fast!*"

Torres stared at the two grim faces while his mind instinctively tried to reject what it was being told. He gazed past them at another large wall screen that was presenting a view being transmitted from ten million miles away in space. He was looking at one of the three enormous G-beam projectors, a cylinder two miles long and a third of a mile across, that had been built in stellar orbit thirty million miles from Iscaris with their axes precisely aligned on the center of the star. Behind the silhouette of the projector Iscaris's blazing globe was still normal in appearance, but even as he looked he imagined that he could see its disk swelling almost imperceptibly but menacingly outward.

For a moment his mind was swamped by emotions —the enormity of the task that suddenly confronted them, the hopelessness of having to think rationally under impossible time pressures, the futility of two years of wasted efforts. And then, as quickly as it had came, the feeling evaporated and the commander in him reasserted itself.

"ZORAC," he called in a slightly raised voice.

"Commander?" The same voice that had spoken in his study answered.

"Contact Garuth on the *Shapieron* at once. Inform him that a matter of the gravest urgency has arisen and that it is imperative for all commanding officers of the expedition to confer immediately. I request that he put out an emergency call to summon them to link in fifteen minutes from now. Also, sound a general alert throughout the base and have all personnel stand by to await further instructions. I'll link in to the conference from the multiconsole in Room 14 of the Main Observatory Dome. That's all."

Just over a quarter of an hour later Torres and the two scientists were facing an array of wall screens that showed the other participants in the conference. Garuth, commander-in-chief of the expedition, sat flanked by two aides in the heart of the mother-ship *Shapieron* two thousand miles above Iscaris III. He listened without interruption to the account of the situation. The chief scientist, speaking from elsewhere in the ship, confirmed that in the past few minutes sensors aboard the *Shapieron* had yielded data similar to that reported by instruments from the surface of Iscaris III, and that the computers had produced the same interpretation. The G-beam projectors had caused some unforeseen and catastrophic change in the internal equilibrium of Iscaris, and the star was in the process of turning into a nova. There was no time to think of anything but escape.

"We have to get everybody off the surface," Garuth said. "Leyel, the first thing I need is a statement of what ships you've got down there at the moment, and how many personnel they can bring up. We'll send down extra shuttles to ferry out the rest as soon as we know what your shortage in carrying capacity is. Monchar . . ." He addressed his deputy on another of the screens. "Do we have any ships more than fifteen hours out from us at maximum speed?"

"No, sir. The farthest away is out near Projector Two. It could make it back in just over ten."

"Good. Recall them all immediately, emergency priority. If the figures we've just heard are right, the only way we'll stand a chance of getting clear is on the *Shapieron*'s main drives. Prepare a schedule of expected arrival times and make sure that preparations for reception have been made."

"Yes, sir."

"Leyel . . ." Garuth switched his gaze back to look straight out of the screen in Room 14 of the Observatory Dome. "Bring all your available ships up to flight-readiness and begin planning your evacuation at once. Report back on status one hour from now. One bag of personal belongings only per person."

"May I remind you of a problem, sir." The chief engineer of the *Shapieron,* Rogdar Jassilane, added from the drive section of the ship.

"What is it, Rog?" Garuth's face turned away to look at another screen.

"We still have a fault on the primary retardation system for the main-drive torroids. If we start up those drives, the only way they'll ever slow down again is at their own natural rate. The whole braking system's been stripped down. We could never put it together again in under twenty hours, let alone trace the fault and fix it."

Garuth thought for a moment. "But we can start them up okay?"

"We can," Jassilane confirmed. "But once those black holes start whirling round inside the torroids, the angular momentum they'll build up will be phenomenal. Without the retardation system to slow them down, they'll take years to coast down to a speed at which the drives can be deactivated. We'd be under main drive all the time, with no way of shutting down." He made a helpless gesture. "We could end up anywhere."

"But we've no choice," Garuth pointed out. "It's fly or fry. We'll have to set course for home and orbit the Solar System under drive until we've dropped to a low enough return velocity. What other way is there?"

"I can see what Rog's getting at," the chief scientist interjected. "It's not quite as simple as that. You see, at the velocities that we would acquire under years of sustained main drive, we'd experience an enormous relativistic time-dilation compared to reference frames moving with the speed of Iscaris or Sol. Since the *Shapieron* would be an accelerated system, much more time would pass back home than would pass on board the ship; we know *where* we'd end up all right . . . but we won't be too sure of *when.*"

"And, in fact, it would be worse than just that,"

Jassilane added. "The main drives work by generating a localized space–time distortion that the ship continuously 'falls' into. This also produces its own time-dilation effect. Hence you'd have the compound effect of both dilations added together. What that would mean with an unretarded main drive running for years, I couldn't tell you—I don't think anything like it has ever happened."

"I haven't done any precise calculations yet, naturally," the chief scientist said. "But if my mental estimates are anything to go by, we could be talking about a compound dilation of the order of millions."

"Millions?" Garuth looked stunned.

"Yes." The chief scientist looked out at them soberly. "For every year that we spend slowing down from the velocity that we'll need to escape the nova, we could find that a million years have passed by the time we get home."

Silence persisted for a long time. At last Garuth spoke in a voice that was heavy and solemn. "Be that as it may, to survive we have no choice. My orders stand. Chief Engineer Jassilane, prepare for deep-space and bring the main drives up to standby readiness."

Twenty hours later the *Shapieron* was under full power and hurtling toward interstellar space as the first outrushing front of the nova seared its hull and vaporized behind it the cinder that had once been Iscaris III.

chapter one

In a space of time less than a single heartbeat in the life of the universe, the incredible animal called Man had fallen from the trees, discovered fire, invented the wheel, learned to fly and gone out to explore the planets.

The history that followed Man's emergence was a turmoil of activity, adventure and ceaseless discovery. Nothing like it had been seen through eons of sedate evolution and slowly unfolding events that had gone before.

Or so, for a long time, it had been thought . . .

But when at last Man came to Ganymede, largest of the moons of Jupiter, he stumbled upon a discovery that totally demolished one of the few beliefs that had survived centuries of his insatiable inquisitiveness: He was not, after all, unique. Twenty-five million years before him, another race had surpassed all that he had thus far achieved.

The fourth manned mission to Jupiter, early in the third decade of the twenty-first century, marked the beginning of intensive exploration of the outer planets and the establishment of the first permanent bases on the Jovian satellites. Instruments in orbit above Ganymede had detected a large concentration of metal some distance below the surface of the moon's ice crust. From a base specially sited for the purpose, shafts were sunk to investigate this anomaly.

The spacecraft that they found there, frozen in its changeless tomb of ice, was huge. From skeletal remains found inside the ship, the scientists of Earth reconstructed a picture of the race of eight-foot-tall giants that had built it and whose level of technology was estimated as having been a century or more ahead of Earth's. They christened the giants the "Ganymeans," to commemorate the place of the discovery.

The Ganymeans had originated on Minerva, a planet that once occupied the position between Mars and Jupiter but which had since been destroyed. The bulk of Minerva's mass had gone into a violently eccentric orbit at the edge of the solar system to become Pluto, while the remainder of the debris was dispersed by Jupiter's tidal effects and formed the Asteroid Belt. Various scientific investigations, including cosmic-ray exposure-tests on material samples recovered from the Asteroid Belt, pinpointed the breakup of Minerva as having occurred some fifty thousand years in the past—long, long after the Ganymeans were known to have roamed the Solar System.

The discovery of a race of technically advanced beings from twenty-five million years back was exciting enough. Even more exciting, but not really surprising, was the revelation that the Ganymeans had visited Earth. The cargo of the spacecraft found on Ganymede included a collection of plant and animal specimens the likes of which no human eye had ever beheld—a representative cross section of terrestrial life during the late Oligocene and early Miocene periods. Some of the samples were well preserved in canisters while others had evidently been alive in pens and cages at the time of the ship's mishap.

The seven ships that were to make up the Jupiter Five Mission were being constructed in Lunar orbit at the time these discoveries were made. When the mission departed, a team of scientists traveled with it, eager to delve more deeply into the irresistibly challenging story of the Ganymeans.

A data manipulation program running in the computer complex of the mile-and-a-quarter-long Jupiter Five mission command ship, orbiting two thousand miles above Ganymede, routed its results to the message-scheduling processor. The information was beamed down by laser to a transceiver on the surface at Ganymede Main Base, and relayed northward via a chain of repeater stations. A few millionths of a second and seven hundred miles later, the computers at Pithead Base decoded the message destination and routed the signal to a display screen on the wall of a small conference room in the Biological Laboratories section. An elaborate pattern of the symbols used by geneticists to denote the internal structures of chromosomes appeared on the screen. The five people seated around the table in the narrow confines of the room studied the display intently.

"There. If you want to go right down to it in detail, that's what it looks like." The speaker was a tall, lean, balding man clad in a white lab coat and wearing a pair of anachronistic gold-rimmed spectacles. He was standing in front and to one side of the screen, pointing toward it with one hand and clasping his lapel lightly with the other. Professor Christian Danchekker of the Westwood Biological Institute in Houston, part of the UN Space Arm's Life Sciences Division, headed the team of biologists who had come to Ganymede aboard *Jupiter Five* to study the early terrestrial animals discovered in the Ganymean spacecraft. The scientists sitting before him contemplated the image on the screen. After a while Danchekker summarized once more the problem they had been debating for the past hour.

"I hope it is obvious to most of you that the expression we are looking at represents a molecular arrangement characteristic of the structure of an enzyme. This same strain of enzyme has been identified in tissue samples taken from many of the species so far examined in the labs up in *J4*. I repeat—*many* of the species . . . many *different* species . . ." Danchekker clasped both hands to his lapels and gazed at his miniaudience expectantly. His voice fell almost to a whisper. "And yet nothing resembling it or suggestive of being in any way related to it has ever been identified in any of today's terrestrial animal species. The problem we are faced with, gentlemen, is simply to explain these curious facts."

Paul Carpenter, fresh-faced, fair-haired and the youngest present, pushed himself back from the table and looked inquiringly from side to side, at the same time turning up his hands. "I guess I don't really see the problem," he confessed candidly. "This enzyme existed in animal species from twenty-five million years back—right?"

"You've got it," Sandy Holmes confirmed from across the table with a slight nod of her head.

"So in twenty-five million years they mutated out of all recognition. Everything changes over a period of time and it's no different with enzymes. Descendant strains from this one are probably still around but they don't look the same. . . ." He caught the expression on Danchekker's face. "No? . . . What's the problem?"

The professor sighed a sigh of infinite patience. "We've been through all that, Paul," he said. "At least, I was under the impression that we had. Let me recapitulate: Enzymology has made tremendous advances over the last few decades. Just about every type has been classified and catalogued, but never anything like this one, which is completely different from anything we've ever seen."

"I don't want to sound argumentative, but is that really true?" Carpenter protested. "I mean . . . we've seen new additions to the catalogues even in the last year or two, haven't we? There was Schnelder and Grossmann at São Paulo with the P273B series and its derivatives . . . Braddock in England with—"

"Ah, but you're missing the whole point," Danchekker interrupted. "Those were new strains, true, but they fell neatly into the known standard families. They exhibited characteristics that place them firmly and definitely within known related groups." He gestured again toward the screen. "That one doesn't. It's completely new. To me it suggests a whole new class of its own—a class that contains just one member. Nothing yet identified in the metabolism of any form of life as we know it has ever done that before." Danchekker swept his eyes around the small circle of faces.

"Every species of animal life that we know belongs to a known family group and has related species and ancestors that we can identify. At the microscopic level the same thing applies. All our previous experiences tell us that even if this enzyme does date from twenty-five million years back, we ought to be able to recognize its family characteristics and relate it to known enzyme strains that exist today. However, we cannot. To me this indicates something very unusual."

Wolfgang Fichter, one of Danchekker's senior biologists, rubbed his chin and stared dubiously at the screen. "I agree that it is highly improbable, Chris," he said. "But can you really be so sure that it is impossible? After all, over twenty-five million years? . . . Environmental factors may have changed and caused the enzyme to mutate into something unrecognizable. I don't know, some change in diet maybe . . . something like that."

Danchekker shook his head decisively. "No. I say it's impossible." He raised his hands and proceeded to count points off on his fingers. "One—even if it did mutate, we'd still be able to identify its basic family architecture in the same way we can identify the fundamental properties of, say, any vertebrate. We can't.

"Two—if it occurred only in one species of Oligocene animal, then I would be prepared to concede that perhaps the enzyme we see here had mutated and given rise to many strains that we find in the world today—in other words this strain represents an ancestral form common to a whole modern family. If such were the case, then perhaps I'd agree that a mutation could have occurred that was so severe that the relationship between the ancestral strain and its descendants has been obscured. But that is not the case. This same enzyme is found in many different and nonrelated Oligocene species. For your suggestion to apply, the same improbable process would have had to occur many times over, independently, and all at the same time. I say that's impossible."

"But . . ." Carpenter began, but Danchekker pressed on.

"Three—none of today's animals possesses such an enzyme in its microchemistry yet they all manage perfectly well without it. Many of them are direct descendants of Oligocene types from the Ganymean ship. Now some of those chains of descent have involved rapid mutation and adaptation to meet changing diets and environments while others have not. In several cases the evolution from Oligocene ancestors to today's forms has been very slow and has produced only a small degree of change. We have made detailed comparisons between the microchemical processes of such ancestral Oligocene ancestors recovered from the ship and known data relating to animals that exist today and are descended from those same ancestors. The results have been very much as we expected— no great changes and clearly identifiable relationships between one group and the other. Every function that appeared in the microchemistry of the ancestor could be easily recognized, sometimes with slight modifications, in the descendants." Danchekker shot a quick glance at Fichter. "Twenty-five million years isn't really so long on an evolutionary time scale."

When no one seemed ready to object, Danchekker forged ahead. "But in every case there was one exception—this enzyme. Everything tells us that if this enzyme were present in the ancestor, then it, or something very like it, should be readily observable in the descendants. Yet in every case the results have been negative. I say that cannot happen, and yet it has happened."

A brief silence descended while the group digested Danchekker's words. At length Sandy Holmes ventured a thought. "Couldn't it still be a radical mutation, but the other way around?"

Danchekker frowned at her.

"How do you mean, the other way around?" asked Henri Rousson, another senior biologist, seated next to Carpenter.

"Well," she replied, "all the animals on the ship had been to Minerva, hadn't they? Most likely they were born there from ancestors the Ganymeans had transported from Earth. Couldn't something in the Mi-

nervan environment have caused a mutation that resulted in this enzyme? At least that would explain why
none of today's terrestrial animals have it. They've
never been to Minerva and neither have any of the
ancestors they've descended from."

"Same problem," Fichter muttered, shaking his
head.

"What problem?" she asked.

"The fact that the *same* enzyme was found in many
different and nonrelated Oligocene species," Danchekker said. "Yes, I'll grant that differences in the Minervan environment could mutate some strain of enzyme
brought in from Earth into something like that." He
pointed at the screen again. "But many different species were brought in from Earth—different species
each with its own characteristic metabolism and particular groups of enzyme strains. Now suppose that
something in the Minervan environment caused those
enzymes—*different* enzymes—to mutate. Are you seriously suggesting that they would *all* mutate independently into the *same* end-product?" He waited for
a second. "Because that is exactly the situation that
confronts us. The Ganymean ship contained many
preserved specimens of different species, but every one
of those species possessed precisely the *same* enzyme.
Now do you want to reconsider your suggestion?"

The woman looked helplessly at the table for a
second, then made a gesture of resignation. "Okay
. . . If you put it like that, I guess it doesn't make
sense."

"Thank you," Danchekker acknowledged stonily.

Henri Rousson leaned forward and poured himself
a glass of water from the pitcher standing in the center of the table. He took a long drink while the others
continued to stare thoughtfully through the walls or at
the ceiling.

"Let's go back to basics for a second and see if
that gets us anywhere," he said. "We know that the
Ganymeans evolved on Minerva—right?" The heads
around him nodded in assent. "We also know that the
Ganymeans must have visited Earth because there's
no other way they could have ended up with terres-

trial animals on board their ship—unless we're going to invent another hypothetical alien race and I'm sure not going to do that because there's no reason to. Also, we know that the ship found here on Ganymede had come to Ganymede from Minerva, not directly from Earth. If the ship came from Minerva, the terrestrial animals must have come from Minerva too. That supports the idea we've already got that the Ganymeans were shipping all kinds of life forms from Earth to Minerva for some reason."

Paul Carpenter held up a hand. "Hang on a second. How do we know that the ship downstairs came here from Minerva?"

"The plants," Fichter reminded him.

"Oh yeah, the plants. I forgot . . ." Carpenter subsided into silence.

The pens and animal cages in the Ganymean ship had contained vegetable feed and floor-covering materials that had remained perfectly preserved under the ice coating formed when the ship's atmosphere froze and the moisture condensed out. Using seeds recovered from this material, Danchekker had succeeded in cultivating live plants completely different from anything that had ever grown on Earth, presumed to be examples of native Minervan botany. The leaves were very dark—almost black—and absorbed every available scrap of sunlight, right across the visible spectrum. This seemed to tie in nicely with independently obtained evidence of Minerva's great distance from the Sun.

"How far," Rousson asked, "have we got in figuring out *why* the Ganymeans were shipping all the animals in?" He spread his arms wide. "There had to be a reason. How far are we getting on that one? I don't know, but the enzyme might have something to do with it."

"Very well, let's recapitulate briefly what we think we already know about the subject," Danchekker suggested. He moved away from the screen and perched on the edge of the table. "Paul. Would you like to tell us your answer to Henri's question." Carpenter scratched the back of his head for a second and screwed up his face.

"Well . . ." he began, "first there's the fish. They're established as being native Minervan and give us our link between Minerva and the Ganymeans."

"Good," Danchekker nodded, mellowing somewhat from his earlier crotchety mood. "Go on."

Carpenter was referring to a type of well-preserved canned fish that had been positively traced back to its origin in the oceans of Minerva. Danchekker had shown that the skeletons of the fish correlated in general arrangement to the skeletal remains of the Ganymean occupants of the ship that lay under the ice deep below Pithead Base; the relationship was comparable to that existing between the architectures of, say, a man and a mammoth, and demonstrated that the fish and the Ganymeans belonged to the same evolutionary family. Thus if the fish were native to Minerva, the Ganymeans were, too.

"Your computer analysis of the fundamental cell chemistry of the fish," Carpenter continued, "suggests an inherent low tolerance to a group of toxins that includes carbon dioxide. I think you also postulated that this basic chemistry could have been inherited from way back in the ancestral line of the fish —right from very early on in Minervan history."

"Quite so," Danchekker approved. "What else?"

Carpenter hesitated. "So Minervan land-dwelling species would have had a low CO_2 tolerance as well," he offered.

"Not quite," Danchekker answered. "You've left out the connecting link to that conclusion. Anybody . . . ?" He looked at the German. "Wolfgang?"

"You need to make the assumption that the characteristics of low CO_2 tolerance came about in a very remote ancestor—one that existed before any land-dwelling types appeared on Minerva." Fichter paused, then continued. "Then you can postulate that this remote life form was a common ancestor to all later land dwellers and marine descendants—for example, the fish. On the basis of that assumption you can say that the characteristic could have been inherited by all the land-dwelling species that emerged later."

"Never forget your assumptions," Danchekker urged. "Many of the problems in the history of science have stemmed from that simple error. Note one other thing too: If the low-CO_2-tolerance characteristic did indeed come about very early in the process of Minervan evolution and survived right down to the time that the fish was alive, then suggestions are that it was a very *stable* characteristic, if our knowledge of terrestrial evolution is anything to go by anyway. This adds plausibility to the suggestion that it could have become a common characteristic that spread throughout all the land dwellers as they evolved and diverged, and has remained essentially unaltered down through the ages—much as the basic design of terrestrial vertebrates has remained unchanged for hundreds of millions of years despite superficial differences in shape, size and form." Danchekker removed his spectacles and began polishing the lenses with his handkerchief.

"Very well," he said. "Let us pursue the assumption and conclude that by the time the Ganymeans had evolved—twenty-five million years ago—the land surface of Minerva was populated by a multitude of its own native life forms, each of which possessed a low tolerance to carbon dioxide, among other things. What other clues do we have available to us that might help determine what was happening on Minerva at that time?"

"We know that the Ganymeans were quitting the planet and trying to migrate someplace else," Sandy Holmes threw in. "Probably to some other star system."

"Oh, really?" Danchekker smiled, showing his teeth briefly before breathing on his spectacle lenses once more. "How do we know that?"

"Well, there's the ship down under the ice here for a start," she replied. "The kind of freight it was carrying and the amount of it sure suggested a colony ship intending a one-way trip. And then, why should it show up on *Ganymede* of all places? It couldn't have been traveling between any of the inner planets, could it?"

"But there's nothing outside Minerva's orbit to colonize," Carpenter chipped in. "Not until you get to the stars, that is."

"Exactly so," Danchekker said soberly, directing his words at the woman. "You said '*suggested* a colony ship.' Don't forget that that is precisely what the evidence we have at present amounts to—a suggestion and nothing more. It doesn't *prove* anything. Lots of people around the base are saying we now know that the Ganymeans abandoned the Solar System to find a new home elsewhere because the carbon-dioxide concentration in the Minervan atmosphere was increasing for some reason which we have yet to determine. It is true that if what we have just said was fact, then the Ganymeans would have shared the low tolerance possessed by all land dwellers there, and any increase in the atmospheric concentration could have caused them serious problems. But as we have just seen, we *know* nothing of the kind; we merely observe one or two suggestions that might add up to such an explanation." The professor paused, seeing that Carpenter was about to say something.

"There was more to it than that though, wasn't there?" Carpenter queried. "We're pretty certain that all species of Minervan land dwellers died out pretty rapidly somewhere around twenty-five million years ago . . . all except the Ganymeans themselves maybe. That sounds like just the effect you'd expect if the concentration did rise and all the species there couldn't handle it. It seems to support the hypothesis pretty well."

"I think Paul's got a point," Sandy Holmes chimed in. "Everything adds up. Also, it fits in with the ideas we've been having about why the Ganymeans were shipping all the animals into Minerva." She turned toward Carpenter, as if inviting him to complete the story from there.

As usual, Carpenter didn't need much encouragement. "What the Ganymeans were really trying to do was redress the CO_2 imbalance by covering the planet with carbon-dioxide-absorbing, oxygen-producing terrestrial green plants. The animals were brought along to provide a balanced ecology that the plants could survive in. Like Sandy says, it all fits."

"You're trying to fit the evidence to suit the answers that you already want to prove," Danchekker cautioned. "Let's separate once more the evidence that is fact from the evidence which is supposition or mere suggestion." The discussion continued with Danchekker leading an examination of the principles of scientific deduction and the techniques of logical analysis. Throughout, the figure who had been following the proceedings silently from his seat at the end of the table farthest from the screen continued to draw leisurely on his cigarette, taking in every detail.

Dr. Victor Hunt had also accompanied the team of scientists who had come with *Jupiter Five* more than three months before to study the Ganymean ship. Although nothing truly spectacular had emerged during this time, huge volumes of data on the structure, design and contents of the alien ship had been amassed. Every day, newly removed devices and machinery were examined in the laboratories of the surface bases and in the orbiting *J4* and *J5* mission command ships. Findings from these tests were as yet fragmentary, but clues were beginning to emerge from which a meaningful picture of the Ganymean civilization and the mysterious events of twenty-five million years before might eventually emerge.

That was Hunt's job. Originally a theoretical physicist specializing in mathematical nucleonics, he had been brought into the UN Space Arm from England to head a small group of UNSA scientists; the group's task was to correlate the findings of the specialists working on the project both on and around Ganymede and back on Earth. The specialists painted the pieces of the puzzle; Hunt's group fitted them together. This arrangement was devised by Hunt's immediate boss, Gregg Caldwell, executive director of the Navigation and Communications Division of UNSA, headquartered in Houston. The scheme had already worked well in enabling them to unravel successfully the existence and fate of Minerva, and first signs were that it promised to work well again.

He listened while the debate between the biologists went full circle to end up focusing on the unfamiliar enzyme that had started the whole thing off.

"No, I'm afraid not," Danchekker said in reply to a question from Rousson. "We have no idea at present what its purpose was. Certain functions in its reaction equations suggest that it could have contributed to the modification or breaking down of some kind of protein molecule, but precisely what molecule or for what purpose we don't know." Danchekker gazed around the room to invite further comment but nobody appeared to have anything to say. The room became quiet. A mild hum from a nearby generator became noticeable for the first time. At length Hunt stubbed his cigarette and sat back to rest his elbows on the arms of his chair. "Sounds as if there's a problem there, all right," he commented. "Enzymes aren't my line. I'm going to have to leave this one completely to you people."

"Ah, nice to see you're still with us, Vic," Danchekker said, raising his eyes to take in the far end of the table. "You haven't said a word since we sat down."

"Listening and learning," Hunt grinned. "Didn't have a lot to contribute."

"That sounds like a philosophical approach to life," Fichter said, shuffling the papers in front of him. "Do you have many philosophies of life . . . maybe a little red book full of them like that Chinese gentleman back in nineteen whatever it was?"

"'Fraid not. Doesn't do to have too many philosophies about anything. You always end up contradicting yourself. Blows your credibility."

Fichter smiled. "You've nothing to say to throw any light on our problem with this wretched enzyme then," he said.

Hunt did not reply immediately but pursed his lips and inclined his head to one side in the manner of somebody with doubts about the advisability of revealing something that he knew. "Well," he finally said, "you've got enough to worry about with that enzyme as things are." The tone was mildly playful, but irresistibly provocative. All heads in the room swung around abruptly to face in his direction.

"Vic, you're holding out on us," Sandy declared. "Give."

Danchekker fixed Hunt with a silent, challenging stare. Hunt nodded and reached down with one hand to operate the keyboard recessed into the edge of the table opposite his chair. Above the far side of Ganymede, computers on board *Jupiter Five* responded to his request. The display on the conference room wall changed to reveal a densely packed columnar arrangement of numbers.

Hunt allowed some time for the others to study them. "These are the results of a series of quantitative analytical tests that were performed recently in the *J5* labs. The tests involved the routine determination of the chemical constituents of cells from selected organs in the animals you've just been talking about —the ones from the ship." He paused for a second, then continued matter-of-factly. "These numbers show that certain combinations of elements turned up over and over again, always in the same fixed ratios. The ratios strongly suggest the decay products of familiar radioactive processes. It's exactly as if radioisotopes were selected in the manufacture of the enzymes."

After a few seconds, one or two puzzled frowns formed in response to his words. Danchekker was the first to reply. "Are you telling us that the enzyme incorporated radioisotopes into its structure . . . selectively?" he asked.

"Exactly."

"That's ridiculous," the professor declared firmly. His tone left no room for dissent. Hunt shrugged.

"It appears to be fact. Look at the numbers."

"But there is no way in which such a process could come about," Danchekker insisted.

"I know, but it did."

"Purely chemical processes cannot distinguish a

radioisotope from a normal isotope," Danchekker pointed out impatiently. "Enzymes are manufactured by chemical processes. Such processes are incapable of selecting radioisotopes to use for the manufacture of enzymes." Hunt had half expected that Danchekker's immediate reaction would be one of uncompromising and total rejection of the suggestion he had just made. After working closely with Danchekker for over two years, Hunt had grown used to the professor's tendency to sandbag himself instinctively behind orthodox pronouncements the moment anything alien to his beliefs reared its head. Once he'd been given time to reflect, Hunt knew, Danchekker could be as innovative as any of the younger generation of scientists seated around the room. For the moment, then, Hunt remained silent, whistling tunelessly and nonchalantly to himself as he drummed his fingers absently on the table.

Danchekker waited, growing visibly more irritable as the seconds dragged by. "Chemical processes cannot distinguish a radioisotope," he finally repeated. "Therefore no enzyme could be produced in the way you say it was. And even if it could, there would be no purpose to be served. Chemically the enzyme will behave the same whether it has radioisotopes in it or not. What you're saying is preposterous!"

Hunt sighed and pointed a weary finger toward the screen.

"I'm not saying it, Chris," he reminded the professor. "The numbers are. There are the facts—check 'em." Hunt leaned forward and cocked his head to one side, at the same time contorting his features into a frown as if he had just been struck with a sudden thought. "*What* were you saying a minute ago about people wanting to fit the evidence to suit the answers they'd already made their minds up about?" he asked.

chapter two

At the age of eleven, Victor Hunt had moved from the bedlam of his family home in the East End of London and gone to live with an uncle and aunt in Worcester. His uncle—the odd man out in the Hunt family—was a design engineer at the nearby laboratories of a leading computer manufacturer and it was his patient guidance that first opened the boy's eyes to the excitement and mystery of the world of electronics.

Some time later young Victor put his newfound fascination with the laws of formal logic and the techniques of logic-circuit design to its first practical test. He designed and built a hard-wired special-purpose processor which, when given any date after the adoption of the Gregorian calendar in 1582, would output a number from 1 to 7 denoting the day of the week on which it had fallen. When, breathless with expectation, he switched it on for the first time, the system remained dead. It turned out that he had connected an electrolytic capacitor the wrong way around and shorted out the power supply.

This exercise taught him two things: Most problems have simple solutions once somebody looks at things the right way, and the exhilaration of winning in the end makes all the effort worthwhile. It also served to reinforce his intuitive understanding that the only sure way to prove or disprove what looked like a good idea was to find some way to test it. As his subsequent career led him from electronics to mathematical physics and thence to nucleonics, these fundamentals became the foundations of his permanent mental makeup. In nearly thirty years he had never lost his addiction to the final minutes of mounting suspense that came when the crucial experiment had been prepared and the moment of truth was approaching.

He experienced that same feeling now, as he watched Vincent Carizan make a few last-minute adjustments to the power-amplifier settings. The attraction in the main electronics lab at Pithead Base that morning was an item of equipment recovered from the Ganymean ship. It was roughly cylindrical, about the size of an oil drum, and appeared to be rather simple in function in that it possessed few input and output connections; apparently it was a self-contained device of some sort, rather than a component in some larger and more complex system.

However, its function was far from obvious. The engineers at Pithead had concluded that the connections were intended as power inlet points. From an analysis of the insulating materials used, the voltage clamping and protection circuits, the smoothing circuits, and the filtering arrangements, they had deduced the kind of electrical supply it was designed to work from. This had enabled them to set up a suitable arrangement of transformers and frequency converters. Today was the day they intended to switch it on to see what happened.

Besides Hunt and Carizan, two other engineers were present in the laboratory to supervise the measuring instruments that had been assembled for the experiment. Frank Towers observed Carizan's nod of satisfaction as he stepped back from the amplifier panel and asked:

"All set for overload check?"

"Yep," Carizan answered. "Give it a zap." Towers threw a switch on another panel. A sharp *clunk* sounded instantly as a circuit breaker dropped out somewhere in the equipment cabinet behind the panel.

Sam Mullen, standing by an instrumentation console to one side of the room, briefly consulted one of his readout screens. "Current trip's functioning okay," he announced.

"Unshort it and throw in some volts," Carizan said to Towers, who changed a couple of control settings, threw the switch again and looked over at Mullen.

"Limiting at fifty," Mullen said. "Check?"

"Check," Towers returned.

Carizan looked at Hunt. "All set to go, Vic. We'll try an initial run with current limiters in circuit, but whatever happens our stuff's protected. Last chance to change your bet; the book's closing."

"I still say it makes music," Hunt grinned. "It's an electric barrel organ. Give it some juice."

"Computers?" Carizan cocked an eye at Mullen.

"Running. All data channels checking normal."

"Okay then," Carizan rubbed the palms of his hands together. "Now for the star turn. Live this time, Frank—phase one of the schedule."

A tense silence descended as Towers reset his controls and threw the main switch again. The readings on the numeric displays built into his panel changed immediately.

"Live," he confirmed. "It's taking power. Current is up to the maximum set on the limiters. Looks like it wants more." All eyes turned toward Mullen, who was scanning the computer output screens intently. He shook his head without looking around.

"Nix. Makes a dodo look a real ball of fire."

The accelerometers, fixed to the outside of the Ganymean device standing bolted in its steel restraining frame on rubber vibration absorbers, were not sensing any internal mechanical motion. The sensitive microphones attached to its casing were picking up nothing in the audible or ultrasonic ranges. The heat sensors, radiation detectors, electromagnetic probes, gaussmeters, scintillation counters, and variable antennas—all had nothing to report. Towers varied the supply frequency over a trial range but it soon became apparent that nothing was going to change. Hunt walked over to stand beside Mullen and inspect the computer outputs, but said nothing.

"Looks like we need to wind the wick up a little," Carizan commented. "Phase two, Frank." Towers stepped up the input voltage. A row of numbers appeared on one of Mullen's screens.

"Something on channel seven," he informed them.

"Acoustic." He keyed a short sequence of commands into the console keyboard and peered at the wave form that appeared on an auxiliary display. "Periodic wave with severe even-harmonic distortion . . . low amplitude . . . fundamental frequency is about seventy-two hertz."

"That's the supply frequency," Hunt murmured. "Probably just a resonance somewhere. Shouldn't think it means much. Anything else?"

"Nope."

"Wind it up again, Frank," Carizan said.

As the test progressed they became more cautious and increased the number of variations tried at each step. Eventually the characteristics of the input supply told them that the device was saturating and seemed to be running at its design levels. By this time it was taking a considerable amount of power but apart from reporting continued mild acoustic resonances and a slight heating of some parts of the casing, the measuring instruments remained obstinately quiet. As the first hour passed, Hunt and the three UNSA engineers resigned themselves to a longer and much more detailed examination of the object, one that would no doubt involve dismantling it. But, like Napoleon, they took the view that lucky people tend to be people who give luck a chance to happen; it had been worth a try.

The disturbance generated by the Ganymean device was, however, not of a nature that any of their instruments had been designed to detect. A series of spherical wave fronts of intense but highly localized space—time distortion expanded outward from Pithead Base at the speed of light, propagating across the Solar System.

Seven hundred miles to the south, seismic monitors at Ganymede Main Base went wild and the data validation programs running in the logging computer aborted to signal a system malfunction.

Two thousand miles above the surface, sensors aboard the *Jupiter Five* command ship pinpointed Pithead Base as the origin of abnormal readings and flashed an alert to the duty supervisor.

Over half an hour had passed since full power had been applied to the device in the laboratory at Pithead. Hunt stubbed out a cigarette as Towers finally shut down the supply and sat back in his seat with a sigh.

"That's about it," Towers said. "We're not gonna get anyplace this way. Looks like we'll have to open it up further."

"Ten bucks," Carizan declared. "See, Vic—no tunes."

"Nothing else, either," Hunt retorted. "The bet's void."

At the instrumentation console Mullen completed the storage routine for the file of meager data that had been collected, shut down the computers and joined the others.

"I don't understand where all that power was going," he said, frowning. "There wasn't nearly enough heat to account for it, and no signs of anything else. It's crazy."

"There must be a black hole in there," Carizan offered. "That's what the thing is—a garbage can. It's the ultimate garbage can."

"I'll take ten on that," Hunt informed him readily.

Three hundred and fifty million miles from Ganymede, in the Asteroid Belt, a UNSA robot probe detected a rapid succession of transient gravitational anomalies, causing its master computer to suspend all system programs and initiate a full run of diagnostic and fault-test routines.

"No kidding—straight out of Walt Disney," Hunt told the others across the table in one corner of the communal canteen at Pithead. "I've never seen anything like the animal murals decorating the walls of that room in the Ganymean spacecraft."

"Sounds crazy," Sam Mullen declared from opposite Hunt.

"What d'you think they are—Minervans or something else?"

"They're not terrestrial, that's for sure," Hunt replied. "But maybe they're not anything . . . anything real that is. Chris Danchekker's convinced they can't be real."

"How d'you mean, *real?*" Carizan asked.

"Well, they don't *look* real," Hunt answered. He frowned and waved his hands in small circles in the air. "They're all kinds of bright colors . . . and clumsy . . . ungainly. You can't imagine them evolving from any real-life evolutionary system—"

"Not selected for survival, you mean?" Carizan suggested. Hunt nodded rapidly.

"Yes, that's it. No adaptation for survival . . . no camouflage or ability to escape or anything like that."

"Mmm . . ." Carizan looked intrigued, but nonplussed. "Any ideas?"

"Well, actually yes," Hunt said. "We're pretty sure the room was a Ganymean children's nursery or something similar. That probably explains it. They weren't supposed to be real, just Ganymean cartoon characters." Hunt paused for a second, then laughed to himself. "Danchekker wondered if they'd named any of them Neptune." The other two looked at him quizzically. "He reasoned that they couldn't have had a Pluto because there wasn't a Pluto then," Hunt explained. "So maybe they had a Neptune instead."

"Neptune!" Carizan guffawed and brought his hand down sharply on the table. "I like it. . . . Wouldn't have thought Danchekker could crack a joke like that."

"You'd be surprised," Hunt told him. "He can be quite a character once you get to know him. He's just a bit stuffy at first, that's all. . . . But you should see them. I'll bring some prints over. One was bright blue with pink stripes down the sides—body like an overgrown pig. And it had a trunk!"

Mullen grimaced and covered his eyes.

"Man . . . The thought's enough to put me off drink for keeps." He turned his head and looked toward the serving counter. "Where the hell's Frank?" As if in answer to the question, Towers appeared behind him carrying a tray with four cups of coffee. He set the tray down, squeezed into a seat and proceeded to pass the drinks round.

"Two white with, a white without, and a black with. Okay?" He settled himself back and accepted a cigarette from Hunt. "Cheers. The man over by the counter there says you're leaving for a spell. That right?"

Hunt nodded. "Only five days. I'm due for a bit of leave on *J5*. Flying up from Main the day after tomorrow."

"On your own?" Mullen asked.

"No—there'll be five or six of us. Danchekker's coming too. Can't say I'll be sorry for a break, either."

"I hope the weather holds out," Towers said with playful sarcasm. "It'd be too bad if you missed the holiday season. This place makes me wonder what the big attraction ever was at Miami Beach."

"The ice comes with scotch there," Carizan suggested.

A shadow fell across the table. They looked up to greet a burly figure sporting a heavy black beard and clad in a tartan shirt and blue jeans. It was Pete Cummings, a structures engineer who had come to Ganymede with the team that had included Hunt and Danchekker. He reversed a chair and perched himself astride it, directing his gaze at Carizan.

"How'd it go?" he inquired. Carizan pulled a face and shook his head.

"No dice. Bit of heat, bit of humming . . . otherwise nothing to shout about. Couldn't get anything out of it."

"Too bad." Cummings made an appropriate display of sympathy. "It couldn't have been you guys that caused all the commotion then."

"What commotion?"

"Didn't you hear?" He looked surprised. "There was a message beamed down from *J5* a little while back. Apparently they picked up some funny waves coming up from the surface . . . seems that the center was somewhere around here. The commander's been calling all around the base trying to find out who's up to what, and what caused it. They're all flappin' around in the tower up there like there's a fox in the hen-house."

"I bet that's the call that came in just when we were leaving the lab," Mullen said. "Told you it could have been important."

"Hell, there are times when a man needs coffee," Carizan answered. "Anyhow, it wasn't us." He turned to face Cummings. "Sorry, Pete. Ask again some other time. We've just been drawing blanks today."

"Well, the whole thing's mighty queer," Cummings declared, rubbing his beard. "They've checked out just about everything else."

Hunt was frowning to himself and drawing on his cigarette pensively. He blew out a cloud of smoke and looked up at Cummings.

"Any idea what time this was, Pete?" he asked. Cummings screwed up his face.

"Lemme see—aw, under an hour." He turned and called across to a group of three men who were sitting at another table: "Hey, Jed. What time did J5 pick up the spooky waves? Any idea?"

"Ten forty-seven local," Jed called back.

"Ten forty-seven local," Cummings repeated to the table.

An ominous silence descended abruptly on the group seated around Hunt.

"How about that, fellas?" Towers asked at last. The matter-of-fact tone did not conceal his amazement.

"It could be a coincidence," Mullen murmured, not sounding convinced.

Hunt cast his eyes around the circle of faces and read the same thoughts on every one. They had all reached the same conclusion; after a few seconds, he voiced it for them.

"I don't believe in coincidences," he said.

Five hundred million miles away, in the radio and optical observatory complex on Lunar Farside, Professor Otto Schneider made his way to one of the computer graphics rooms in answer to a call from his assistant. She pointed out the unprecedented readings that had been reported by an instrument designed to measure cosmic gravitational radiation, especially that believed to emanate from the galactic center. These signals were quite positively identified, but had not come from anywhere near that direction. They originated from somewhere near Jupiter.

Another hour passed on Ganymede. Hunt and the engineers returned to the lab to reappraise the experiment in light of what Cummings had told them. They called the base commander, reported the situation, and agreed to prepare a more intensive test for the Ganymean device. Then, while Towers and Mullen reexamined the data collected earlier, Hunt and Carizan toured the base to beg, borrow or steal some seismic monitoring equipment to add to their instruments. Suitable detectors were finally located in one of the warehouses, where they were kept as spares for a seismic outstation about three miles from the base, and the team began planning the afternoon's activities. By this time their excitement was mounting rapidly, but even more their curiosity; if, after all, the machine was an emitter of gravity pulses, what purpose did it serve?

One thousand five hundred million miles from Ganymede, not far from the mean orbit of Uranus, a communications subprocessor interrupted the operation of its supervisory computer. The computer activated a code-conversion routine and passed a top-priority message on to the master-system monitor.

A transmission had been received from a standard Model 17 Mark 3B Distress Beacon.

chapter three

The surface transporter climbed smoothly above the eternal veil of methane-ammonia haze that cloaked Pithead Base and leveled out onto a southerly course. For nearly two hours it skimmed over an unchanging wilderness of a stormy sea sculptured in ice and half immersed in a sullen ocean of mist. Occasional outcrops of rock added texture to the scene, standing black against the ghostly radiance induced by the serene glow of Jupiter's enormous rainbow disk. And then the cabin view screen showed a tight group of perhaps half a dozen silver spires jutting skywards from just over the horizon ahead—the huge thermonuclear Vega shuttles that stood guard over Ganymede Main Base.

After taking refreshments at Main, Hunt's party joined other groups bound for J5 and boarded one of the Vegas. Soon afterward they were streaking into space and Ganymede rapidly became just a smooth, featureless snowball behind them. Ahead, a pinpoint of light steadily elongated and enlarged, and then resolved itself into the awe-inspiring, majestic, mile-and-a-quarter-long Jupiter Five mission command ship, hanging alone in the void; *Jupiter Four* had departed the week before, bound for Callisto where it would take up permanent orbit. The computers and docking radars guided the Vega gently to rest inside the cavernous forward docking bay, and within minutes the arrivals were walking into the immense city of metal.

Danchekker promptly disappeared to discuss with the J5's scientists the latest details of their studies of the terrestrial animal samples from Pithead. Without

31

shame or conscience Hunt spent a glorious twenty-four hours totally relaxing, doing nothing. He enjoyed many rounds of drinks and endless yarns with *Jupiter Five* crew members he had become friendly with on the long voyage out from Earth, and found unbounded pleasure in the almost forgotten sense of freedom that came with simply sauntering unencumbered along the seemingly interminable expanses of the ship's corridors and vast decks. He felt intoxicated with well-being —exuberant. Just being back on *Jupiter Five* again seemed to bring him nearer to Earth and to things that were familiar. In a sense he was home. This tiny, manmade world, an island of light and life and warmth drifting through an infinite ocean of emptiness, was no longer the cold and alien shell that he had boarded high above Luna more than a year ago. It now seemed to him a part of Earth itself.

Hunt spent the second day paying social calls on some of *J5*'s scientific personnel, exercising in one of the ship's lavishly equipped gymnasiums and cooling off afterward with a swim. A little while later, enjoying a well-earned beer in one of the bars and debating with himself what to do about dinner, he found himself talking to a medical officer who was snatching a quick refresher after coming off duty. Her name was Shirley. To their mutual surprise it turned out that Shirley had studied at Cambridge, England, and had rented a flat not two minutes' walk from Hunt's own student-day lodgings. Before very long one of those instant friendships that springs up out of nowhere was bursting into full bloom. They dined together and spent the rest of the evening talking and laughing and drinking, and drinking and laughing and talking. By midnight it had become evident that there would be no sudden parting of the ways. Next morning he felt better than he had for what he was sure was an unhealthily long time. That, he told himself, was surely what medical officers were supposed to make people feel like.

On the following day he rejoined Danchekker. The results of the two years of work that Hunt and Danchekker had spearheaded was by now a subject of worldwide acclaim, and the names of the two scientists had been in the limelight as a consequence. The Jupiter Five mission director, Joseph B. Shannon, an Air Force colonel prior to world demilitarization fifteen years earlier, had been informed of their presence on the ship and had invited them to join him for lunch. Accordingly, halfway through the official day, they found themselves sitting at a table in the director's dining room, savoring the mellow euphoria that comes with cigars and brandy after the final course and obliging Shannon with their personal accounts of the other sensational discovery that had rocked the scientific world during those two years—the discovery of Charlie and the Lunarians. It ranked in sensationalism with that of the Ganymeans.

The Ganymeans had turned up later, when the shafts driven down into the ice below Pithead had penetrated to the Ganymean spacecraft. Some time before that discovery, exploration of the Lunar surface had yielded traces of yet another technologically advanced civilization that had flourished in the Solar System long before that of Man. This race was given the name "Lunarians," again to commemorate the place where the first finds had been made, and was known to have reached its peak some fifty thousand years before—during the final cold period of the Pleistocene Ice Age. Charlie, a spacesuited corpse found well-preserved beneath debris and rubble not far from Copernicus, had constituted the first find of all and had provided the clues that marked the starting point from which the story of the Lunarians was eventually reconstructed.

The Lunarians had proved to be fully human in every detail. Once this fact was established, the problem that presented itself was that of explaining where the Lunarians had come from. Either they had originated on Earth itself as a till-then unsuspected civilization that had emerged prior to the existence of modern Man, or they had originated somewhere else. There were no other possibilities open to consideration.

But for a long time both possibilities seemed to be ruled out. If an advanced society had once flourished on Earth, surely centuries of archaeological excavation should have produced abundant evidence of it. On the other hand, to suppose that they had originated else-where would require a process of parallel evolution—a violation of the accepted principles of random mutation and natural selection. The Lunarians therefore, being neither from Earth nor from anywhere else, couldn't exist. But they did. The unraveling of this seemingly insoluble mystery had brought Hunt and Danchekker together and had occupied them, along with hundreds of experts from just about all the world's major scientific institutions, for over two years.

"Chris insisted right from the beginning that Charlie, and presumably all the rest of the Lunarians too, could only have descended from the same ancestors as we did." Hunt spoke through a swirling tobacco haze while Shannon listened intently. "I didn't want to argue with him on that, but I couldn't go along with the conclusion that seemed to go with it—that they must, therefore, have originated on Earth. There would have to be traces of them around, and there weren't."

Danchekker smiled ruefully to himself as he sipped his drink. "Yes, indeed," he said. "As I recall, our meetings in those early days were characterized by what might be described as, ah, somewhat direct and acrimonious exchanges."

Shannon's eyes twinkled briefly as he pictured the months of heated argument and dissent that were implied by Danchekker's careful choice of euphemisms.

"I remember reading about it at the time," he said, nodding. "But there were so many different reports flying around and so many journalists getting their stories confused, that we never could get a really clear idea of exactly what was going on behind it all. When did you first figure out for sure that the Lunarians came from Minerva?"

"That's a long story," Hunt answered. "The whole thing was an unbelievable mess for a long time. The more we found out, the more everything seemed to contradict itself. Let me see now . . ." He paused and rubbed his chin for a second. "People all over were getting snippets of information from all kinds of tests on the Lunarian remains and relics that started to turn up after Charlie. Then too, there was Charlie himself, his spacesuit, backpack and so on, and all the things with them . . . then the other bits and pieces from around Tycho and places. The clues eventually started fitting together and out of it all we gradually built up a surprisingly complete picture of Minerva and managed to work out fairly accurately where Minerva must have been."

"I was with UNSA at Galveston when you joined Navcomms," Shannon informed Hunt. "That part of the story received a lot of coverage. *Time* did a feature on you called 'The Sherlock Holmes of Houston.' But tell me something—what you've just said doesn't seem to sort out the problem; if you managed to track them down to Minerva, how did that answer the question of parallel evolution? I'm afraid I still don't see that."

"Quite right," Hunt confirmed. "All it proved was that a planet existed. It didn't prove that the Lunarians evolved on it. As you say, there was still the problem of parallel evolution." He flicked his cigar at the ashtray and shook his head with a sigh. "All kinds of theories were in circulation. Some talked about a civilization from the distant past that had colonized Minerva and had somehow gotten cut off from home; others said they had evolved there from scratch by some kind of convergent process that wasn't properly understood. . . . Life was becoming crazy."

"But at that point we encountered an extraordinary piece of luck," Danchekker came in. "Your colleagues from *Jupiter Four* discovered the Ganymean spaceship—here, on Ganymede. Once the cargo was identified as terrestrial animals from about twenty-five million years ago, an explanation suggested itself that could account adequately for the whole situation. The conclusion was incredible, but it fitted."

Shannon nodded vigorously, indicating that this answer had confirmed what he had already suspected.

"Yes, it had to be the animals," he said. "That's what I thought. Until you established that the ancestors of the Lunarians had been shipped from Earth to Minerva by the Ganymeans, you had no way of connecting the Lunarians with Minerva. Right?"

"Almost, but not quite," Hunt replied. "We'd already managed to connect the Lunarians with Minerva —in other words we knew they'd been involved with the planet somehow—but we couldn't account for how they could have *evolved* there. You're right, though, in saying that the animals that the Ganymeans shipped there long before solved that one in the end. But first we had to connect the Ganymeans with Minerva. At first, you see, all we knew was that one of their ships conked out on Ganymede. No way of knowing where it came from."

"Of course. That's right. There wouldn't have been anything to indicate that the Ganymeans had anything to do with Minerva, would there? So what finally pointed you in the right direction?"

"Another stroke of luck, I must confess," Danchekker said. "Some perfectly preserved fish were found among the food stocks in the remains of a devastated Lunarian base on Luna. We succeeded in proving that the fish were native to Minerva and had been brought to Luna by the Lunarians. Furthermore, the fish were shown to be anatomically related to Ganymean skeletons. This, of course, implied that the Ganymeans too must have evolved from the same evolutionary line as the fish. Since the fish were from Minerva, the Ganymeans also had to be from Minerva."

"So that was where the ship must have come from," Hunt pointed out.

"And where the animals must have come from," Danchekker added.

"And the only way they could have got there is if the Ganymeans took them there," Hunt finished.

Shannon reflected on these propositions for a while. "Yes . . . I see," he said finally. "It all makes sense. And the rest everybody knows. Two isolated populations of terrestrial animals resulted—the one that had always existed on Earth, and the one established on Minerva by the Ganymeans, which included advanced primates. During the twenty-five million years that followed, the Lunarians evolved from them, on Minerva, and that's how they came to be human in form." Shannon stubbed his cigar, then placed his hands flat on the table and looked up at the two scientists. "And the Ganymeans," he said. "What happened to them? They vanished completely twenty-five million years back. Are you people anywhere near answering that one yet? How about leaking a little bit of information in advance? I'm interested."

Danchekker made an empty-handed gesture.

"Believe me, I would like nothing better than to be able to comply. But honestly, we haven't made any great strides in that direction yet. What you say is correct; not only the Ganymeans, but also all the land-dwelling forms of life native to Minerva died out or disappeared in a very short space of time, relatively speaking, at about that time. The imported terrestrial species flourished in their place and eventually the Lunarians emerged." The professor showed his palms again. "What happened to the Ganymeans and why? That remains a mystery. Oh . . . we have theories, or should I say we can offer possible explanations. The most popular seems to be that an increase in atmospheric toxins, particularly carbon dioxide, proved lethal to the natives but not to the immigrant types. But to be truthful, the evidence is far from conclusive. I was talking to your molecular biologists here on J5 only yesterday; some of their more recent work makes me less confident in that theory than I was two or three months ago."

Shannon looked mildly disappointed but accepted the situation philosophically. Before he could comment further, a white-jacketed steward approached the table and began collecting the empty coffee cups and dusting away the specks of ash and bread crumbs. As they sat back in their chairs to make room, Shannon looked up at the steward.

"Good morning, Henry," he said casually. "Is the world treating you well today?"

"Oh, mustn't grumble, sir. I've worked for worse firms than UNSA in my time," Henry replied cheerfully. Hunt was intrigued to note his East London accent. "A change always does you good; that's what I always say."

"What did you do before, Henry?" Hunt inquired.

"Cabin steward for an airline."

Henry moved away to begin clearing the adjacent table. Shannon caught the eyes of the two scientists and inclined his head in the direction of the steward.

"Amazing man, Henry," he commented, his tone lowered slightly. "Did you get to meet him at all on the way out from Earth?" The other two shook their heads. "*Jupiter Five*'s reigning chess champion."

"Good Lord," Hunt said, following his gaze with a new interest. "Really?"

"Learned to play when he was six," Shannon told them. "He's got a gift for it. He could probably make a lot of money out of it if he chose to take the game seriously, but he says he prefers keeping it as a hobby. The first navigation officer studies up day and night just to take the title away from Henry. Between us though, I think he's going to need an awful lot of luck to do it, and that's supposed to be the one game that luck doesn't come in to. Right?"

"Precisely," Danchekker affirmed. "Extraordinary."

The mission director glanced at the clock on the dining-room wall, then spread his arms along the edge of the table in a gesture of finality.

"Well, gentlemen," he said. "It's been a pleasure meeting you both at last. Thank you for a most interesting conversation. We must make a point of keeping in touch regularly from now on. I have to attend an appointment shortly, but I haven't forgotten that I promised to show you the ship's command center. So, if you're ready, we'll go there now. I'll introduce you to Captain Hayter who's to show you around. Then, I'm afraid, you'll have to excuse me."

Fifteen minutes later, after riding a capsule through one of the ship's communications tubes to reach another section of the vessel, they were standing surrounded on three sides by a bewildering array of consoles, control stations and monitor panels on the bridge; below them stretched the brilliantly lit panorama of *Jupiter Five*'s command center. The clusters of operator stations, banks of gleaming equipment cubicles and tiers of instrument panels were the nerve center from which ultimately all the activities of the mission and all the functions of the ship were controlled. The permanent laser link that handled the communications traffic to Earth; the data channels to the various surface installations and the dispersed fleet of UNSA ships nosing around the Jovian system; the navigation, propulsion and flight-control systems; the heating, cooling, lighting, life-support systems and ancillary computers and machinery, and a thousand and one other processes—all were supervised and coordinated from this stupendous concentration of skills and technology.

Captain Ronald Hayter stood behind the two scientists and waited as they took in the scene below the bridge. The mission was organized and its command hierarchy structured in such a way that operations were performed under the ultimate direction of the Civilian Branch of the Space Arm; supreme authority lay with Shannon. Many functions essential to UNSA operations, such as crewing spaceships and conducting activities safely and effectively in unfamiliar alien environments, called for standards of training and discipline that could only be met by a military-style command structure and organization. The Uniformed Branch of the Space Arm had been formed in response to these needs; also, not entirely fortuitously, it went a long way toward satisfying peacefully the longing for adventure of a significant proportion of the younger generation, to whom the idea of large-scale, regular armed forces belonged to a past that was best forgotten. Hayter was in command of all uniformed ranks present aboard *J5* and reported directly to Shannon.

"It's quiet at the moment compared to what it can be like," Hayter commented at last, stepping forward to stand between them. "As you can see, a number of sections down there aren't manned; that's because lots of things are shut down or just under automatic supervision while we're parked in orbit. This is just a skeleton crew up here too."

"Seems to be some activity over there," Hunt said. He pointed down at a group of consoles where the operators were busily scanning viewscreens, tapping intermittently into keyboards and speaking into microphones and among themselves. "What's going on?"

Hayter followed his finger, then nodded. "We're hooked into a cruiser that's been in orbit over Io for a while now. They've been putting a series of probes in low-altitude orbits over Jupiter itself and the next phase calls for surface landings. The probes are being prepared over Io right now and the operation will be controlled from the ship there. The guys you're looking at are simply monitoring the preparation." The captain indicated another section further over to the right. "That's traffic control . . . keeping tabs on all the ship movements around the various moons and in between. They're always busy."

Danchekker had been peering out over the command center in silence. At last he turned toward Hayter with an expression of undisguised wonder on his face.

"I must say that I am very impressed," he said. "Very impressed indeed. On several occasions during our outward voyage, I'm afraid that I referred to your ship as an infernal contraption; it appears that I am now obliged to eat my words."

"Call it what you like, Professor," Hayter replied with a grin. "But it's probably the safest contraption ever built. All the vital functions that are controlled from here are fully duplicated in an emergency command center located in a completely different part of the ship. If anything wiped out this place we could still get you home okay. If something happened on a large enough scale to knock out both of them— well . . ." he shrugged, "I guess there wouldn't be much of the ship left to get home anyhow."

"Fascinating," Danchekker mused. "But tell me—"

"Excuse me, sir." The watch officer interrupted from his station a few feet behind them. Hayter turned toward him.

"What is it, Lieutenant?"

"I have the radar officer on the screen. Unidentified

object detected by long-range surveillance. Approaching fast."

"Activate the second officer's station and switch it through. I'll take it there."

"Aye aye, sir."

"Excuse me," Hayter muttered. He moved over to the empty seat in front of one of the consoles, sat down and flipped its main screen into life. Hunt and Danchekker took a few paces to bring them a short distance behind him. Over his shoulder they could see the features of the ship's radar officer materialize.

"Something unusual going on, Captain," he said. "Unidentified object closing on Ganymede. Range eighty-two thousand miles; speed fifty miles per second but reducing; bearing two-seven-eight by oh-one-six solar. On a direct-approach course. ETA computed at just over thirty minutes. Strong echoes at quality seven. Reading checked and confirmed."

Hayter stared back at him for a second. "Do we have any ships scheduled in that sector?"

"Negative, sir."

"Any deviations from scheduled flight plans?"

"Negative. All ships checked and accounted for."

"Trajectory profile?"

"Inadequate data. Being monitored."

Hayter thought for a moment. "Stay live and continue reporting." Then he turned to the watch officer: "Call the duty bridge crew to stations. Locate the mission director and alert him to stand by for a call to the bridge."

"Yes, sir."

"Radar." Hayter directed his gaze back at the screen on the panel in front of him. "Slave optical scanners to LRS. Track on UFO bearing and copy onto screen three, B5." Hayter paused for a second, then addressed the watch officer again. "Alert traffic control. All launches deferred until further notice. Arrivals scheduled at J5 within the next sixty minutes are to stand off and await instructions."

"Do you want us to leave?" Hunt asked quietly. Hayter glanced around at him.

"No, that's okay," he said. "Stick around. Maybe you'll see some action."

"What is it?" Danchekker asked.

"I don't know." Hayter's face was serious. "We've never had anything like this before."

Tension rose as the minutes ticked by. The duty crew appeared quickly in ones and twos and took up their positions at the consoles and panels on the bridge. The atmosphere was quiet but charged with suspense as the well-oiled machine readied itself . . . and waited.

The telescopic image resolved by the optical scanners was distinct, but impossible to interpret: circular overall, it appeared to possess four thin protuberances in cruciform, with one pair somewhat long and slightly thicker than the other. It could have been a disk, or a spheroid, or perhaps it was something else seen end-on. There was no way of telling.

Then the first view came in via the laser link to *Jupiter Four,* orbiting Callisto. Because of the relative positions of Ganymede and Callisto, and of the rapidly diminishing range of the intruder, the telescopes on the *Jupiter Four* obtained an oblique view from a position some distance from its projected course, to Ganymede.

The observers aboard *J5* gasped as the picture being transmitted from *J4* appeared on the screen. Vegas, the only ships intended for flight through planetary atmospheres, were the only UNSA vessels in the vicinity that were constructed to a streamlined design; this ship was clearly not a Vega. Those sweeping lines and delicately curved, gracefully balanced fins had not been conceived by any designer of Earth.

Some of the color drained from Hayter's face as he stared incredulously at the screen and the full implications of the sight dawned on him. He swallowed hard, then surveyed the astounded faces surrounding him.

"Man all stations on the command floor," he ordered in a voice approaching a whisper. "Summon the mission director to the bridge immediately."

chapter four

Framed in the large wall display screen on the bridge of *Jupiter Five,* the alien craft hung in a void against a background of stars turning almost imperceptibly. It was almost an hour since the new arrival had slowed down to rest relative to the command ship and had gone into a parallel orbit over Ganymede. The two ships were standing just over five miles apart and every detail of the craft was now easily discernible. There was little to interrupt the sleek contours of its hull and fin surfaces and no identification markings or insignia of any kind. There were, however, several patches of discoloration that might have been the remnants of markings which had been abraded, or perhaps, scorched. In fact the whole appearance of the craft somehow gave the impression of wear and deterioration suffered in the course of a long, hard voyage. Its outer skin was rough and pitted and was from end to end disfigured by indistinct streaks and blotches, as if the whole ship had at some time been exposed to severe heat.

Jupiter Five had been the scene of frenzied activity ever since the first meaningful pictures came in. There had been no indication so far of whether or not the craft carried a crew or, if it did, what the intentions of that crew might be. *Jupiter Five* carried no weapons or defensive equipment of any kind; this was one eventuality the mission planners had not considered seriously.

Every position on the command floor was now manned and throughout the ship every crew member was at his assigned emergency station. All bulkheads had been closed and the main drives brought to a state of standby readiness. Communications with the bases on the surface of Ganymede and from other UNSA ships in the vicinity had ceased, in order to avoid revealing their existence and their locations. Those daughter ships of J5 capable of being made flight-ready within the time available had dispersed into the surrounding volume of space; a few were under remote control from J5, to be used as ramships if necessary. Signals beamed at the alien craft evoked a response, but J5's computers were unable to decode it into anything intelligible. Now there was nothing else to do but wait.

Throughout all the excitement, Hunt and Danchekker had stood virtually dumbstruck. They were the only people present on the bridge who were privileged to enjoy a grandstand view of everything that happened, without the distraction of defined duties to perform. They were, perhaps, the only ones able to reflect deeply on the significance of the events that were unfolding.

After the discoveries of first the Lunarians and then the Ganymeans, the notion that other races besides Man had evolved to an advanced technological level was firmly accepted. But this was something different. Just five miles away from them was not some leftover relic from another age or the hulk of an ancient mishap. There was a functional, working machine that had come from another world. Right at that moment, it was under the control and guidance of some form of intelligence; it had been maneuvered surely and unhesitatingly to its present orbit and it had responded promptly to J5's signals. Whether it contained occupants or not, these events added up to the first-ever interaction between modern Man and an intelligence that was not of his planet. The moment was unique; however long history might continue to unfold, it could never be repeated.

Shannon stood in the center of the bridge gazing up at the main screen. Hayter was standing beside him, running his eye over the data reports and other images being presented on the row of auxiliary screens below it. One of them showed a view of Gordon

Storrel, the deputy mission director, standing by in the emergency command center with his own staff of officers. The outgoing signal to Earth was still operating, carrying complete details of everything that happened.

"Analyzers have just detected a new component," the communications officer called out from his station on one side of the bridge. Then he announced a change in the pattern of signals being picked up from the alien craft. "Tight-beam transmission resembling K-Band radar. PRF twenty-two point three four gigahertz. Unmodulated."

Another minute or so dragged endlessly by. Then, another voice: "New radar contact. Small object has separated from alien ship. Closing on *J5*. Ship maintaining position."

A wave of alarm, felt rather than sensed directly, swept over the observers on the bridge. If the object was a missile there was little that they could do; the nearest ramship was fifty miles away and would require half a minute, even under maximum acceleration, to intercept. Captain Hayter did not have time to juggle with arithmetic.

"Fire *Ram One* and engage," he snapped.

A second later the reply came to confirm. *"Ram One* fired. Locked on target."

Beads of perspiration showed on some of the faces staring at the screens. The main display had not yet resolved the object, but one of the auxiliary screens displayed a plot of the two large vessels and a small but unmistakable blip beginning to close the gap between them.

"Radar reports steady approach speed of ninety feet per second."

"Ram One closing. Impact at twenty-five seconds."

Shannon licked his dry lips as he scanned the data on the screens and digested the flow of reports. Hayter had done the right thing and placed the safety of his ship above all other considerations. What to do now was a problem that lay solely with the mission director.

"Thirty miles. Fifteen seconds to impact."

"Object holding course and speed steady."

"That's no missile," Shannon said in a tone that was

decisive and final. "Captain, call off the interception."

"Abort *Ram One*," Hayter ordered.

"*Ram One* disengaged and turning away."

Long exhalations of breath and sudden relaxing of postures signaled the release of the tensions that had been building up. The Vega streaking in from deep-space made a shallow turn that took it into a pass at twenty miles' distance and vanished once more into the infinite cosmic backdrop.

Hunt turned to Danchekker, talking in a low voice, "You know, Chris, it's a funny thing. . . . I've got an uncle who lives in Africa. He says there are some places where it's customary to greet strangers by intimidating them with screams and shouts and brandishings of spears. It's the accepted way of establishing your status."

"Perhaps they regard that as no more than a sensible precaution," Danchekker said drily.

At last the optical cameras distinguished a bright speck in the middle-distance between *J5* and the alien ship. A zoom-in revealed it to be a smooth, silver disk devoid of any appendages; as before, the view gave no clue of its true shape. It continued its unhurried pace until it was a half-mile from the command ship; there it came to rest and turned itself broadside-on to present a simple, unadorned egg-shaped profile. It was just over thirty feet long and appeared to be of entirely metallic construction. After a few seconds it began showing a bright and slowly flashing white light.

The consensus arrived at in the debate that followed was that the egg was requesting permission to enter the ship. The communication time lag to Earth did not allow immediate consultation with higher authority. After sending a full report Earthward via the laser link, Shannon announced his decision to grant the request.

A reception party was hurriedly organized and dispatched to one of *Jupiter Five*'s docking bays. The docking bay, designed for maintenance work on *J5's* assorted daughter vessels, carried a pair of enormous outer doors which were normally left open, but which could be closed when circumstances dictated that the bay be filled with air. Access from the main body of the ship was gained through a number of smaller ancillary airlocks positioned at intervals along the inner side of the bay. Clad in spacesuits, the reception party emerged onto one of the vast working platforms in the docking bay and set up a beacon adjusted to flash at the same frequency as that still pulsing on the egg.

On the bridge of *Jupiter Five,* an expectant semicircle formed around the screen showing the docking bay. The silver ovoid drifted into the center of the starry carpet separating the gaping shadows of the outer doors. The egg descended slowly, its light now extinguished, then hovered some distance above the platform as if cautiously surveying the situation. A close-up showed that in several places on its surface, circular sections of its skin had risen above the overall outline, forming a series of squat, retractable turrets which rotated slowly, presumably to scan the inside of the bay with cameras and other instruments. The egg then resumed its descent and came gently to rest about ten yards from where the reception party was standing in a tight, apprehensive huddle. Overhead an arc-light came on to bathe it in a pool of white.

"Well, it's down." The voice of Deputy Mission Director Gordon Storrel, who had volunteered to lead the reception party, announced on an audio channel. "Three landing pads have come out from underneath. There's no other sign of life."

"Give it two minutes," Shannon said into his microphone. "Then move forward to the halfway point, slowly. Stop there."

"Roger."

After sixty seconds another light was turned on to illuminate the group of Earthmen; somebody had suggested that to have the party seen as shadowy forms lurking in the gloom could give an undesirably sinister impression. The action produced no response from the egg.

At last Storrel turned to his men. "Okay, time's up. We're moving in."

The screen showed the knot of ungainly, helmeted figures walking slowly forward; at their head was the one bearing Storrel's golden shoulder-flashes, and on either side of him a senior UNSA officer. They halted. Then, a panel in the side of the egg slid aside smoothly to reveal a hatch about eight feet high and at least half that wide. The figures in the spacesuits stiffened visibly and the watchers on the bridge braced themselves, but nothing further happened.

"Maybe they're hung up about protocol or something," Storrel said. "They've come into our den. Could be they're telling us it's our turn."

"Could be," Shannon agreed. In a quieter voice he asked Hayter: "Anything to report from up top?" The captain activated another channel to speak to two UNSA sergeants positioned on a maintenance catwalk high above the platform in the docking bay.

"Come in, Catwalk. What can you see?"

"We've got a fair angle down inside it. The inside's in shadow but we've got an image on the intensifier. Just pieces of equipment and fittings . . . seems crammed pretty full. No movement or signs of life."

"No signs of life visible, Gordon," Shannon relayed to the bay. "It looks as if you can stay there forever or have a look. Good luck. Don't think twice about backing off if anything's even slightly suspicious."

"No chance of that," Storrel told him. "Okay, fellas, you heard. Never say UNSA doesn't live up to its job ads. Miralski and Oberman, come with me; the rest of you, stay put."

Three figures moved forward from the group and paused near a small ramp that had telescoped from the bottom of the hatch. Another screen came to life on the bridge to show the view picked up by a hand-held camera operated by one of the UNSA officers. For a second it held a shot of the yawning hatch and the top of the ramp, and then a back view of Storrel filled the screen.

Storrel's commentary came through on audio. "I'm at the top of the ramp now. There's a drop of about a foot down to the deck inside. There's an inner door on the other side of the entrance compartment and it's open. Looks like an airlock." The TV picture closed in as the camera operator moved up beside Storrel; it confirmed his description and the general impression of cramped and cluttered surroundings that had been gained from the catwalk. A glow of warm, yellowy light penetrated the lock from beyond the inner door.

"I'm going through into the inner compartment. . . ." A pause. "This looks like the control cabin. It has seats for two occupants sitting side by side, facing forward. Could be pilot and copilot stations—all kinds of controls and instruments . . . No sign of anybody, though . . . just one other door, leading aft, closed. The seats are very large, in scale with everything else about the general design. Must be big guys . . . Oberman, come on through and get a shot of it for the folks back home."

The view showed the scene as Storrel had described, then began sweeping slowly around the cabin to record close-ups of the alien equipment. Suddenly Hunt pointed toward the screen.

"Chris!" he exclaimed, catching Danchekker's sleeve. "That long gray panel with the switches on . . . did you notice it? I've seen those same markings before! They were on—"

He abruptly stopped speaking as the camera swung sharply upward and focused on a large display screen that was set directly in front of the egg's two empty seats. Something was happening on it. A second later they were staring speechlessly at the image of three alien beings. Every pair of eyes on the bridge of *Jupiter Five* opened wide in stunned disbelief.

There was not a man present who had not seen that form before—the long, protruding lower face broadening into the elongated skull . . . the massive torsos and the incredible six-fingered hand with two thumbs. . . . Danchekker himself had constructed the first eight-feet-tall, full-scale model of that same form, not long after *Jupiter Four* had sent back details of its finds. Everybody had seen the artist's impressions of what the shapes that had contained those skeletons must have looked like.

The artists had done a fine job . . . as everybody could now see.

The aliens were Ganymeans!

chapter five

The evidence amassed to that time indicated that the
Ganymean presence in the Solar System had ceased
some twenty-five million years in the past. Their home
planet no longer existed, except as an ice ball beyond
Neptune and the debris that constituted the Asteroid
Belt, and had not for fifty thousand years. So how
could Ganymeans appear on the screen in the egg?
The first possibility to flash through Hunt's mind was
that they were looking at an ancient recording
that had been triggered when the egg was entered.
This idea was quickly dispelled. Behind the three
Ganymeans, they could see a large display screen not
unlike the main display on *J5*'s bridge; it held a view
of *Jupiter Five*, seen from the angle at which the large
alien ship was lying. The Ganymeans were out there,
now, inside that ship . . . just five miles away. Then
things began happening inside the egg that left no time
for more philosophic speculation as to the meaning of
it all.

Nobody could be sure what the changes of expression on the alien faces meant, but the general impression was that they were every bit as astonished as
the Earthmen. The Ganymeans began gesticulating,
and at the same time meaningless speech issued from
the audio grille. There was no air inside the egg to
carry sound. Evidently the Ganymeans had been
monitoring the transmissions from the reception party
and were now using the same frequencies and modu-
lation.

The picture of the aliens focused on the middle one
of the trio. Then an alien voice spoke again, pronounc-
ing just two syllables. It said something that sounded

51

like "Gar-ruth." The figure on the screen inclined its head slightly, in a way that unmistakably conveyed a combination of politeness and dignity rarely seen on earth. "Gar-ruth," the alien voice repeated. Then again, "Garuth." A similar process took place to introduce the other two, at which point the view widened out to embrace all three. They remained unmoving, staring from the screen, as if waiting for something.

Catching on quickly, Storrel moved to stand directly in front of the screen. "Stor-rel. Storrel." Then, on impulse, he added: "Good afternoon." He admitted later that it sounded stupid, but claimed that his brain hadn't been thinking too coherently at the time. The view on the egg's screen changed momentarily to show Storrel looking back at himself.

"Storrel," the alien voice stated. The pronunciation was perfect. A number of those watching had believed at the time that it was Storrel himself, who had spoken.

Miralski and Oberman were introduced in turn, an exercise in shuffling and clambering that was not helped by the restricted confines of the cabin. Then a series of pictures was flashed on the screen, to each of which Storrel replied with an English noun: *Ganymean, Earthman, spaceship, star, arm, leg, hand, foot.* That went on for a few minutes. Evidently the Ganymeans were accepting the onus of doing all the learning; it soon became apparent why—whoever was doing the talking showed an ability to absorb and remember information with astonishing speed. He never asked for a repeat of a definition and he never forgot a detail. His mistakes were frequent to begin with but once corrected they never recurred. The voice did not synchronize with the mouths of the three visible Ganymeans; presumably the speaker was one of the others aboard the alien ship who must have been monitoring the proceedings.

A small screen alongside the egg's main display, suddenly presented a diagram: a small circle adorned with a wreath of radial spikes, and around it a set of nine concentric circles.

"What the hell's this?" Storrel's voice murmured.

Shannon's brow creased into a frown. He looked inquiringly at the faces around him.

"Solar System," Hunt suggested. Shannon passed the information on to Storrel, who advised the Ganymean. The picture switched to that of just an empty circle.

"Who is this?" the Ganymean voice asked.

"Correction," Storrel said, employing the convention that had already been adopted. *"What* is this?"

"Where 'who'? Where 'what'?"

" 'Who' for Ganymeans and Earthmen."

"Ganymeans and Earthmen—collective?"

"People."

"Ganymeans and Earthmen people?"

"Ganymeans and Earthmen *are* people."

"Ganymeans and Earthmen are people."

"Correct."

" 'What' for not-people?"

"Correct."

"Not-people—general?"

"Things."

" 'Who' for people; 'what' for things?"

"Correct."

"What is this?"

"A circle."

A dot then appeared in the middle of the circle.

"What is this?" the voice inquired.

"The center."

" 'The' for one; 'a' for many?"

" 'The' *when* one; 'a' *when* many."

The diagram of the Solar System reappeared as before, but with the symbol at the center flashing on and off.

"What is this?"

"The Sun."

"A star?"

"Correct."

Storrel proceeded to name the planets as their respective symbols were flashed in turn. The dialogue was still slow and clumsy but it was improving. During the exchange that followed, the Ganymeans managed to convey their bewilderment at the absence of any planet between Mars and Jupiter, a task that proved to be not too difficult since the Earthmen had been expecting it. It took a long time to get the message across that Minerva had been destroyed, and that all that remained of it was some rubble and Pluto, the latter already named and the source, understandably, of further mystery to the aliens.

When, after repeated questioning and double-checking, the Ganymeans at last accepted that they had not misunderstood, their mood became very quiet and subdued. Despite the fact that none of the gestures and facial expressions were familiar to them, the Earthmen watching were overcome by the sense of utter despair and infinite sadness apparent on the alien ship. They could feel the anguish that was written into every movement of those long, now somehow sorrowful, Ganymean faces, as if their very bones were being touched by a wail that came from the beginning of time.

It took a while for the aliens to become communicative again. The Earthmen, noting that the Ganymean expectations had been based on a knowledge of the Solar System that belonged to the distant past, concluded that they must after all, as had been suspected for some time, have migrated to another star. Very probably then, their sudden reappearance represented a sentimental journey to the place where their kind had originated millions of years before and which none of them had ever seen except, perhaps, as carefully preserved records that had been handed down for longer than could be remembered. Small wonder they were dismayed at what they had come so far to find.

But when the Earthmen introduced the notion that the Ganymeans had journeyed from another star, and sought an indication of its position, they were greeted with what appeared to be a firm denial. The aliens seemed to be trying to tell them that their journey had begun long ago from Minerva itself, which of course was ridiculous. By this time, however, Storrel had got himself into a hopeless grammatical tangle and the whole subject was dismissed as the result of a short-term communications problem. No doubt it would be resolved later, when the linguistic skills of the interpreter had improved.

The Ganymean interpreter had spotted the implied connection between "Earth" and "Earthmen," and returned to the subject to obtain confirmation that the beings he was talking to had indeed come from the third planet from the Sun. The Ganymeans visible on the screen appeared very agitated when informed that this was correct, and they went off into a lengthy exchange of remarks among themselves which were not audible on radio. Why that revelation should cause such a reaction was not explained. The question was not asked.

The aliens concluded by indicating that they had been voyaging for a great length of time and had endured much illness and many deaths among their numbers. They were short of supplies, their equipment was in poor condition with much of it unserviceable, and they were all suffering from total physical, mental, emotional and spiritual exhaustion. They gave the impression that only the thought of returning to their home had given them the will to carry on against impossible difficulties; now that hope had been shattered, they were at their end.

Leaving Storrel to continue talking to the aliens, Shannon moved away from the screen and beckoned some of the others, including the two scientists, to gather round for a short, impromptu conference.

"I'm going to send a party across to their ship," he informed them in a lowered voice. "They need help over there and I guess we're the only ones around here that can give it. I'll recall Storrel from the bay and have him lead it; he seems to be getting along fine with them." Then he glanced at Hayter. "Captain, make ready a bus for immediate flight. Detail ten men to go with Storrel, including at least three officers. I'd like everybody in the party to be assembled for a briefing in the lock antechamber to whichever bus can leave soonest, let's say . . . thirty minutes from now. Everyone to be fully supplied, of course."

"Right away," Hayter acknowledged.

"Any other points from anybody?" Shannon asked the assembly.

"Do you want sidearms issued," one of the officers inquired.

"No. Anything else?"

"Just one thing." The speaker was Hunt. "A request. I'd like to go too." Shannon looked at him and hesitated, as if the question had taken him by surprise. "I was sent here specifically to investigate the Ganymeans. That's my official assignment. What better way could there be of helping me do it?"

"Well, I really don't know." Shannon screwed up his face and scratched the back of his head as he sought for possible objections. "There's no reason why not, I suppose. Yeah—I guess that'd be okay." He turned to Danchekker. "How about you, Professor?"

Danchekker held up his hands in protest. "You are most kind to offer, but thank you, no. I'm afraid I've already had quite enough excitement for one day. And besides that, it has taken me more than a year to feel safe inside *this* contraption. What an alien one must be like, I dread to think."

Hayter grinned and shook his head, but said nothing.

"Fine then." Shannon cast his gaze around one more time to invite further comments. "That's it. Let's get back to our man out front." He walked back to the screen and drew toward him the microphone that connected him with Storrel. "How's it going down there, Gordon?"

"Okay. I'm teaching them to count."

"Good. But get one of the others to take over, would you? We're sending you out on a little trip. Captain Hayter will provide the details in a second. You're going to be an ambassador for Earth."

"What do they pay one of those?"

"Give us time, Gordon. We're still working on the matter." Shannon smiled. It was the first time he had felt relaxed for what seemed like a very long while.

chapter six

The bus—a small personnel carrier normally used for ferrying passengers between satellites or orbiting spacecraft—was drawing near to the Ganymean ship. From where he was sitting, squeezed between the bulky shapes of two other spacesuited figures on one of the benches that ran along the sides of the cabin, Hunt could see the ship closing in toward them on the small viewscreen set into the end wall.

From close range, the impression of age and wear was even more vivid than it had been previously. The patterns of discoloration covering the ship from nose to tail, not fully resolved from *J5* even under quite high magnification, were now distinct and in places suggested camouflage patterns reminiscent of movies. The outer skin was peppered irregularly with round holes of various sizes, none of them very large, each of which was surrounded by a raised rim of rounded grayish metal and looked like a miniature Lunar crater; it was as if the ship had been bombarded by thousands of tiny particles moving at enormous speed—sufficient to puncture the skin and dissipate enough energy to melt the surrounding material. Either the ship had traveled an enormous distance, Hunt told himself, or there were conditions outside the Solar System that UNSA had yet to encounter.

A rectangular aperture, easily large enough to admit the bus, had opened in the side of the *Shapieron,* as they now knew the Ganymean ship to be called. A soft orange glow illuminated the inside and a white beacon flashed near the center of one of the longer sides.

As the bus turned gently to home in on it, the pi-

lot's voice came over the intercom. "Hold on to your
seats back there. We're going in without any docking
radar so it's gonna have to be a purely visual approach. Leave all helmets in their racks until after
touchdown."

With its maneuvering jets nudging delicately, the
bus inched its way through the opening. Inside the
bay a bulbous craft with a blue-black sheen was
secured against the inner bulkhead, taking up most of
the available space. Two large and sturdy-looking
platforms, constructed perpendicular to the main axis
of the ship, projected into the volume that remained;
a pair of silver eggs lay side by side on one of them
but the other was clear except for a beacon that had
been positioned well over to one side to allow ample
unobstructed landing space. The bus lined itself up,
moved in to hover ten feet or so above the platform,
eased itself gingerly downward and came to rest.

Hunt knew immediately that there was something
strange about the situation but it took him a few seconds to realize just what it was. There were puzzled
expressions on a couple of the faces around him too.

The seat was pressing up against him. He was experiencing an approximately normal weight, but he had
seen no evidence of any mechanism whereby such an
effect could have been achieved. *Jupiter Five* had sections that simulated normal gravity by means of con-
tinual rotation, although some parts of the ship were
designated zero-*G* areas for special purposes. Instruments that needed to be trained on fixed objects, for
example the camera that had been holding the *Shapieron* for the previous few hours, were mounted on
projecting booms which could be counterrotated to
compensate—similar in principle to ground-based as-
tronomic telescopes. But the view of the Ganymean
ship presented on the screens back at *J5* had given no
suggestion that the vessel, or any part of it, was rotat-
ing. Furthermore, as the bus had positioned itself for
its final approach into the landing bay, thus maintaining a fixed position relative to the door, the background
stars had been stationary; this meant that the pilot had
not been obliged to synchronize his approach run with

any rotational motion of his target. Thus, the sensation of weight could only mean that the Ganymeans were employing some revolutionary technology to produce an artificial gravity effect. Intriguing.

The pilot spoke again to confirm this conclusion.

"Well, I guess I'm having one of my lucky days. We made it." The slow Southern drawl was a godsend. "Some of you people have probably noticed the gravity. Don't ask me how they do it but it sure ain't centrifugal. The outer hatch has closed and we're reading a pressure buildup outside, so it looks like they're turning on the air or whatever they use. I'll tell you if you need helmets or not when we've done some tests. Won't take more'n a minute. We still have contact with J5 here. Guess our friends are picking up our transmissions and relaying them on. J5 says the emergency status has been relaxed and communications have been resumed with other locations. Message from J4 reads: *Tell 'em we waved as they went past.*"

The air was breathable—almost normal. Hunt had expected as much; the ship's atmosphere would probably resemble that of Minerva, and terrestrial life had flourished there. The figures in the cabin stayed outwardly calm, but here and there fidgeting and last-minute fiddling with pieces of equipment betrayed the rising air of impatience and expectancy.

The honor of placing the first human foot on an alien spacecraft was to be Storrel's. He rose from his seat near the rear of the cabin and waited for the inner door of the lock to swing aside; then he moved through into the chamber and peered through the transparent port of the outer door.

After a short wait he reported his findings to the rest of the party. "A door is opening in the wall at the edge of the platform we're on. There are guys standing inside it—the big guys. They're coming out . . . one, two, three . . . five of them. Now they're coming across . . ." Heads in the cabin turned instinctively toward the wall screen, but it was showing another part of the structure.

"Can't get a scanner on them," the pilot said, as if reading their thoughts. "It's a blind spot. You're in command now, sir." Storrel continued looking out of the port but said nothing further for a while. Then he turned back to face the cabin and took a deep breath.

"Okay, this is it. No change from plan; play it as briefed. Open her up, pilot."

The outer door of the bus slid into its recess and a short metal stairway unfolded onto the platform. Storrel moved forward to stand framed in the entrance for a second, then disappeared slowly outside. The UNSA officer who was to be second, already waiting at the inner door, followed him while, farther back in the cabin, Hunt took his place in the slowly shuffling line.

Hunt's impression as he emerged was one of a vastness of space that had not been apparent from inside the bus; it was like walking suddenly out of a side chapel and into the nave of a cathedral. Not that he found himself surrounded by a large unused area—this was, after all, a spacecraft—but beyond the tail assembly of the *Shapieron*'s daughter ship, now seen as a sweeping, metallic, geometrical sculpture above their heads, the perspective lines of the docking bay's interior converged in the distance to add true proportion to the astronautic wonder in which they were now standing.

But these were just sensations that flitted across the background of Hunt's perceptions. Before him, history was being made: the first face-to-face meeting between Man and an intelligent, alien species was taking place. Storrel and the two officers were standing slightly in front of the rest of the party, who had formed into a single rank; just a few feet away, facing Storrel, stood what appeared to be the leader of the Ganymean reception committee and, behind him, his four companions.

Their skins were light gray and appeared somewhat coarse compared to that of humans. All five displayed dense hair covering their heads and hanging to their shoulders though there was no hint of any facial growth. On three of them, including the leader, the hair was jet black; one of the others had gray, almost white, hair while the fifth's was a very dark coppery hue, enhancing the subtle reddish tint of his complexion.

Their clothes were a mixture of colors and shared nothing in common except a basic style, which was that of a simple, loose-fitting, shirtlike garment worn with plain trousers gathered into some kind of band at the ankle; there was certainly no suggestion of any sort of uniform. All were wearing glossy, thick-soled boots, again in various colors, and some had ornate belts around their waists. In addition, each sported a thin, gold headband supporting what looked like a disk-shaped jewel in the center of his forehead and wore a flat, silver box, at a distance not unlike a cigarette case, on a metallic wrist bracelet. There was nothing to distinguish the leader visually.

For a few momentous seconds the two groups faced each other in silence. In the doorway behind the Earthmen, the copilot of the bus was recording the scene for posterity, using a hand camera. Then the Ganymean leader moved forward a pace and made the same head-inclining gesture they had seen earlier on the screen in *Jupiter Five*. Wary of anything that might unwittingly give offense, Storrel replied with a crisp, regulation UNSA salute. To the delight of the Earthmen, all five Ganymeans promptly copied him, though with a trace of uncertainty and an appalling lack of timing that would have brought tears to the eyes of a UNSA drill sergeant.

Slowly and haltingly, the Ganymean leader spoke. "I am Mel-thur. Good af-ter-noon."

That simple statement would go down among history's immortal moments. Later it became a standard joke, shared equally by Earthmen and Ganymeans alike. The voice was deep and gravelly, nothing like that of the interpreter who had spoken previously via the egg; in the latter case, the diction, and even the accent, had been flawless. Evidently this was not the interpreter; it made the fact that he had taken the trouble to offer an opening greeting in the native tongue of his guests an even nicer gesture.

Melthur went on to deliver a brief recitation in his own language while the visitors listened respectfully.

Then it was Storrel's turn. All the way over from J5 he had been anticipating and dreading this moment, wishing that there was something in the UNSA training manuals to cover a situation like this. After all, weren't mission planners paid to exhibit a modicum of foresight? He straightened up and delivered the short speech that he had mentally prepared, hoping that the historians of years to come would be lenient in their judgment and appreciative of the circumstances.

"Fellow travelers and neighbors, greetings from the people of Planet Earth. We come in peace and in a spirit of friendship to all beings. May this meeting prove to be the beginning of a long and lasting coexistence between our races, and from it may there grow a mutual understanding and an accord that will benefit both our kinds. Henceforth let Ganymeans and Earthmen together continue to expand that common frontier of knowledge that has brought them both away from their worlds and into this universal realm that belongs to all worlds."

The Ganymeans in their turn showed respect by remaining motionless and silent for a few seconds after Storrel had finished. Then, the formalities over, the leader beckoned to them to follow and turned back toward the door through which he and his companions had appeared. Two of the other Ganymeans followed him to lead the party of Earthmen, and the remaining pair fell in behind.

They proceeded along a broad, white-walled corridor onto which many doors opened from both sides. Every place was brilliantly lit by a uniform diffuse glow that seemed to emanate from every part of the ceiling and from many of the panels that made up the walls. The floor was soft and yielding beneath their feet and made no sound. The air was cold.

Along the way, groups and small lines of Ganymeans had gathered to watch the procession. Most of them were as tall as those who had met the bus, but several were much smaller and looked more delicate in build and complexion; they appeared to be children at various stages of growth. The variations in clothing on the bystanders was even more pronounced than before, but everyone was wearing the same type of jeweled headband and wrist unit. Hunt began to suspect that these served more than purely decorative purposes. Many of the clothes showed signs of wear and general deterioration, contributing to the overall atmosphere of weariness and demoralization that he sensed on every side. The walls and doors bore scars that had been left by countless scrapings of passing objects; away from the walls the floors had been worn thin by feet that had passed to and fro for longer than he could imagine; and the sagging postures of some of the figures, several of them being supported by companions, told their own story.

The corridor was quite short and brought them to a second, slightly wider one that ran transversely; this second corridor curved away from them to left and right and seemed to be part of a continuous circular thoroughfare that encompassed the core of the vessel. Immediately in front of them, in the curving wall that formed the outer shell of the core, was a large open door. The Ganymeans ushered them through into the bare circular room beyond—it was about twenty feet in diameter—and the door slid silently shut. A vague whine of unseen machinery issued from an unidentifiable source and meaningless symbols flashed on and off on a panel set into the wall near the door. Hunt guessed after a few seconds that they were inside a large elevator that moved along a shaft contained within the ship's core. There had been no sensation of acceleration whatsoever—another example, perhaps, of the Ganymean mastery of gravitic engineering.

They emerged from the elevator and crossed another circular corridor to pass through what seemed to be a control or instrumentation room; on both sides of the central throughway the walls were lined with console stations, indicator panels and displays, and Ganymeans were seated at a number of the positions. The general lines of the room were cleaner and less cluttered than those aboard UNSA vessels. The instruments and equipment seemed to be integrated into the decor rather than added afterward. At least as much thought had been devoted to aesthetics as to function.

The color scheme, a subtle balance of yellows, oranges and greens, formed a single, organic, curviform design that flowed from end to end of the room, making it as much an object for appreciative contemplation as an operational part of the *Shapieron*. By comparison the command center of *Jupiter Five* seemed stark and utilitarian.

The door at the far end brought them to their destination. It was a large trapezoidal room, presumably as a consequence of its position between the core of the ship and the outer hull, predominantly white and gray. The wall at the wide end was dominated by an enormous display screen, below which stood a row of crew stations and instrument facia, all encumbered by noticeably fewer switches and buttons than would be normal for equivalent equipment on J5. Some desklike working surfaces and a number of unidentifiable devices occupied the central area of the room and the narrow end was raised to form a dais that carried three large, unoccupied chairs, standing behind a long console and facing the main display screen. This was almost certainly the place from which the captain and his lieutenants supervised operation of the ship.

Four Ganymeans were waiting in the large open area before the dais. The Earthmen drew up facing them and the ritual exchange of short speeches was repeated. As soon as the formalities had been concluded the Ganymean spokesman, Garuth as he had just identified himself, directed their attention to a collection of items arrayed along the top of one of the tables. For each of the Earthmen present there was a headband and wrist unit identical to those worn by all the Ganymeans, plus some smaller articles. One of the UNSA officers reached hesitantly toward them and then, reassured by gestures from the aliens that were obviously meant to convey encouragement, picked a headband to examine it more closely. One by one the others followed suit.

Hunt selected one and picked it up, only to find that it was practically weightless. What had seemed from a distance to be a jewel in the middle of the piece turned out in fact to be a flat, shiny disk of silvery metal about the size of a quarter, with a tiny dome of what appeared to be black glass mounted in the center. The band itself was far too short to encircle a Ganymean head and the metal showed signs of having been broken and crudely repaired—clearly the result of the device having been hastily modified to human proportions.

A huge, gray six-fingered hand with broad nails as well as flexible horn pads on the knuckles moved into Hunt's field of vision and gently took hold of the headband. He looked up and found himself staring into the eyes of one of the alien giants, who was now standing right beside him. The eyes were dark blue and contained enormous, circular pupils; Hunt could have sworn that they were twinkling with good-natured laughter. Before he had time to collect his reeling thoughts, the headband had been secured snugly in place. The Ganymean then picked up one of the smaller items, a rubbery disk attached to a padded clip, and attached it with a simple movement to the lobe of Hunt's right ear; it fitted quite comfortably in such a way that the disk rested lightly against the bony protrusion above the side of his neck. A similar device was fastened to the neck of his shirt collar, just visible inside the rim of the helmet-seating of his spacesuit. The gadget's disk in contact with his throat. Hunt realized that the aliens were mingling freely and that all his colleagues were being assisted in a similar manner. Before he could observe any more, his own giant held up the last item, the wrist unit, and demonstrated the ingenious adjustment method of the bracelet a few times before securing it on Hunt's suit forearm. The face of the unit was taken up almost entirely by what had to be a miniature display screen, although nothing was visible on it at that moment. The giant pointed to one of the tiny buttons set in a row beneath the screen and made a series of head movements and facial expressions that didn't mean very much. Then he turned away to an unattended Earthman who was having trouble fitting his earpiece into place.

Hunt looked around him. The unoccupied Ganymeans gathered round the room to witness these proceedings seemed to be waiting patiently for something to happen. Above them, framed in panorama on the main viewing screen, was the image of *Jupiter Five*, still riding five miles off. The sudden sight of something familiar and reassuring among all these strange surroundings at once swept away the dreamlike paralysis that had slowly been creeping over him. He looked down at the wrist unit again, shrugged, and touched the button that the giant had indicated.

"I am ZORAC. Good afternoon."

Hunt looked up again and turned to see who had spoken, but nobody was even looking at him. A puzzled frown formed on his face.

"You are who?" He heard the same voice again. Hunt looked from side to side and behind him again, completely bewildered. He noticed that one or two of the other Earthmen were acting in the same strange manner, and that a couple of them had started to mumble, apparently to themselves. And then he realized that the voice was coming from the earpiece he was wearing. It was the voice of the Ganymean interpreter that he had first heard on *J5*. In the same split second it dawned on him that the throat-piece was a microphone. Feeling, for a moment, slightly self-conscious at the thought of appearing as ridiculous as his colleagues, he replied, "Hunt."

"Earthmen talk to me. I talk to Ganymeans. I translate."

Hunt was taken completely by surprise. He had not expected to have to play so active a role in whatever developed, having seen himself more as an observer; now he was being invited to participate directly in the dialogue. For a moment he was nonplused because no intelligent continuation suggested itself.

Then, not wishing to give an impression of rudeness, he asked: "Where are you?"

"Different parts in different places in the *Shapieron*. I am not a Ganymean. I am a machine. I believe the Earth word is *computer* . . ." A short pause followed, then: "Yes. I was correct. I am a computer."

"How did you manage to check that out so fast?" Hunt queried.

"I am sorry. I do not understand that question yet. Can you say it more simply please?"

Hunt thought for a second.

"You did not understand the word computer the first time. You did understand it the second time. How did you know?"

"I asked the Earthman who is talking to me in the egg inside *Jupiter Five*."

Hunt marveled as he realized that ZORAC was no mere computer, but a supercomputer. It was capable of conducting and learning from independent and simultaneous conversations. That went a long way toward explaining the phenomenal progress it was making in its comprehension of English and accounted for its ability to memorize every detail of information without need for repetition. Hunt had seen some of Earth's most advanced language-translation machines in action on several occasions; compared to them ZORAC was staggering.

For the next few minutes the Ganymeans remained silent spectators while the Earthmen familiarized themselves with ZORAC and with the facilities that they now enjoyed for communicating both with it and through it. The headbands were miniature TV cameras through which the scene perceived by a wearer could be transmitted directly into the machine. The view from any headband could be presented on any wrist screen, as could any other item of information capable of graphic representation and available from the ship's computer complex. ZORAC—a collective name for this complex—provided not only a versatile mechanism enabling individuals to access and interact with the ship's many facilities, but also an extremely sophisticated means for individuals to communicate among themselves. And all this was merely a sideline; ZORAC's prime function was that of supervising and controlling just about everything in the *Shapieron*. That was why the instrument panels and consoles were so simple and straightforward in general appearance; most operations were carried out by means of vocal commands to ZORAC.

Once ZORAC had introduced itself to all the newcomers, the serious business of the day resumed once more with Storrel conducting a more productive dialogue with Garuth, the Ganymean mission commander. From the discussion it appeared that the *Shapieron* had indeed come from another star system to which it had gone long before for the purpose of conducting a scientific mission of some complexity. A catastrophe had befallen the expedition and forced them to depart in haste, without time to prepare for a long voyage; the situation was exacerbated by technical problems relating to the ship itself, though their precise nature remained obscure. The voyage had been long and was beset with difficulties, resulting in the predicament that the giants now found themselves facing, and which had already been described to the Earthmen. Garuth concluded by stressing again the poor physical and mental condition of his people, and their need to find somewhere to land their ship in order to recuperate and appraise their situation.

Throughout the proceedings, a running commentary on both sides of the conversation was radioed back to the crew remaining on the bus, whose Ganymean relay gave Shannon and the others on the bridge of the *J5* a minute-by-minute report of what was happening.

Even before Garuth had finished speaking, Shannon had contacted Ganymede Main Base and instructed the commander there to begin preparations to receive a shipload of unexpected and very weary guests.

chapter seven

"One of the other Earthmen has just instructed me to get lost and switched his unit off," ZORAC said. "I could only do that by taking the *Shapieron* away into space and I'm certain that he didn't intend that. What did he mean?"

Hunt grinned to himself as he allowed his head to sink back into the pillow while he contemplated the ceiling. He had been back on board *Jupiter Five* for several hours and was relaxing in his cabin after a strenuous day while experimenting further with his Ganymean communications kit.

"It's an Earth saying," he replied. "It doesn't mean what the words mean literally. It's what people sometimes say when they're not interested in listening to somebody. Probably he was tired and needed to sleep. But don't you say it when you talk to Earthmen. It conveys irritation and is a little insulting."

"I see. Okay. Is there a word or phrase for a saying that doesn't mean what it says literally?"

Hunt sighed and rubbed the bridge of his nose wearily. Suddenly he had nothing but admiration for the patience of schoolteachers.

"I suppose we'd call it a figure of speech," he said.

"But surely speech is formed from words, not figures, or have I made a mistake somewhere?"

"No, you're right. That's just another saying."

"A figure of speech is a figure of speech then. Right?"

"Yes. ZORAC, I'm getting tired too. Could you save any more questions about English until I'm ready for it again. There are some questions I'd still like to ask you."

"Otherwise you'll instruct me to get lost and switch off?"

"Correct."

"Okay. What are your questions?"

Hunt hoisted his shoulders up against the end of his bunk and clasped his hands behind his head. After a moment's reflection, he was ready. "I'm interested in the star that your ship came from. You said that it had a system of several planets."

"Yes."

"Your ship came from one of those planets?"

"Yes."

"Did all the Ganymean people move from Minerva and go live on that planet a long time ago?"

"No. Only three large ships went and their carried-ships. Also there were three very large machines that propelled themselves like spaceships. The Ganymeans went there to test a scientific idea. They did not go there to live. All came back in the *Shapieron* but many have died."

"When you went to the star, where did you travel from?"

"From Minerva."

"Where were the rest of the Ganymean people—the ones who didn't go with you to the star?"

"They remained on Minerva, naturally. The work to be done at the star needed only a small number of scientific people."

Hunt's incredulity could no longer be contained. The thing that he had been beginning to suspect for some time was really true.

"How long ago was it when you left the star?" he asked, his voice catching slightly as he formed the words.

"Approximately twenty-five million Earth years ago," ZORAC informed him.

For a long time Hunt said nothing. He just lay there, his mind struggling to comprehend the enormity of what he had learned. Just a few hours before he had been standing face to face with beings who had been alive long before the species called *Homo sapiens* had ever begun to emerge. And they were still alive now, and had been through the unimaginable epochs between. The very thought of it was stupefying.

He did not imagine for one moment that this could represent anything like a normal Ganymean life span and he guessed it to be the result of relativistic time-dilation. But to produce an effect of such magnitude they must have sustained a phenomenal velocity for an incredible length of time. What could possibly have induced the Ganymeans to journey the vast distance that this implied? And, equally strange, why should they willingly inflict upon themselves what they must have known would be a permanent forfeiture of their world, their way of life and all the things that were familiar to them? What significance could their expedition have had, since nothing they could have achieved at their destination could possibly have affected their civilization in any way whatsoever—not with that discrepancy in time scales? But hadn't Garuth said something about everything not having gone according to plan?

Having sorted his thoughts into something resembling order once more, Hunt had another question. "How far from the sun was this star?"

"The distance that light would travel in nine point three Earth years," ZORAC answered.

The situation was getting crazy. Allowing for the speed that would have been necessary to produce the time-dilation, such a journey should have taken hardly any time at all . . . astronomically speaking.

"Did the Ganymeans know that they would return after twenty-five million years?" Hunt asked, determined to get to the bottom of it.

"When they left the star, they knew. But when they left Minerva to go to the star, they did not know. They did not have a reason to believe that the journey from the star would be longer than the journey to the star."

"How long did it take them to get there?"

"Measured from the sun, twelve point one years."

"And the journey back again took twenty-five million?"

"Yes. They could not avoid traveling very fast. I

believe that the results of this are familiar to you. They orbited the sun far away many times."

Hunt replied with the obvious question. "Why didn't they just slow down?"

"They could not."

"Why?"

ZORAC seemed to hesitate for a fraction of a second.

"The electrical machines could not be operated. The points-that-destroy-all-things and move in circles could not be stopped. The space-and-time-joining blendings could not be unbent."

"I don't understand that," Hunt said, frowning.

"I can't be more clear without asking more questions about English," ZORAC warned him.

"Leave it for now." Hunt remembered the stir caused by speculations about the propulsion system of the Ganymean ship beneath Pithead, which dated from about the same period as the *Shapieron*. Although the UNSA scientists and engineers could not be certain, many of them suspected that motion had been produced not by reactive thrust, but by an artificially induced zone of localized space–time distortion into which the vessel "fell" continuously. Hunt felt that such a principle could allow the kind of sustained acceleration needed for the *Shapieron* to attain the speeds implied by ZORAC's account. No doubt other scientists were putting similar questions to ZORAC; he would discuss the matter with them tomorrow, he decided, and not press the matter further for the time being.

"Do you remember that time," he asked casually. "Twenty-five million years ago, when your ship left Minerva?"

"Twenty-five million years by Earth time," ZORAC pointed out. "It has been less than twenty years by *Shapieron* time. Yes. I remember all things."

"What kind of world did you leave?"

"I don't fully understand. What kind of *kind* do you mean?"

"Well, for example, what was the place on Minerva like that you departed from? Was the land flat? Was there water? Were there structures that the Ganymean people had built? Can you describe a picture of it?"

"I can show a picture," ZORAC offered. "Please observe the screen."

Intrigued, Hunt reached out to pick up the wrist unit from where he had placed it on the top of the bedside locker. As he turned it over in his hand the screen came to life with a scene that immediately drew an involuntary whistle of amazement from his lips. He was looking down on the *Shapieron,* or at least on a vessel that was indistinguishable from it, but this was not the scarred and pitted hulk that he had seen from the bus a few hours before; it was a clean, gleaming, majestic tower of flawless mirror-silver, standing proudly on its tail in a vast open space that was occupied by strange constructions—buildings, cylinders, tubular structures, domes, masts and curves, all interconnected and fused into a single, contiguous synthetic landscape. Two other ships were standing there on either side of the first, both just as grand, but somewhat smaller.

The air above the spaceport—for that was what the picture suggested—was alive with all manner of flying vehicles ranging from the very large to the very small, the majority of which moved in well-defined lanes like processions of disciplined skywalking ants.

Behind it all, soaring up for what must have been miles to dominate the skyline, was the city. It was nothing like any city that Hunt had ever seen, but there was nothing else that it could have been. Tier upon tier, level after level, the skyscrapers, terraces, sweeping ramps, and flying bridges clung together in a fantastic composite pattern that seemed to leap into the sky in a series of joyous bounds that defied gravity. The whole construction might have been sculpted by some infinitely skillful cosmic artist from a single monolith of gleaming marble, and yet there were parts of it that seemed to float detached like ivory islands in the sky. Only a knowledge that transcended Man's could have conceived such a feat; it had to be yet another instance of a Ganymean science that remained to be stumbled upon by the scientists of Earth.

"That is the *Shapieron* as it was before it left Minerva," ZORAC informed him. "The other two ships that traveled with it are there too. The place behind was called *Gromos*. I don't know what the word is for a place constructed for many Ganymeans to live in."

"A city," Hunt supplied, at the same time feeling an acute inadequacy in the description. "Were the Ganymeans fond of their city?"

"Sorry?"

"Did they like their city? Did they wish very much to be home again?"

"Very much. The Ganymeans were fond of all things on Minerva. They were fond of their home." ZORAC seemed to possess a well-developed ability to sense when further information was needed. "When they left the star, they knew then that their journey home would take a long time. They did not expect all things to be not changed. But they did not expect to find that their home did no longer exist. They are very sad." Hunt had already seen enough to know this. Before he could ask another question, ZORAC spoke up. "Is it okay if I ask questions that are not about English?"

"Yes, all right," Hunt answered. "What do you want to know?"

"The Ganymeans are very unhappy. They believe that the Earthmen destroyed Minerva. Is this true, and if it is, why did they destroy it?"

"No!" Hunt reacted instinctively, with a start. "No. That's not true. Minerva was destroyed fifty thousand years ago. There were no men on Earth then. We came later."

"Did the Lunarians destroy Minerva then?" ZORAC asked. Evidently it had broached this same subject with others on *Jupiter Five* already.

"Yes. How much do you know about them?"

"Twenty-five million years ago, the Ganymeans took kinds of Earth life from Earth to Minerva. In a short time afterward, the Ganymeans and all kinds of life that were of Minerva and lived on land died.

The life kinds from Earth did not die. The Lunarians grew from them and looked like Earthmen now. Other scientific people on *Jupiter Five* have told me this. This is all I know."

This told Hunt something that he hadn't realized before and hadn't really thought about. Prior to the last few hours, it seemed, ZORAC had been completely ignorant of the Ganymeans having imported large numbers of terrestrial animal species to their own planet. Just to be sure, he had one other question. "The Ganymeans had not brought any Earth life to Minerva before you left to go to the star?"

"No."

"Do you know if they intended to?"

"If they did, I was never told."

"Do you know of any reason why they should wish to?"

"No."

"So whatever the problem was, it must have cropped up later."

"Sorry?"

"The reason must have happened after you left Minerva."

"I think the phrase is 'I suppose so.' I can compute no alternative."

Hunt realized with growing excitement that the mystery of what had happened to the Ganymean civilization was one that posed a challenge to both races. Surely, he told himself, their combined knowledge would prove capable of producing the answers. He decided it was time to complete the story of the Lunarians for ZORAC's benefit—the story that had uncovered the most astounding revelations of recent years, even, perhaps, of all time. This story involved a change in our understanding of the structure of the Solar System and required a complete rewriting of the very origins of Mankind.

"Yes, you are right," Hunt said, after a while. "The Lunarians grew—we would say 'evolved'—from the forms of Earth life that were left on Minerva after the Ganymeans and other Minervan kinds died out. It took twenty-five million years for them to evolve. By fifty thousand years ago, they had become an advanced race; they built spaceships, machines and cities. Has anybody told you what happened after that?"

"No. But I was intending to ask."

"Is it true that Minerva possessed a moon?"

"A satellite that orbited the planet?"

"Correct."

"Yes."

Hunt nodded to himself in satisfaction. It was as he and the other scientists of Earth had deduced from their investigations of the Lunarian finds.

"And tell me," he asked as a check. "Did Earth possess a moon . . . twenty-five million years ago?"

"No. Earth had no satellite then." Hunt could have been mistaken, but he was sure that ZORAC was learning to convey emotional colorations by the inflection of its voice. He could have sworn that there was surprise in that response.

"Today, Earth has a moon," he said. "It has had a moon for approximately fifty thousand years."

"Since the time when the Lunarians became an advanced race."

"Exactly."

"I see. A connection is clearly implied. Please explain."

"When the Lunarians destroyed Minerva, the planet exploded . . . broke into pieces. The largest piece now orbits the sun as its most distant planet, Pluto. The other pieces, or most of them, still orbit the sun between Mars and Jupiter. I assume you know this, since the Ganymeans were surprised when they found that the Solar System had changed."

"Yes, I know about Pluto and the asteroids," ZORAC confirmed. "I knew that the Solar System had changed and that Minerva was not present. But I did not know about the process by which it had changed."

"Minerva's moon fell toward the Sun. Lunarians were still alive on the moon. It came near to Earth and was captured. It became Earth's moon, and still is now."

"The Lunarians who were alive must have traveled

to Earth," ZORAC interrupted. "During the time that followed, they increased their numbers. Earthmen have evolved from Lunarians. That is why they look the same. I can compute no alternative. Am I right?"

"Yes, you're right, ZORAC." Hunt shook his head in admiration. With hardly any data at all to go by, the machine had unerringly arrived at the same conclusion that had taken the scientists of Earth more than two years to piece together, after some of the most vigorous argument and dissent for many decades. "At least, we believe that that is right. We cannot prove it conclusively."

"Sorry. Conclusively?"

"Finally . . . for certain."

"I see. I reason that the Lunarians must have traveled to Earth in spaceships. They must have taken machines and other things. I suggest that Earthmen should look for these things on the surface of the Earth. This would prove what you believe is true. My conclusion is that you haven't tried, or alternatively you have tried but have not succeeded."

Hunt was flabbergasted. Had ZORAC been around two years earlier the whole puzzle would have been solved in a week.

"Have you been talking to an Earthman called Danchekker?" he asked.

"No. I have not met the name. Why?"

"He is a scientist and reasons the same things as you. We have not yet found any traces of things that the Lunarians might have brought with them. Danchekker predicts that such things will be found one day."

"Did the Earthmen not know where they had come from?" ZORAC inquired.

"Not until very recently. Before that it was believed that they evolved only on Earth."

"The life kinds that they evolved from on Minerva had been taken from Earth by the Ganymeans. The same life kinds were left to live on Earth also.

"The Lunarians who did not die and went to Earth were an advanced race. The Earthmen of now did not know of them until recently. Therefore they had forgotten where they came from. I reason that there must have been very few Lunarians who did not die. They became unadvanced and forgot their knowledge. After fifty thousand years they became advanced again, but they had forgotten the Lunarians. As they found new knowledge, they would see remains of life kinds from many years ago everywhere on Earth. They would see the sameness as their own life kind. They would reason that they evolved on Earth. Recently Earthmen have discovered Lunarians and Ganymeans. Now they have deduced the true events. Otherwise they would not be able to explain why Lunarians looked the same as them."

ZORAC had the whole thing figured out. Admittedly the machine had been able to start out with a number of key items of information that had taken Hunt and his colleagues a long time to uncover, but nevertheless it was a staggering piece of logical analysis.

Hunt was still marveling at the achievement when ZORAC spoke again. "I still do not know *why* the Lunarians destroyed Minerva."

"They didn't intend to," Hunt explained. "There was a war on Minerva. We believe the planet's crust was thin and unstable. The weapons used were very powerful. The planet exploded in the process."

"Sorry. War? Crust? Weapon? Don't follow."

"Oh God . . ." Hunt groaned. He paused to select and light a cigarette from a pack lying on the locker. "The outside of a planet is cold and hard—near the surface. That's its crust."

"Like a skin?"

"Yes, but brittle . . . it breaks into pieces easily."

"Okay."

"When many people fight in large groups, that's war."

"Fight?"

"Oh hell . . . violent action between one group of people and another group. When they organize themselves to kill."

"Kill what?"

"The other group of people."

ZORAC gave one distinct impression of confusion. For a second the machine seemed to be having difficulty in believing its microphone.

"Lunarians organized themselves to kill other Lunarians," it said, slowly and carefully as if anxious not to be misunderstood. "They did this deliberately?" The turn of conversation had caught Hunt somewhat unprepared. He began to feel uneasy and even a little embarrassed, like a child being insistently cross-examined over some transgression that it would sooner forget.

"Yes," was all he could manage.

"Why did they wish to do such a thing?" The emotional inflection was there again, now registering undisguised incredulity.

"They fought because . . . because . . ." Hunt wrestled for something to say. The machine, it seemed, had no comprehension whatsoever of such matters. What way was there to summarize the passions and complexities of millennia of history in a few sentences? "To protect themselves . . . to defend their own group from other groups . . ."

"From other groups who were organized to kill them?"

"Well, the matter is very complicated . . . but yes, you could say that."

"Then logically the same question still applies—why did the other groups wish to do such things?"

"When one group made another group angry about something . . . or when two groups both wanted the same thing, or when one group wanted another group's land, maybe . . . sometimes they would fight to decide." What he was saying didn't seem an adequate explanation, Hunt admitted to himself, but it was the best he could do. A short silence ensued; even ZORAC, it seemed, had to think hard about this one.

"Did all the Lunarians have brain problems?" it asked at last, having evidently deduced what it considered the most probable common factor.

"They were naturally a very violent race, we believe," Hunt replied. "But at the time they lived, they faced the prospect of extinction—all dying out. Minerva was freezing all over fifty thousand years ago. They wanted to go to a warmer planet to live. We think they wanted to go to Earth. But there were many Lunarians, few resources, and little time. The situation made them afraid and angry . . . and they fought."

"They killed each other to prevent them from dying? They destroyed Minerva to protect it from freezing?"

"They didn't intend to do such a thing," Hunt said again.

"What did they intend?"

"I suppose they intended that the group that was left after the war would go to Earth."

"Why couldn't all groups go? The war must have needed resources that would have been used better for other things. All Lunarians could have used their knowledge. They wanted to live but did everything to make certain that they would not. They had brain problems." The tone of ZORAC's final pronouncement was definite.

"All this was not something they had planned deliberately. They were driven by emotions. When men feel strong emotions, they do not always do the most logical things."

"Men . . . Earthmen . . . ? Earthmen feel strong emotions too, that make them fight like the Lunarians did?"

"Sometimes."

"And Earthmen make wars too?"

"There have been many wars on Earth, but there have been none for a long time."

"Do the Earthmen wish to kill the Ganymeans?"

"No! No . . . of course not. There is no reason . . ." Hunt protested violently.

"There can never be a reason," ZORAC stated. "The Lunarians had no reason. The things that you said are not reasons since they do the opposite to what is wanted—so they are not reasonable. The Earthmen must have evolved brain problems from the Lunarians. Very sick."

Danchekker had theorized that the extraordinary

aggressiveness and powers of determination exhibited by Man, compared to other terrestrial species, had originated as a mutation among the anthropoids left on Minerva after the decline of the Ganymeans. It had accounted for the startling rapidity of the emergence and development of the Lunarian civilization, which had attained spaceflight while the most advanced species on Earth were represented only by primitive stone-working cultures. As ZORAC had surmised, this formidable Lunarian trait had indeed been passed on to their terrestrial descendants (although becoming somewhat diluted in the process), and had in turn constituted the most potent factor in the subsequent emergence and rise of the human race. Could that trait after all turn out to be the unique aberration that Danchekker had sometimes speculated?

"Were there never wars on Minerva?" Hunt asked. "Even in the early history of the Ganymean people, did groups never fight?"

"No. There can be no reason. Such ideas would never occur."

"Individuals—did they never fight? Were they never violent?"

"Sometimes a Ganymean would try to harm another Ganymean, but only if he was very sick. Brain problems did occur. Very sad. On most occasions the doctors could fix the problems. Sometimes one with problems would have to be kept away from other Ganymeans and helped. But very few were like that."

Mercifully, ZORAC did not seem disposed to pass moral judgments, but all the same Hunt was beginning to feel distinctly uncomfortable, like a Papuan headhunter facing a missionary.

ZORAC quickly made the situation worse. "If all Lunarians were sick and the doctors were sick too, anything could happen. It then becomes computable that they blew the planet up. If Earthmen are all sick and can make machines and come to Ganymede, they can make a war and blow up planets too. I must warn Garuth of the possibility. He might not want to stick around. Other places would be safer than a Solar System full of sick Earthmen."

"There will be no war," Hunt told ZORAC firmly. "Those things happened a long time ago. Earthmen are different now. We do not fight today. The Ganymeans are safe here—they are our friends."

"I see." The machine sounded unconvinced. "To compute the probability of the truth of that, I must know more about the Earthmen and how they have evolved. Can I ask more questions?"

"Ask them some other time," Hunt said, suddenly feeling weary of it all. He had much to think about and discuss with others before taking the conversation any further. "I think we've talked enough for now. I need some sleep."

"I must get lost then?"

"Yes, I'm afraid so, ZORAC old pal. I'll talk to you tomorrow."

"Very well. In that case, good afternoon."

"You got that wrong. I'm going to bed. It's night now."

"I know. It was a joke."

"Good afternoon," Hunt smiled as he pressed a button on the wrist unit to break the connection. A computer with a sense of humor; now he had seen everything. He carefully arranged the various items that made up the communications kit on top of his locker and settled back to finish his cigarette while he reflected on the astonishing conversation. How ludicrous and tragically comical all their fears and precautions seemed now. The Ganymeans not only had no word for war, they had not the faintest concept of it. He was beginning to feel like something that had lived its whole grubby life beneath a stone that had just been turned over.

He was just about to switch off the light when the chime of the bedside wall panel sounded. Absently he reached out and flipped a switch to accept the call. It was an announcement via the audio channel.

"This is Director Shannon speaking. I just thought you'd all like to know that a message was received from Earth at 2340 hours local. After an all-night emergency meeting at UN Headquarters, the decision to allow the *Shapieron* to land at Ganymede Main Base has been endorsed. The Ganymeans have been informed and preparations are going ahead. That's all. Thank you."

chapter eight

And so, the incredible voyage of twenty-five million years came at last to an end.

Hunt was among the observers in the spacious transparent dome of the Operations Control Tower at Ganymede Main who watched in silence as the huge shape of the *Shapieron* slid slowly down toward the space prepared for it just beyond the edge of the base. It came to rest standing upright on the tips of the four sharply swept fins that formed its tail assembly, with the stern end of the main body of the ship still one hundred feet or more above the ice, dwarfing the platoon of Vegas that stood on one side like a welcoming guard of honor.

The small fleet of vehicles that had been waiting just outside the area at once began crawling forward; the leading three stopped just in front of the nearest supporting fin and disgorged figures clad in standard-issue UNSA spacesuits, while the rest formed up into waiting lines on either side. The figures assembled into straight ranks facing the ship; three stood a short distance ahead of the rest—Commander Lawrence Foster, in charge of Main, his deputy, and one of the several senior officers from *Jupiter Five* who had come down to observe. The diminutive sun was very low in the sky, accentuating the bleakness of the Ganymedian landscape and painting sinister streaks of bottomless shadow across the frozen crags and the shattered cliffs of ice that had survived unchanging from meteorite impacts as old as time itself.

Then, as they watched, the stern section of the *Shapieron* detached itself from the main hull of the vessel and began to move vertically downward. After a few seconds they could see that it was still connected by three steadily lengthening bright silver tubes, the tubes clustered tightly around the central axis of the ship. The stern section touched the ice, and stopped; a number of doors slid open all around it and short access ramps extended downward to connect them to the surface. Watching from the dome, Hunt remembered the elevator shaft through which he and his companions had been conveyed after leaving the bus when they had visited the *Shapieron*. If his estimations were accurate, the shaft had been about as far in from the outer hull of the ship as were the three tubes that were visible now. Presumably then, the shaft extended on inside one of the tubes and each of the tubes was an extension of an identical shaft. That meant that traffic up and down the length of the ship traveled via a three-elevator system that could be extended to ground level when required; the whole tail end of the structure moved down as well to afford a "lobby." Very neat. But his further study of the vessel was interrupted as a stir spread through the dome. The Ganymeans were coming out.

Looking more gigantic than ever in their suits, a party of aliens descended one of the ramps slowly and approached the waiting Earthmen, who immediately snapped into saluting posture. In the next few minutes an exchange of formalities similar to that which Hunt had already witnessed was reenacted. The loudspeaker inside the dome broadcast Foster's welcome to the Ganymeans on behalf of all the governments of Earth and reiterated a desire for friendship between all races for all time. He made reference to the plight of the voyagers and indicated that, though sparse, whatever resources and assistance the Earthmen could offer was theirs.

Garuth, who had elected to lead his people personally from the ship, replied through ZORAC, a channel from which had been linked into the dome's communications circuits. He echoed Foster's sentiments dutifully, though in a way that sounded somehow mechanical and artificial, as if he could not fully comprehend why such sentiments need be voiced.

Garuth gave the impression of doing his best to comply with an unfamiliar ritual that served no obvious purpose. Nevertheless his audience appreciated the gesture. He went on to express the gratitude of his people that fate, while taking their brothers from them, had left them new brothers to take their place when they came home. The two races, he concluded, had much to learn from each other.

Then the waiting vehicles moved toward the ramps to transport the Ganymeans to the quarters that had been made ready for them. The vehicles could not manage more than a few Ganymeans at one time, even stripped of seats and removable fittings, so they concentrated primarily on moving the sick and enfeebled, of whom there were many. The rest, guided by the spacesuited pygmy figures now dotting the scene, began a slow trek on foot toward the buildings waiting for them. Before long a broken procession of huddled groups and stragglers stretched across the ice from the ship to the base proper. Above it all, in the harshness of seminight, the stars stared down in stony-eyed indifference.

The dome had become very quiet. Grim faces looked out over the scene, each one an impenetrable mask preserving the privacy of thoughts that were not for sharing. No video record would ever recapture the feelings of this moment, whatever it might show, however many times it might be seen.

After a while, a sergeant who was standing next to Hunt turned his head a fraction. "Man, I don't know," he muttered quietly. "What a hell of a way to come home."

"What a hell of a home to come home to," Hunt replied.

The accommodations available at Main were not sufficient to hold all the Ganymeans, who numbered more than four hundred, so the majority were obliged to remain in the *Shapieron*. Nevertheless, just being on a firm surface again, even if it was only the frozen ball of rubble called Ganymede, and among other beings seemed to provide the aliens with a badly needed psychological tonic. Earthmen showed them the facilities and amenities that were available in their new quarters, pointed out the stocks of supplies and food-suffs provided for experimentation, and the various other items which, it was hoped, would help to make life reasonably comfortable. Meanwhile other UNSA crews delivered similar loads, hurriedly ferried from one of the orbiting freighters, to the Ganymeans still inside their ship. Then the new arrivals were left in peace and to their own devices.

After a much-needed rest, they announced that they were ready to resume their dialogue with their hosts. Accordingly, an evening conference was arranged between the leaders and certain other individuals of the two races, to be held in the officers' mess and to be followed by a formal welcoming dinner. Hunt was among those invited to attend; so was Danchekker.

chapter nine

The temperature had originally been lowered to make the Ganymeans feel more at home, but by the time everybody had been crammed into the officers' mess for an hour or more and palls of tobacco smoke were hanging sullenly beneath the lights, it turned out to be just as well for all. Danchekker finished what he had been saying into the microphone of the headset that he was wearing over his sweater then resumed his seat. Garuth replied from the far end of the room, where the Ganymean contingent was concentrated.

"I think I'd better let a scientist answer a scientist on that one, Professor." He looked down and behind him at one of the other Ganymeans. "Shilohin, will you respond?" All the Earthmen present who did not possess Ganymean kits had been equipped with headsets similar to Danchekker's and could thus follow ZORAC's translation of the proceedings. The machine's ability in this respect was now quite passable although, mainly as a result of having conversed with many and varied individuals, it had not yet fully established a way to disentangle formal English constructions from American colloquialisms, a defect that sometimes yielded hilarious results.

Shilohin, the chief scientist of the Ganymean expedition, had already been introduced to the company. As Garuth sat down to make room, she rose to her feet and spoke. "First, I must congratulate the scientists of Earth for their superb piece of figuring out. Yes, as Professor Danchekker has just suggested, we Ganymeans do not enjoy a high tolerance to carbon dioxide. He and his colleagues were also absolutely correct in the picture that they had deduced of conditions on Minerva at the time of our departure—a planet that they had not even seen."

Shilohin paused a moment, waiting for that much to sink in. Then she continued. "The average concentration of radioactive, heat-producing substances in Minervan rocks was somewhat higher than is found on Earth. The interior of Minerva was thus hotter and molten to a greater degree, and the crust was thinner. The planet was therefore more active volcanically than Earth, a tendency that was further complicated by the strong tidal forces induced in the crust by Luna, which orbited closer to Minerva than it does to Earth today. This high level of volcanic activity released large quantities of carbon dioxide and water vapor into the atmosphere, resulting in a greenhouse effect that sustained a high enough surface temperature for the oceans to remain liquid and life to emerge. By terrestrial standards it was still sure-as-hell cold, but not nearly as cold as it would have been otherwise.

"This situation had always existed throughout the history of Minerva. By the time that our civilization was at its peak, however, a new epoch of tectonic activity was just beginning. The level of carbon dioxide in the atmosphere began showing a measurable increase. It soon became clear that it would only be a matter of time before the level grew beyond the point we could tolerate. After that our world would become, for us, uninhabitable. What could we do?" Shilohin let the question hang and cast her eyes around the room, apparently inviting the Earthmen to start a discussion.

After a few seconds a UNSA engineer at the back responded. "Well, we've seen some pretty remarkable examples of the kind of technology that you people had. I wouldn't have thought you'd have found it much of a problem to figure out some way of simply winding the level back down again . . . some kinda planetwide climatic control, I guess . . . sump'n like that."

"Commendably on the ball," she said, with something that they took to be the equivalent of an approving nod. "We did in fact employ planetary climatic control to some degree, primarily to limit the extent of the Minervan ice caps. But when it came to tinkering with the chemical composition of the atmosphere, we were less certain of our ability to keep everything sufficiently under control; the balance was very delicate." She looked directly at the questioner. "A scheme along the lines you suggest was in fact proposed, but mathematical models indicated that there was too high a risk of destroying the greenhouse effect completely, and so of guaranteeing the end of life on Minerva even more quickly. We are a cautious people and do not take risks readily. Our government threw the idea out."

She remained silent and allowed them time to think of other possibilities. Danchekker didn't bother to raise the notion that they might have tried importing terrestrial plant life as an attempt at introducing a compensatory mechanism. He already knew full well that the Ganymeans knew nothing of such a venture. Presumably that solution had been tried after Garuth's expedition had departed. Further analyses by his scientists and discussions with ZORAC had indicated if that had been the objective of the exercise, it would not have succeeded anyway—a point that would surely not have escaped the Ganymean scientists at the time. For the moment this event was still as much a mystery as ever.

Eventually Shilohin spread her arm wide as if appealing to a class of children who were being a little slow that day. "Logically it's very simple," she said. "If we left the carbon-dioxide level to rise, we would die. Therefore we could not allow it to rise. If we prevented the rise, as we could have done, there would have been too much of a risk of freezing the whole planet solid because the carbon dioxide kept Minerva warm through the greenhouse effect. We needed the results of the greenhouse effect to keep us warm because we were a long way from the Sun. Hence, we wouldn't need it at all if we were nearer the Sun, or if the Sun were warmer."

Some of the faces in front of her remained blank;

some suddenly looked incredulous. "It's easy then," a voice called from near Hunt. "All you had to do was move Minerva in a bit or heat up the sun." He meant that as a joke but the Ganymean began nodding her head in imitation of the human mannerism.

"Exactly," she said. "And those were the two conclusions we arrived at too." A few gasps of amazement came from various parts of the room. "Both possibilities were studied extensively. Eventually a team of astrophysicists convinced the government that warming up the sun was the more practicable. Nobody could find a flaw in the calculations, but, as always, our government was cautious and elected not to blow a wad on fooling around with the sun. They wanted to see some proof first that the plan would work . . . Yes, Dr. Hunt?" She had noticed his hand half raised to attract attention.

"Could you give us a few details on how they proposed to do such a thing?" he asked. "I think even the idea of contemplating something like that has astonished a few of us here." Mutters of agreement from all around echoed his sentiments.

"Certainly," she replied. "The Ganymeans, as most of you know by now, had developed a branch of technology that is not yet understood in your own world—a technology based on the principles of artificially generating and controlling the effect termed 'gravity.' The proposal of the Ganymean astrophysicists involved placing three very large and very powerful projectors in orbit around the sun, which would concentrate beams of space–time distortion—'gravity intensification' if you like, although that describes the effect of the process rather than its nature—at the Sun's center. Theory predicted that this would induce an increase, effectively, in the Sun's self-gravitation and produce a slight collapse of the star, which would cease when the radiation pressure again balanced the gravitational pressure. At the new equilibrium the Sun would radiate more strongly and, provided that all the right quantities were chosen, would just compensate for the loss of Minerva's greenhouse effect. In other words we could now risk tampering with the carbon-dioxide level since, if we blew it and we started to freeze, we could put things right again by adjusting the solar constant. Does that answer the question sufficiently, Dr. Hunt?"

"Yes . . . very much so. Thank you." There were a thousand other questions that he could have asked at that moment, but he decided to leave them all for ZORAC later; for the time being he was having enough trouble even trying to visualize engineering on such a scale, yet Shilohin made the whole thing sound as routine as putting up an apartment block.

"As I said a moment ago," Shilohin resumed, "our government insisted on testing the theory first. Our expedition was formed for that purpose—to carry out a full-scale trial experiment on a Sunlike star elsewhere." She paused and made a gesture that was not familiar. "As it turned out, I guess they did the right thing. The star became unstable and went nova. We barely escaped with our lives. Garuth has just told you of the problem with the *Shapieron*'s propulsive system that resulted in the situation we have now—although we have aged less than twenty years since leaving Iscaris, on your time scale this all happened twenty-five million years ago. So here we are."

A chorus of mutterings broke out around the room. Shilohin waited for a few moments before continuing. "It's a bit cramped in here and difficult to change places. Does anybody else have any questions for me before I sit down again and hand this back to Garuth?"

"Just one." The speaker was Lawrence Foster, commander of Main. "A few of us have been wondering . . . You developed a technology that was way ahead of ours—interstellar travel for instance. So you must have explored the Solar System pretty thoroughly in the course of all that. Somebody here's taking bets that at least some Ganymeans got to Earth at some time. Care to comment on that?"

Shilohin seemed to flinch slightly for some reason . . . although it was difficult to be sure. She did not answer at once, but turned to exchange a few briefly muttered words with Garuth. Then she looked up again.

"Yes . . . you are correct . . ." The words coming through the headphones and earpieces of the listeners sounded hesitant, as if faithfully reproducing an uncertainty from the original utterances. "The Ganymeans came . . . to Earth."

A stir of excitement broke out across the room. This was something that nobody wanted to miss.

"Before your expedition went to Iscaris, I guess," Foster said.

"Yes, naturally . . . in the hundred Earth years or so before that time." She paused. "In fact a few of the crew of the *Shapieron* went to Earth before being recruited for the Iscaris expedition. None of them is here at the moment though."

The Earthmen were keen to hear more about their own world from beings who had actually been there long before they themselves had even existed. Questions began pouring spontaneously from all around the room.

"Hey, when can we talk to them?"

"Do you have any pictures stored away someplace?"

"How about maps or something?"

"I bet they built that city high up in that place in South America."

"You're crazy. It's not near old enough."

"Were these the expeditions to Earth to bring back the animals?"

The sudden increase in the enthusiasm of her audience seemed only to add to Shilohin's confusion. She picked up the last question, the answer to which they already knew, as if hoping for some reason that it would divert attention from the rest.

"No, there were no shipments of animals to Minerva then, neither was there any talk of such a plan. That must have happened later on. Like you, we do not know why that was done."

"Okay, but about the——" Foster stopped speaking as ZORAC sounded in his ear.

"This is ZORAC speaking only to the Earthmen; I am not interpreting for Shilohin. I do not believe that the Ganymeans really wish to elaborate further for the time being. It might be a good idea to change the subject. Excuse me."

The puzzled frowns that immediately appeared all over the room confirmed that all the Earthmen had heard the same thing: apparently the message had not, however, been transmitted to the Ganymeans, who showed none of the reactions that it would, without a doubt, have elicited. An awkward silence reigned for just a second before Foster took firm control and steered them all into calmer waters.

"These things can wait until another time," he said. "Time's getting on and we must be near dinner. Before we finish here, we ought to agree on our more immediate plans. The biggest problem seems to me to be the trouble you've got with your ship. How do you plan tackling that, and is there anything we can do to help?"

Shilohin conferred briefly with her companions and then sat down, giving a distinct impression of relief at getting out of the firing line. Her place was taken by Rogdar Jassilane, chief engineer of the *Shapieron*.

"We've had twenty years to figure out what the problem is, and we know how to fix it," he told them. "Garuth has described the effect of the trouble, which involved being unable to slow down the system of circulating black holes upon which the physics of the drive is based. All the time that drive was running, there was nothing we could do about it. We're able to fix it now, but some key components were wrecked and to attempt replacing them from scratch would be difficult, if not impossible. What we really need to do is have a look at the Ganymean ship that's under the ice at Pithead. From the pictures you've shown us, it seems to be a somewhat more advanced design than the *Shapieron*. But I'm hopeful we will be able to find what we need there. The basic concepts of the drive appear to be the same. That's the first thing we have to do—go to Pithead."

"No problem there," Foster said. "I'll arrange . . . oh, excuse me a second . . ." He turned to throw an inquiring look at a steward, who had appeared in the doorway. "I see . . . thanks. We'll be right along." He looked back toward Jassilane. "Sorry about that, but dinner's ready now. Yes, in answer to your question, we can arrange that expedition for as early as you like tomorrow. We can talk about the details later tonight, but in the meantime, shall we all go through?"

"That will be fine," Jassilane said. "I will select some of our own engineers for the visit. In the meantime as you say, let's all go through." He remained standing while the rest of the Ganymeans hoisted themselves to their feet behind him, forming a hopeless crush at the end of the room.

As the Earthmen also stood up and began moving back to make more space for the giants, Garuth made one final comment. "The other reason we wish to see the ship at Pithead is also very important to us. There is a chance that we might find some clues there which support your theory that the Ganymeans eventually migrated to another star system. If that is true, we might perhaps find something to identify which star it was."

"I think the stars can wait until tomorrow too," Jassilane said as he moved past. "Right now I'm more interested in that Earth food. Have you tried that stuff they call pineapple yet? It's delicious—never anything like that on Minerva."

Hunt found himself standing beside Garuth in the crowd forming around the door. He looked up at the massive features. "Would you really do it, Garuth . . . go all the way to still another star, after all this time?"

The giant stared down and seemed to be weighing the question in his mind.

"Perhaps," he replied. "Who knows?" Hunt sensed from the tone of the voice in his ear that ZORAC had ceased operating in public-address mode and was now handling separately the different conversations taking place on either side. "For years now my people have lived on a dream. At this time more than any other, it would be wrong to destroy that dream. Today they are tired and think only of rest; tomorrow they will dream again."

"We'll see what tomorrow brings at Pithead then,"

Hunt said. He caught the eye of Danchekker, who was standing immediately behind them. "Are you going to sit with us at dinner, Chris?"

"With pleasure, provided you are prepared to tolerate my being unsociable," the professor replied. "I absolutely refuse to eat with this contraption hanging round my head."

"Enjoy your meal, Professor," Garuth urged. "Let the socializing wait until afterward."

"I'm surprised you heard that," Hunt said. "How did ZORAC know we were talking in a group of three? I mean, it must have known that to put it through on your audio as well."

"Oh, ZORAC is very good at things like that. It learns fast. We're quite proud of ZORAC."

"It's an amazing machine."

"In more ways than you perhaps imagine," Garuth agreed. "It was ZORAC that saved us at Iscaris. Most of us were overcome by the heat when the ship was caught by the fringe of the nova; that was what caused many of the deaths among us. It was ZORAC that got the *Shapieron* clear."

"I really must stop calling its brethren contraptions," Danchekker murmured. "Wouldn't want to upset it or anything if it's sensitive about such matters."

"That's okay by me." A different voice came through on the circuit. "As long as I can still call *your* brethren monkeys."

That was when Hunt learned to recognize when a Ganymean was laughing.

When they all sat down to dinner, Hunt was mildly surprised to note that the menu was completely vegetarian. Apparently the Ganymeans had insisted on this.

chapter ten

The period of leave that Hunt and Danchekker had
originally intended to spend on *Jupiter Five* had ex-
pired anyway, so the two scientists traveled the next
day with the mixed party of Earthmen and Ganymeans to Pithead Base. The journey was indeed a
mixed affair, with some Ganymeans squeezing into
the UNSA medium-haul transporters while the luckier
Earthmen traveled as passengers in one of the
Shapieron's daughter vessels.

The first thing the aliens were shown at Pithead
was the distress beacon that had brought them across
the Solar System to Ganymede; already that event
seemed a long time ago. The aliens explained that
ordinary electromagnetic transmissions could not be
received inside the zone of localized space–time distortion that was generated by the standard form of
Ganymean drive, and for this reason most long-range
communications were effected by means of modulated
gravity pulses instead; the beacon used precisely this
principle. The Ganymeans had picked up the signal
after they had at last shut down their main drives and
entered the Solar System under auxiliary power, which
was fine for flitting around between planets but not
much good for interstellar marathons. Their subsequent bewilderment at what they found—Minerva
gone and an extra planet where there shouldn't have
been one—could well be imagined; and then they had
picked up the signals. As one UNSA officer said to
Hunt: "Imagine coming back in twenty-five million
years' time and hearing something out of today's hit
parade. They must have wondered if they hadn't

really been anywhere at all and had dreamed the whole thing."

The party continued on through a metal-walled underground corridor which brought them to the laboratories where preliminary examinations were normally made of items brought up from the ship below. The room that they found themselves in was a large one divided by half-height partitions into a maze of work bays, each a clutter of machinery, test instruments, electronics racks and tool cabinets. Above it all, the roof was barely visible behind the tangles of piping, ducts, cables and conduits that spanned the room.

Craig Patterson, the lab supervisor for that section, ushered the group into one of the bays and gestured at a workbench on which lay a squat metal cylinder, about a foot high and three feet or more across, surrounded by an intricate arrangement of brackets, webs and flanges, all integral with the main body. The whole assembly looked heavy and solid and had evidently been removed from a mounting in some larger piece of equipment; there were several ports and connections that suggested inlet and outlet points, possibly electrical.

"Here's something that's had us baffled," Patterson said. "We've brought a few of these up so far—all identical. There are hundreds more down there, all over the ship. They're mounted under the floors at intervals everywhere you go. Any ideas?"

Rogdar Jassilane stepped forward and stooped to study the object briefly.

"It resembles a modified *G*-pack," Shilohin commented from the doorway where she was standing next to Hunt. The Ganymeans were able to converse via ZORAC, still at Main, seven hundred miles away. Jassilane ran a finger along the casing of the object, examined some of the markings still visible in places, and then straightened up, apparently having seen all he needed.

"That's what it is, all right," he announced. "It

seems to have a few extras to the ones I'm used to, but the basic design's the same."

"What's a G-pack?" asked Art Stelmer, one of Patterson's engineers.

"An element in a distributed node field," Jassilane told him.

"Great." Stelmer replied with a shrug, still mystified.

Shilohin went on to explain. "I'm afraid it's to do with a branch of physics that hasn't been discovered by your race yet. In your space vessels, such as *Jupiter Five,* you simulate gravity by arranging for most portions of the structure to rotate, don't you?" Hunt suddenly remembered the inexplicable sensation of weight that he had felt on entering the *Shapieron.* The implication of what Shilohin had just said became clear.

"You don't simulate it," he guessed. "You manufacture it."

"Quite," she confirmed. "Devices like that were standard fittings in all Ganymean ships."

The Earthmen present were not really surprised since they had suspected for some time that the Ganymean civilization had mastered technologies that were totally unknown to them. All the same they were intrigued.

"We've been wondering about that," Patterson said, turning to face Shilohin. "What kind of principles is it all based on? I've never heard of anything like this before." Shilohin did not answer at once but seemed to pause to collect her thoughts.

"I'm not really sure where to begin," she replied at last. "It would take rather a long time to explain meaningfully. . . ."

"Hey, there's a booster collar from a transfer tube," one of the other Ganymeans broke in. He was staring over the partition into the adjoining bay and pointing to another, larger piece of Ganymean machinery that was lying there partially dismantled.

"Yes, I believe you're right," Jassilane agreed, following his companion's gaze.

"What the hell's a booster collar?" Stelmer pleaded.

"And a transfer tube?" Patterson added, forgetting his question of a few seconds before.

"There were tubes running all over the ship that were used for moving objects, and people, from place to place," Jassilane answered. "You must know them because I've seen them on the plans of the ship that your engineers have drawn."

"We kind of half-guessed what they were," Hunt supplied. "But we were never really sure about how they worked. Is this another *G*-trick?"

"Right," Jassilane said. "Local fields inside the tubes provided the motive force. That collar next door is simply a type of amplifier that was fitted around the tube to boost and smooth the field strength. There'd be one—oh—every thirty feet or so, depending on how wide the tube was."

"You mean people went hurtling through these things?" Patterson sounded distinctly dubious.

"Sure. We've got them in the *Shapieron* too," Jassilane replied nonchalantly. "The main elevator that some of your people have already been in runs in one. That one uses an enclosed capsule running inside, but the smaller ones don't. In those you just free-fall."

"How do you avoid colliding with somebody?" Stelmer asked. "Or are they strictly one-way?"

"Two-way," Jassilane told him. "A tube would usually carry a split field, half up and half down. The traffic can be segregated without problems. The collar contributes to that too—part of it is what we call a 'beam edge delimiter.' "

"So how d'you get out?" Stelmer persisted, still clearly fascinated by the idea.

"You decelerate through a localized pattern of standing waves that's triggered as you approach the drop-out point you've selected," Jassilane said. "You enter in much the same way . . ."

The conversation degenerated into a long discussion on the principles of operation and traffic control employed in the networks of transfer tubes built into Ganymean spacecraft and, as it turned out, most Ganymean buildings and cities. Throughout it all, Patterson's question as to how it worked never did get answered.

After spending some time examining a few more items from the ship, the party left that section of the base to continue their tour. They followed another corridor to the subsurface levels of the Site Operations Control Building and ascended several flights of stairs to the first floor. From there an elevated walkway carried them into an adjacent dome, constructed over the head of number-three shaft. Eventually, after negotiating a labyrinth of walkways and passages, they were standing in the number-three high-level airlock anteroom. A capsule was waiting beyond the airlock to take the first half-dozen of them down to the workings below the surface. By the time the capsule had returned and made its third descent, the whole party was together again deep inside the ice crust of Ganymede.

Accompanied by Jassilane, two other Ganymeans, and Commander Hew Mills, the senior officer of the uniformed UNSA contingent at Pithead, Hunt emerged from the capsule into number-three low-level anteroom. From there a short corridor brought them at last to the low-level control room, where the rest of the party was already gathered. Nobody took any notice of the new arrivals; all eyes were fixed on the view that confronted them from beyond the expanse of glass that constituted the far wall of the control room.

They were looking out over a vast cavern hewn and melted from the solid ice, shining a hundred different hues from gray to brilliant white in the light from a thousand arc lamps. The far side of the cavern was lost to view behind a forest of huge steel jacks and columns of ice left intact to support the roof. There, immediately before them, stretching away into the distance and cutting a clean swath through the forest, was the Ganymean ship.

Its clean, graceful lines of black metal were broken at scores of points where sections of the hull had been removed to gain access or to remove selected parts of the internal machinery. In some places the ship resembled the skeleton of a whale stranded on a beach, just a series of curving ribs soaring toward the cavern roof, to mark where whole sections of the ship had been stripped down. Latticeworks of girders and metal tubing adorned its sides in irregular and untidy clusters, in some places extending fully from floor to roof, supporting a confusion of catwalks, ladders, platforms, ramps, rigs, and winches wreathed intermittently in bewildering tangles of hydraulic and pneumatic feed tubes ventilator pipes and electrical supply lines.

Scores of figures labored all across the panorama up on the scaffolding by the hull, down among the maze of stacked parts and fittings that littered the floor, high on the walkways clinging to the rough-hewn walls of ice and standing on the top of the hull itself. In one place a gantry was swinging clear a portion of the outer skin; in another, the sporadic flashing of an oxyacetylene torch lit up the interior of an exposed compartment; further along, a small group of engineers was evidently in conference, making frequent gestures at information being presented on a large, portable viewscreen. The site was a bustle of steady, deliberate earnest activity.

The Earthmen waited in silence while the Ganymeans took in the scene.

Eventually Jassilane said, "It's quite a size . . . certainly as large as we expected. The general design is definitely a few steps ahead of anything that was flying when we left Minerva. ZORAC, what do you make of it?"

"Torroidal sections protruding from the large cutaway portion three hundred feet along from where you're standing are almost certainly differential resonance stress inductors to confine focus of the beam point for the main drive," ZORAC answered. "The large assembly on the floor immediately below you, with the two Earthmen standing in front of and underneath it is unfamiliar, but suggests an advanced design of an aft compensating reactor. If so, propulsion was probably by means of standard stress-wave propagation. If I am correct, there should be a forward compensating reactor in the ship too. The Earthmen at Main have shown me diagrams of a device that looks like one, but to be sure we should make a point of looking inside the nose end to check it firsthand. I would also like an opportunity to view the primary energy-convertor section and its layout."

"Mmm . . . it could be worse," Jassilane murmured absently.

"What was that all about, Rog?" Hunt asked him. The Giant half turned and raised an arm toward the ship.

"ZORAC has confirmed my own first impressions," he said. "Although that ship was built some time after the *Shapieron,* the basic design doesn't seem to have altered too much."

"There's a good chance it might help you get yours fixed then, huh?" Mills chimed in.

"Hopefully," Jassilane agreed.

"We'd need to see it close-up to be sure," Shilohin cautioned.

Hunt turned to face the rest of the party and spread his arms with palms upturned. "Well, let's go on down and do just that," he said.

They moved away from the viewing window and threaded their way through and between the equipment racks and consoles of the control room to a door on the opposite side to descend to the lower floor. After the door had closed behind the last of the party, one of the duty operators at the consoles half turned to one of his colleagues.

"See Ed, I told ya," he remarked cheerfully. "They didn't eat anybody."

Ed frowned dubiously from his seat a few feet away.

"Maybe they're just not hungry today," he muttered.

On the floor of the cavern, immediately below the window, the mixed group of Ganymeans and Earthmen emerged through an airlock and began making their way across the steel-mesh flooring and through the maze of assorted engineering toward the ship.

"It's quite warm," Shilohin commented to Hunt as

they walked. "And yet there's no sign of melting on the walls. How come?"

"The air-circulation system's been carefully designed," he informed her. "The warmer air is confined down here in the working area and screened off from the ice by curtains of cold air blowing upward all round the sides to extractors up in the roof. The way the walls are shaped to blend into the roof produces the right flow pattern. The system works quite well."

"Ingenious," she murmured.

"What about the explosion risk from dissolved gases being released from the ice?" another Ganymean asked. "I'd have thought there'd be a hazard there."

"When the excavations were first started it was a problem," Hunt answered. "That was when most of the melting was being done. Everybody had to work in suits down here then. They were using an argon atmosphere for exactly the reason you just mentioned. Now that the ventilation's been improved there's not really a big risk anymore so we can be a bit more comfortable. The cold-air curtains help a lot too; they keep the rate of gas-escape down pretty well to zero and what little there is gets swept away upward. The chances of a bang down here are probably less than the base up top getting clobbered by a stray meteorite."

"Well, here we are," Mills announced from the front. They were standing at the foot of a broad, shallow metal ramp that rose from the floor and disappeared through a mass of cabling up into a large aperture cut in the hull. Above them, the bulging contour of the ship's side soared in a monstrous curve that swept over and out of sight toward the roof. Suddenly they were like mice staring up at the underside of a garden roller.

"Let's go in then," Hunt said.

For the next two hours they walked every inch of the labyrinth of footways and catwalks that had been built inside the craft, which had come to rest on its side and offered few horizontal surfaces of its own upon which it was possible to move easily. The Giants followed the cable-runs and the ducting with eyes that obviously knew what they were looking for. Every now and then they stopped to dismantle an item of particular interest with sure and practiced fingers or to trace the connections to a device or component. They absorbed every detail of the plans supplied by UNSA scientists, which showed as much as the Earthmen could deduce of the vessel's design and structure.

After a long dialogue with ZORAC to analyze the results of these observations, Jassilane announced, "We are optimistic. The chances of restoring the *Shapieron* to a fully functional condition seem good. We'd like to conduct a far more detailed study of certain parts of this ship, however—one that would involve more of our technical experts from Main. Could you accommodate a small group of our people here for, say, two or three weeks?" He addressed these last words to Mills. The commander shrugged and opened his hands.

"Whatever you want. Consider it done," he replied.

Within an hour of the party's return to the surface for a meal, another UNSA transporter was on its way north from Main bringing more Ganymeans and the necessary tools and instruments from the *Shapieron*.

Later on, they went to the biological laboratories section of the base and admired Danchekker's indoor garden. They confirmed that the plants he had cultivated were familiar to them and represented types that were widespread in the equatorial regions of the Minerva they had known. At the professor's insistence they accepted some cuttings to be taken back to the *Shapieron* and grown there as mementoes of their home. The gesture seemed to affect them deeply.

Danchekker then led the party down into a large storage room excavated out of the solid ice below the biological labs. They emerged into a spacious, well-lit area, the walls of which were lined with shelving that carried a miscellany of supplies and instruments; there were rows of closed storage cupboards all painted a uniform green, unrecognizable machines draped in dustcovers, and in places stacks of unopened packing cases reaching almost to the ceiling. But the sight that immediately captured every eye was that of the beast towering before them about twenty feet from the doorway.

It stood over eighteen feet high at the shoulder on four tree-trunklike legs, its massive body tapering at the front into a long sturdy neck to carry its relatively small but ruggedly formed head high and well forward. Its skin was grayish and appeared rough and leathery, twisting into deep, heavy wrinkles that girded the base of its neck and the underside of its head below its short, erect ears. Over two enormous flared nostrils and a yawning parrot-beaklike mouth, the eyes were wide and staring. They were accentuated by thick folds of skin above, and directed straight down to stare at the door.

"This is one of my favorites," Danchekker informed them breezily as he walked forward at the head of the party to pat the beast fondly on the front of one of its massive forelegs.

"*Baluchitherium*—a late-Oligocene to early-Miocene Asian ancestor of modern rhinoceroses. In this species the front feet have already lost their fourth toe and adopted a three-toed structure similar to the hind feet—a trend which had become well pronounced in the Oligocene. Also, the strengthening of the upperjaw structure here is quite developed, although this particular breed did not evolve into a true horned variety, as you can see. Another interesting point is the teeth, which—" Danchekker stopped speaking abruptly as he turned to face his audience and realized that only the Earthmen had followed him into the room to stand around the specimen he was describing. The Ganymeans had come to a standstill in a close huddle just inside the door, where they stood staring speechless up at the towering shape of *Baluchitherium*. Their eyes were opened wide as if frozen in disbelief. They were not exactly cowering at the sight, but the expressions on their faces and their tense stances signaled uncertainty and apprehension.

"Is something the matter?" Danchekker asked, puzzled. There was no response. "It's quite harmless, I assure you," he went on, making his voice reassuring.

"And very, very dead . . . one of the samples preserved in the large canisters that were found in the ship. It's been very dead for at least twenty-five million years."

The Ganymeans slowly returned to life. Still silent and somehow subdued, they began moving cautiously toward the spot where the Earthmen were standing in a loose semicircle. For a long time they gazed at the immense creature, absorbing every detail in awed fascination.

"ZORAC," Hunt muttered quietly into his throat mike. The rest of the Earthmen were watching the Ganymeans silently, waiting for some signal to resume their dialogue and not sure yet what exactly it was that was affecting their guests so strongly.

"Yes, Vic?" the machine answered in his ear.

"What's the problem?"

"The Ganymeans have not seen an animal comparable to *Baluchitherium* before. It is a new and unexpected experience."

"Does it come as a surprise to you too?" Hunt asked.

"No. I recognize it as being very similar to other early terrestrial species recorded in my archives. The information came from Ganymean expeditions to Earth that took place before the time of the *Shapieron*'s departure from Minerva. None of the Ganymeans with you at Pithead has ever been to Earth, however."

"But surely they must know something about what those expeditions found," Hunt insisted. "The reports must have been published."

"True," ZORAC agreed. "But it's one thing to read a report about animals like that, and another to come face to face with one suddenly, especially when you're not expecting it. I suppose that if I were an organic intelligence that had evolved from a survival-dominated organic evolutionary system, and possessed all the conditioned emotional responses that implies, I'd be a bit shocked too."

Before Hunt could reply, one of the Ganymeans—Shilohin—finally spoke up.

"So . . . that is an example of an animal of Earth,"

she said. Her voice was low and hesitant, as if she were having difficulty articulating the words.

"It's incredible!" Jassilane breathed, still keeping his eyes fixed on the huge beast. "Was that thing really alive once . . . ?"

"What's *that?*" Another Ganymean was pointing beyond *Baluchitherium* to a smaller but more ferocious-looking animal posed with one paw raised and lips curled back to reveal a set of fearsome, pointed teeth. The other Ganymeans followed his finger and gasped.

"*Cynodictis,*" Danchekker answered with a shrug. "A curious mixture of feline and canine characteristics from which both our modern cat and dog families eventually emerged. The one next to it is *Mesohippus,* ancestor of all modern horses. If you look carefully you can see . . ." He stopped in midsentence and seemed to switch his line of thought abruptly. "But why do these things seem so strange to you? Surely you have seen animals before . . . There were animals on Minerva, weren't there?"

Hunt observed intently. The reactions that he had witnessed seemed odd from a race so advanced and which, until then, had seemed so rational in everything they said and did.

Shilohin took it upon herself to answer. "Yes . . . there were animals . . ." She began looking from side to side at her companions as if seeking support in a difficult situation. "But they were . . . *different* . . ." she ended, vaguely. Danchekker seemed intrigued.

"Different," he repeated. "How interesting. In what way do you mean? Weren't there any as big as this for instance?"

Shilohin's anxiety seemed to increase. She was showing the same inexplicable reluctance to discuss Oligocene Earth as on earlier occasions. Hunt sensed a crisis approaching and saw that Danchekker, in his enthusiasm, was not getting the message. He turned away from the rest of the party. "ZORAC, give me a private channel to Chris Danchekker," he said in a lowered voice.

"You've got it," ZORAC responded a second later, sounding almost relieved.

"Chris," Hunt whispered. "This is Vic." He observed a sudden change in Danchekker's expression and went on. "They don't want to talk about it. Maybe they're still nervous about our links with the Lunarians or something—I don't know but something's bugging them. Wrap up and let's get out of here."

Danchekker caught Hunt's eye, blinked uncomprehendingly for a second, then nodded and abruptly changed the subject. "Anyway, I'm sure all that can wait until we are in more comfortable surroundings. Why don't we go back upstairs. There are some more experiments being conducted in the labs that I think might interest you."

The group began shuffling back toward the door. Behind them, Hunt and Danchekker exchanged mystified glances.

"What was the meaning of all that, may I ask?" the professor inquired.

"Search me," Hunt replied. "Come on or we'll get left behind."

Many hundreds of millions of miles from Pithead, the news of the meeting with an intelligent alien race broke over an astounded world. As recordings of the first face-to-face contact aboard the *Shapieron* and the arrival of the aliens at Ganymede Main Base were replayed across the world's viewscreens, a wave of wonder and excitement swept around the planet, exceeding even that which had greeted the discoveries of Charlie and the first Ganymean spaceship. Some of the reactions were admirable, some deplorable, some just comical—but all of them predictable.

At a high, official level, Frederick James McClusky, senior United States delegate to the extraordinary session that had been called by the United Nations, sat back in his chair and stared around the packed circular auditorium while Charles Winters, the UK representative from US Europe, delivered the final words of his forty-five-minute address:

". . . In summary it is our contention that the location at which the first landing is to be effected should obviously be selected from within the boundaries of the British Isles. The English language is now established as the standard means of communication for social, business, scientific, and political dialogue between all the races, peoples and nations of Earth. It has come to symbolize the dissolution of the barriers that once divided us, and the establishment of a new order of harmony, trust and mutual cooperation across the surface of the globe. And so it is particularly appropriate that the English tongue should have been the vehicle by which the first words between our alien friends and ourselves were exchanged. Might I also remind you that at present, the speech of the British Isles is the only human language that has been assimilated by the Ganymean machine. What then, gentlemen, could be more fitting than that the first Ganymean to set foot upon our planet should do so on the soil where that language originated?"

Winters concluded with a final appealing look around the auditorium and sat down among a mixed murmuring of lowered voices and rustling of papers. McClusky jotted a few notes on his pad and cast an eye over the collection that he had already made.

In a rare show of agreement, the governments of Earth had released a joint statement declaring that the homeless wanderers from the past would be welcome to settle there if they so wished. The present meeting was called after the public announcement had been released, and had degenerated into a heated wrangle in camera over which nation should enjoy the prestige of receiving the aliens first.

Initially, McClusky, following his brief from the Presidential Advisory Committee and the State Department in Washington, had made first claim by drawing attention to the predominantly American flavor of the UNSA operations being staged around Jupiter. The Americans had found them, he had said in effect, and the Americans therefore had a right to keep them. The Soviets had taken two hours to say that since their nation occupied a larger portion of the

Earth's land surface than any other, it represented the majority of the planet and that was what counted. China had countered by pointing out that she represented more people than any other nation and therefore, making an expedient appeal to democratic principles, China offered a more meaningful interpretation of "majority." Israel had taken the view that it had more in common with homeless minority groups and that considerations of such kind would more accurately reflect the true nature of the situation. Iraq had lodged a claim on the grounds of its being the site of the oldest known nation, and one of the African republics on the grounds of its being the youngest.

By then McClusky was getting fed up with the whole business. Irritated he threw his pen down onto his pad and stabbed a finger at the button that caused his request light to come on. A few minutes later an indicator on his panel informed him that the Chairman had acknowledged the request. McClusky leaned to his microphone. "The Ganymeans haven't even said they want to come to Earth yet, let alone settle here. Wouldn't it be a good idea to ask them about it first before we spend more time on all this?"

The remark prompted a further debate during which the opportunity for diplomatic procrastination proved impossible to resist. In the end the matter was duly *Deferred, Pending Further Information.*

The delegates did, however, agree on one small item.

They were concerned that the UNSA spacecrews, officers, scientists and other on-the-spot personnel at Ganymede had not been schooled in the subtle arts of diplomacy and found the risks implicit in their enforced status as representatives and ambassadors for the whole of Earth worrisome. Accordingly they drafted a set of guidelines impressing upon all UNSA personnel the seriousness and importance of their responsibilities and, among other things, urged them to ". . . desist from any thoughtless or impulsive statements or actions that might conceivably be interpreted as provocative by unfamiliar beings of uncertain disposition and intent. . . ."

When the message was transmitted and dutifully read to the UNSA crews and scientists on Ganymede, it produced some amusement. Such was the Earthmen's uncertainty of the "dispositions and intent . . ." that they read the message to the Ganymeans, too.

The Giants thought it was funny.

chapter eleven

Compared to Main, Pithead was small and spartan, offering only limited accommodations and restricted amenities. During the days that Ganymean experts were conducting a more intensive examination of the ship there, the two races found themselves intermingling more freely than before and getting to know one another better. Hunt made the most of this opportunity to observe the aliens at close hand and to gain a deeper insight to their ways and temperaments.

The single most striking thing that set them apart from Earthmen was, as he already knew, their total ignorance of the very concept of war or willful violence in any form. At Pithead he gradually came to attribute this to a common factor that he noticed in all of them—something which, he realized, represented a fundamental difference in their mental makeup. Not once had he detected a hint of aggressiveness in a Ganymean. They never seemed to argue about anything, show signs of impatience, or give any evidence of possessing tempers that could be frayed. That in itself did not surprise him unduly; he would hardly have expected less from an extremely advanced and civilized people. But the point that did strike him was the complete absence of emotional traits of the kind that would provide alternate outlet for such instincts in a socially acceptable manner. They exhibited no sense of competitiveness among themselves, no sense of rivalry, even in the harmless, subtle, friendly ways that men accept as part of living and frequently find enjoyable.

The notion of losing face meant nothing to a Ganymean. If he were proved wrong in some matter he would readily concede the fact; if he were proved right he would feel no particular self-satisfaction. He could stand and watch another perform a task that he knew he could do better, and say nothing—a feat almost impossible for most Earthmen. In the reverse situation he would prompty ask for help. He was never arrogant, authoritative or disdainful, yet at the same time never visibly humble, servile or apologetic; nothing in his manner ever sought to intimidate, and neither did it acknowledge implied intimidation from others. There was simply nothing in anything they said or did, or in the way that they said and did them, that signaled any instinctive desire to seek status or superiority. Many psychologists believed this aspect of human social behavior constituted a set of substitute rituals that permitted release of underlying aggressive instincts which communal patterns of living required to be suppressed. If this was so, then the only conclusion Hunt could draw from his observations was that for some reason these underlying instincts just didn't exist in the Ganymeans.

All this was not to say that the Ganymeans were a cold and unemotional people. As their reactions to the destruction of Minerva had shown, they were warm, friendly and deeply sentimental, at times to a degree that an Earthman reared in the "old school" might have considered unbecoming. And they possessed a well-developed, though very subtle and sophisticated, sense of humor, not a little of which was evident in the basic design of ZORAC. Also as Shilohin had indicated, they were a cautious people, cautious not in the sense of being timid, but of premeditating every move and action. They never did anything without knowing exactly what they were trying to achieve, why they wanted to achieve it, how they were going to do it, and what they would do if the expected failed to materialize. To the average engineer from Earth the disaster of Iscaris would have been shrugged off as just one of those things to be forgotten or tried again with hopes for better luck; to the Ganymeans it was inexcusable that such a thing should ever have happened and they had not yet fully come to terms with it, even after twenty years.

Hunt saw them as a dignified and proud race, moderate in speech and noble in bearing, yet underneath it all sociable and approachable. They exhibited none of the suspicion and mistrust of strangers that was typical through much of the society of Earth. They were quiet, reserved, self-assured, and above all they were rational. As Danchekker remarked to Hunt one day in the bar at Pithead: "If the whole universe went insane and blew itself up, I'm sure the Ganymeans would still be there at the end of it to put the pieces together again."

The bar at Pithead became the main focus of social activity between the small group of Ganymeans and the Earthmen. Every evening after dinner, ones and twos of both races would begin trickling in until the room was filled to capacity and every square foot of horizontal space, including the floor, was covered by a sprawling body of one kind or the other, or littered with glasses. The discussions rambled on to touch every subject conceivable and usually went through to the early hours of the morning; for anybody not disposed to seek solitude and privacy, there was little else to do after work at Pithead.

The Ganymeans developed a strong partiality for scotch whiskey, which they preferred neat, by the tumblerful. They reciprocated by bringing in a distillation of their own from the *Shapieron*. A number of the Earthmen experimented with it and found it to be pleasant, warming, slightly sweet . . . and of devastating potency, but not until about two hours after beginning to drink it. Those who had learned the hard way christened it GTB—Ganymean Time Bomb.

It was during one of these evenings that Hunt decided to broach directly the subject that had been puzzling more than a few of the Earthmen for some time. Shilohin was present, so was Monchar, Garuth's second-in-command, together with four other Ganymeans; on the Earth side were Danchekker, Vince

Carizan the electronics engineer, and a half-dozen others.

"There is a point that's been bothering some of us," he said, by that time having come to appreciate the Ganymean preference for direct speech. "You must know that having people around today who can describe how Earth was in the distant past makes us want to ask all kinds of questions, yet you never seem to want to talk about it. Why?" A few murmurs from all around endorsed the question. The room suddenly became very quiet. The Ganymeans seemed ill at ease again and looked at each other as if hoping someone else would take the lead.

Eventually Shilohin replied. "We know very little about your world. It's a delicate issue. You have a culture and history that are completely strange. . . ." She gave the Ganymean equivalent of a shrug. "Customs, values, manners . . . accepted ways of saying things. We wouldn't want to offend somebody by unwittingly saying the wrong thing, so we tend to avoid the subject."

Somehow the answer was not really convincing.

"We all believe there's a deeper reason than that," Hunt said candidly. "We in this room might come from different origins, but first and foremost we are all scientists. Truth is our business and we shouldn't shy away from the facts. This is an informal occasion and we all know each other pretty well now. We'd like you to be frank. We're curious."

The air became charged with expectancy. Shilohin looked again toward Monchar, who quietly signaled his acquiescene. She downed the last of her drink slowly as she collected her thoughts, then looked up to address the room.

"Very well. Perhaps, as you say, we would do better without any secrets. There was one crucial difference between the patterns of natural evolution that unfolded on your world and on our world—on Minerva there were no carnivores." She paused as if waiting for a response, but the Earthmen continued to sit in silence; obviously there was more to come. She felt a twinge of sudden relief inside. Perhaps the

Ganymeans had been overapprehensive of the possible reactions of these unpredictable and violently inclined dwarves after all.

"The basic reason for this difference, believe it or
not, lay in the fact that Minerva was much farther
away from the Sun." She went on to explain. "Life
could never have developed on Minerva at all without the greenhouse effect, which you already know
about. Even so, it was a cold planet, certainly in comparison to Earth.

"But this greenhouse effect kept the Minervan
oceans in a liquid state and, as on Earth, life first appeared in the shallower parts of the oceans. Conditions there did not favor progression toward higher
forms of life as much as on the warmer Earth; the
evolutionary process was relatively slow."

"But intelligence appeared there much earlier than
it did on Earth," somebody tossed in. "Seems a little
strange."

"Only because Minerva was further from the Sun
and cooled more quickly," Shilohin replied. "That
meant that life got off to an early start there."

"Okay."

She resumed. "The patterns of evolution on the two
worlds were remarkably similar to start with. Complex
proteins appeared, leading eventually to self-replicating
molecules, which in time led to the formation of living
cells. Unicellular forms came first, then colonies of
cells and after them multicelled organisms with specialized features—all of them variations on the basic
marine invertebrate form.

"The point of departure at which the two lines
went their own way, each in response to the conditions prevailing on its own planet, was marked by the
appearance of marine vertebrates—boned fishes. This
stage marked a plateau beyond which the Minervan
species couldn't progress toward anything higher until
they had solved a fundamental problem that was not
faced by their counterparts on Earth. The problem was
simply their colder environment.

"You see, as improvements appeared in the Minervan fish species, the improved body processes and

more highly refined organs demanded more oxygen. But the demand was already high because of the lower temperature. The primitive circulatory systems of the early Minervan fish couldn't cope with the dual workload of carrying enough oxygen to the cells, and of carrying wastes and toxins away from the cells—not if progress toward anything more advanced was going to be made, anyway."

Shilohin paused again to invite questions. Her listeners were too intrigued, however, to interrupt her story at that point.

"As always happens in situations like that," she continued, "Nature tried a number of alternatives to find a way around the problem. The most successful experiment took the form of a secondary circulation system developing alongside the first to permit load-sharing—a completely duplicated network of branching ducts and vessels; thus, the primary system concentrated exclusively on circulating blood and delivering oxygen, while the secondary took over fully the job of removing the toxins."

"How extraordinary!" Danchekker could not help from exclaiming.

"Yes, I suppose that when judged by the things you're used to it was, Professor."

"One thing—how did the different substances find their way in and out of the right system?"

"Osmotic membranes. Do you want me to go into detail now?"

"No, er, thank you." Danchekker held up a hand. "That can wait until another time. Please continue."

"Okay. Well, after this basic architecture had become sufficiently refined and established, evolution toward higher stages was able to resume once more. Mutations appeared, the environment applied selection principles, and life in the Minervan seas began diverging and specializing into many and varied species. After a while, as you would expect, a range of carnivorous types established themselves. . . ."

"I thought you said there weren't any," a voice queried.

"That came later. I'm talking about very early times."

"Okay."

"Fine. So, carnivorous fish appeared on the scene and, again as you would expect, Nature immediately commenced looking for ways of protecting the victims. Now the fish that had developed the double-circulatory-system architecture, who tended to be more advanced forms anyway because of this, hit on a very efficient means of defense: the two circulatory systems became totally isolated from one another, and the concentration of toxins in the secondary system increased to lethal proportions. In other words, they became poisonous. The isolation of the secondary system from the primary prevented poison from entering the bloodstream. That would have been fatal for the owner itself, naturally."

Carizan was frowning about something. He caught her eye and gestured for her to hold the conversation there a moment.

"Can't really say I see that as being much protection at all," he said. "What's the good in poisoning a carnivore after it's eaten you? That'd be too late, wouldn't it?"

"To the individual who was unfortunate enough to encounter one that hadn't learned yet, yes," she agreed. "But don't forget that Nature can afford to be very wasteful when it comes to individuals; it's the preservation of the species as a whole that matters. When you think about it, the survival or extermination of a species can depend on whether or not a strain of predators becomes established that has a preference for them as a diet. In the situation I've described, it was impossible for such a strain of predators to emerge; if a mutation appeared that had a tendency in that direction, it would promptly destroy itself the first time it experimented in following its instinct. It would never get a chance to pass its characteristic on to any descendants, so the characteristic could never be reinforced in later generations."

"Another thing too," one of the UNSA biologists interjected. "Young animals tend to imitate the feeding habits of their parents . . . on Earth anyway. If that was true on Minerva too, the young that managed to get born would naturally tend to pick up the habits of parents that avoided the poisonous species. It would have to be that way since any mutant that didn't avoid them wouldn't live long enough to become a parent in the first place."

"You can see the same thing in terrestrial insects, for example," Danchekker threw in. "Some species mimic the coloring of wasps and bees, although they are quite harmless. Other animals leave them alone completely—it's the same principle."

"Okay, that makes sense." Carizan motioned for Shilohin to continue.

"So marine life on Minerva developed into three broad families: carnivorous types; nonpoisonous noncarnivores, with specialized alternative defense mechanisms; and poisonous noncarnivores, which possessed the most effective defense and were left free to carry on their development from what was already an advanced and privileged position."

"This didn't alter their resistance to cold then?" somebody asked.

"No, the secondary system in these species continued to perform its original function as well as ever. As I said, the only differences that had occurred were that the toxin concentration was increased and it became isolated from the primary."

"I got it."

"Fine. Now, the two types of noncarnivores had to eat, so they competed between themselves for what was available—plants, certain rudimentary invertebrate organisms, water-borne organic substances and so on. But Minerva was cold and did not offer an abundance of things like that—nothing like what is found on Earth, for instance. The poisonous species were efficient competitors and gradually became overwhelmingly dominant. The nonpoisonous noncarnivores declined and, since they constituted the food supply for the carnivores, the numbers and varieties of carnivores declined with them. Eventually two distinct groups segregated out of all this and from that time on lived separate lives: the nonpoisonous types moved out into the oceans away from the competition, and the carnivores naturally followed them. Those two groups evolved into a pattern of deep-sea life that eventually found its own balance and stabilized. The poisonous types retained the shallower, coastal waters as their sole preserve, and it was from them that land dwellers subsequently emerged."

"You mean that all the land-dwelling species that developed later inherited the basic pattern of a double system?" Danchekker said, fascinated. "They were all poisonous?"

"Precisely," she replied. "By that time the trait had become firmly established as a fundamental part of their basic design—much as many vertebrate characteristics on your own world. It was faithfully passed on to all later descendants, essentially unchanged. . . ."

Shilohin paused as a few mutterings and murmurs of surprise arose from the listeners; the implication of what she was saying was beginning to dawn on them. Somebody at the back finally put it into words.

"That explains what you said at the start—why there were no carnivores on Minerva later on. They could never become established for all the reasons you've been talking about, even if they appeared spontaneously from time to time."

"Quite so," she confirmed. "Occasionally an odd mutation in that direction would appear but, as you point out, it could never gain a foothold again. The animals that evolved on Minerva were exclusively herbivorous. They did not follow the same lines of development as terrestrial animals because the selective factors operating in their natural environment were different. They evolved no fight-or-flight instincts since there was nothing to defend against and nothing to flee from. They did not develop behavior patterns based on fear, anger or aggression since such emotions had no survival value to them, and hence were not selected and reinforced. There were no fast runners since there were no predators to run from, and there was no need for natural camouflage. There were no birds, since there was nothing to stimulate their appearance."

"Those murals in the ship!" Hunt turned to Danchekker as the truth suddenly hit him. "They weren't children's cartoons at all, Chris. They were real!"

"Good Lord, Vic." The professor gaped and blinked through his spectacles in surprise, wondering why the same thought hadn't struck him. "You're right. Of course . . . you're absolutely right. How extraordinary. We must study them more closely. . . " Danchekker seemed about to say something else but stopped abruptly, as if another thought had just occurred to him. He frowned and rubbed his forehead but waited until the hubbub of voices had died away before he spoke.

"Excuse me," he called when normality had returned. "There is something else . . . If there were no predators in existence at all, what kept the numbers of the herbivores in check? I can't see any mechanism for preserving a natural balance."

"I was just coming to that," Shilohin answered. "The answer is: accidents. Even slight cuts or abrasions would allow poison to seep from the secondary system into the primary. Most accidents were fatal to Minervan animals. Natural selection favored natural protection. The species that survived and flourished were those with the best protection—leathery outer skins, thick coverings of fur, scaly armor plating, and so on." She held up one of her hands to display extensive nails and knuckle pads, and then shifted the collar of her shirt slightly to uncover part of the delicate, overlapping, scaly plates that formed a strip along the top of her shoulder. "Many remnants of ancestral protection are still detectable in the Ganymean form today."

Hunt realized now the reasons for the Ganymeans' temperament being the way it was. From the origins that Shilohin had just described, intelligence had emerged not in response to any need to manufacture weapons or to outwit foe or prey, but as a means of anticipating and avoiding physical damage. Learning and the communication of knowledge would have assumed a phenomenal survival value among the primitive Ganymeans. Caution in all things, prudence, and the ability to analyze all possible outcomes of an action would have been reinforced by selection; haste and rashness would be fatal.

Evolving from such ancestors, what else could they be but instinctively cooperative and nonaggressive? They would know nothing of violent competition in any form or of the use of force against a rival; hence they exhibited none of the types of complex behavior patterns which, in a later and more civilized society, would "normally" afford symbolic expression of such instincts. Hunt wondered what was "normal." Shilohin, as if reading his thoughts, supplied a definition from the Ganymean point of view.

"You can imagine then how, when civilization eventually began to develop, the early Ganymean thinkers looked upon the world that they saw about them. They marveled at the way in which Nature, in its infinite wisdom, had imposed a strict natural order upon all living things: the soil fed the plants and the plants fed the animals. The Ganymeans accepted this as the natural order of the universe."

"Like a divinely ordained plan," somebody near the bar suggested. "Sounds like a religious outlook."

"You're right," Shilohin agreed, turning to face the speaker. "In the early history of our civilization religious notions did prevail widely. Before scientific principles were better understood, our people attributed many of the mysteries that they were unable to explain to the workings of some omnipotent agency . . . not unlike your God. The early teachings held that the natural order of living things was the ultimate expression of this guiding wisdom . . . I suppose you would say: The will of God."

"Except in the deep-ocean basins," Hunt commented.

"Well, that fitted in quite well too," Shilohin replied. "The early religious thinkers of our race saw that as a punishment. In the seas, way back before history, the law had been defied. As a punishment for that, the lawbreakers had been banished permanently to the deepest and darkest depths of the oceans and never emerged to enjoy sunlight."

Danchekker leaned toward Hunt and whispered, "Rather like the Fall from Eden. An interesting parallel, don't you think?"

"Mmm . . . with a T-bone steak in place of an apple," Hunt murmured.

Shilohin paused to push her glass across the bar and waited for the steward to refill it. The room remained quiet while the Earthmen digested the things she had been saying. At last she sipped her drink, and then resumed.

"And so, you see, to the Ganymean, Nature was indeed perfect in all its harmony, and beautiful in its perfection. As the sciences were discovered and the Ganymeans learned more about the universe in which they lived; they never doubted that however far among the stars their knowledge might take them and however far they might one day probe toward infinity, Nature and its natural law would everywhere reign supreme. What reason had they even to imagine otherwise? They were unable even to conceive how things could be otherwise."

She stopped for a moment and swept her eyes slowly around the room, as if trying to weigh up the expressions on the circle of faces.

"You asked me to be frank," she said, then paused again. "At last, we realized a dream that we had been nurturing for generations—to go out into space and discover the wonders of other worlds. When at last the Ganymeans, still with their idyllic convictions, came to the jungles and savagery of Earth, the effect on them was shattering. We called it the Nightmare Planet."

chapter twelve

The Ganymean engineers announced that the ship beneath Pithead would provide the parts needed to repair the drive system of the *Shapieron* and that the work would take three to four weeks. A shuttle service between Pithead and Main came into being as technicians and scientists of both races cooperated in the venture. The Ganymeans, of course, directed and carried out the technical side of the operation while the Earthmen took care of the transportation, logistics, and domestic arrangements. Parties of UNSA experts were invited aboard the *Shapieron* to observe the work in progress and to stand in spellbound fascination as some of the mysteries and intricacies of Ganymean science were explained. One eminent authority on nuclear engineering from *Jupiter Five* declared later that the experience made him feel like "an unapprenticed plumber's mate being shown around a fusion plant."

While all this was going on, a team of UNSA specialists at Main worked out a schedule to give ZORAC a crash course on terrestrial computer science and technology. The result of this exercise was the construction of a code-conversion and interface system, most of the details of which were worked out by ZORAC itself, to couple the Ganymean computer directly into the communications network at Main and thus into the computer complex of *J5*. This gave ZORAC, and through it the Ganymeans as well, direct access to *J5*'s data banks and opened up a mine of information on many aspects of the ways of life, history, geography and sciences of Earth—for which the aliens had insatiable appetites.

One day, in the communications room of the Mission Control Center at UNSA Operational Command Headquarters, Galveston, there was consternation when a strange voice began speaking suddenly and unexpectedly over the loudspeaker system. It was another of ZORAC's jokes. The machine had composed its own message of greeting to Earth and injected it into the outgoing signal stream of the laser link from Jupiter.

Earth was, of course, clamoring to know more about the Ganymeans. In a press conference staged specifically for broadcast over the world news grid, a panel of Ganymeans answered questions put to them by scientists and reporters who had traveled with the J5 mission. A large local audience was expected for the event and, since none of the facilities available at Main seemed to be large enough, the Ganymeans readily agreed to the idea of holding the event inside the *Shapieron*. Hunt was a member of the group that flew down from Pithead to take part.

The first questions concerned the concepts and principles behind the design of the *Shapieron,* especially its propulsive system. In reply, the Ganymeans stated that the speculations of the UNSA scientists had been partly right, but did not tell the whole story. The arrangement of massive torroids containing tiny black holes that spun in closed circular paths did indeed generate very high rates of change of gravity potential which resulted in a zone of intense space–time distortion, but this did not propel the ship directly; it created a focal point in the center of the torroids at which a trickle of ordinary matter was induced to annihilate out of existence. The mass-equivalent appeared in the form of gravitational energy, though not in any way as simple as the classical notion of a force directed toward a central point; the Ganymeans described the resultant effect as resembling "a stress in the structure of space–time surrounding the ship. . . ." It was this stress wave that propagated through space, carrying the ship with it as it went.

The idea of being able to cause matter to annihilate

at will was astonishing, and that the annihilation should result in artificial gravity phenomena was a revelation. But to learn that all this merely represented a means of bringing under control something that went on naturally anyway all over the universe . . . was astounding. For this, apparently, was exactly the way in which gravity originated in Nature; all forms of matter were all the time decaying away to nothing, albeit at an immeasurably slow rate, and it was the tiny proportion of basic particles that were annihilating at any given moment that gave rise to the gravitational effect of mass. Every annihilation event produced a microsopic, transient gravity pulse, and it was the additive effect of millions of these pulses occurring every second which, when perceived at the macroscopic level, produced the illusion of a steady field. Thus, gravity ceased to be something static and passive that existed wherever a quantity of mass happened to be; now, no longer an oddity standing apart, it fell into line with all the other field phenomena of physics and became a quantity that depended on the rate of *change* of something—in this case, the rate of change of mass. This principle, together with the discovery of a means of artificially generating and controlling the process, formed the basis of Ganymean gravitic engineering technology.

This account caused consternation among the scientists from Earth who were present. Hunt voiced their reactions by asking how some of the fundamental laws of physics—conservation of mass-energy and momentum, for example—could be reconciled with the notion of particles being able to vanish spontaneously whenever they chose. The cherished fundamental laws, it turned out, were neither fundamental nor laws at all. Like the Newtonian mechanics of an earlier age, they were just approximations that would be revealed with the development of more precise theoretical models and improved measurement techniques, similar to the way in which careful experiments with light waves had demonstrated the untenability of classical physics and resulted in the formulation of special relativity. The Ganymeans illustrated the point by mentioning that the rate at which matter decayed was such that one gram of water would require well over ten billion years to disappear completely—utterly undetectable by any experiment that could be devised within the framework of contemporary terrestrial science. While that remained true, the established laws that Hunt had referred to would prove perfectly adequate since the errors that resulted from them would make no practical difference. In the same way, classical Newtonian mechanics continued to suffice for most day-to-day needs although relativity provided the more accurate description of reality. The history of Minervan science had shown the same pattern of development; when terrestrial science had progressed further, no doubt, similar discoveries and lines of reasoning would lead to the same reexamination of basic principles.

This led to the question of the permanency of the universe. Hunt asked how the universe could still exist at all let alone still be evolving if all the matter in it was decaying at the rate that the Ganymeans had indicated, which was not slow on a cosmic time scale; there ought not to have been very much of the universe left. The universe went on forever, he was told. All the time, throughout the whole volume of space, particles were appearing spontaneously as well as vanishing spontaneously, the latter process taking place predominantly inside matter—naturally, since that was where there were more of them to vanish from in the first place. Thus the evolution of progressively more complex mechanisms of creating order out of chaos—basic particles, interstellar clouds, stars, planets, organic chemicals, then life itself and after that intelligence—formed a continuous cycle, a perpetual stage where the show never stopped but individual actors came and went. Underlying it all was a unidirectional pressure that strove always to bring high levels of organization from lower ones. The universe was the result of a conflict of two opposing, fundamental trends; one, represented by the second law of thermodynamics, was the tendency for disorder to increase, while the other—the evolutionary principle—

produced local reversals by creating order. In the Ganymean sense, the term evolution was not something that applied only to the world of living things, but one that embraced equally the whole spectrum of increasing order, from the formation of an atomic nucleus from stellar plasma to the act of designing a supercomputer; within this spectrum, the emergence of life was reduced to just another milestone along the way. They compared the evolutionary principle to a fish swimming upstream against the current of entropy; the fish and the current symbolized the two fundamental forces in the Ganymean universe. Evolution worked the way it did because selection worked; selection worked because probability worked in a particular way. The universe was, in the final analysis, all a question of statistics.

Basic particles thus appeared, lived out their mortal spans, and then vanished. Where did they come from and where did they go to? This question summed up the kinds of problem that had existed at the frontier of Ganymean science at the time of the *Shapieron*'s departure. The whole universe perceived by the senses was compared to a geometric plane through which a particle passed, to be observable for a while as it made its contribution to the evolving histories of the galaxies. But in what kind of superuniverse was this plane embedded? Of what kind of truer reality was everything that had ever been observed just a pale and insignificant shadow? These were the secrets that the researchers of Minerva had been beginning to probe and which, they had confidently believed, would eventually yield the key not only to practicable intergalactic travel, but also to movement in domains of existence that even they were incapable of imagining. The scientists from the *Shapieron* wondered how much their descendants had learned in the years, decades, or even centuries, that had elapsed after their departure from Minerva. Could the abrupt disappearance of a whole civilization have a connection with some undreamed of universe that they had discovered?

The newsmen present were interested in the cultural basis of the Minervan civilization, particularly the means of conducting everyday commercial transactions between individuals and between organizations. A freely competing economy based on monetary values seemed incompatible with the noncompetitive Ganymean character and raised the question of what alternative system the aliens used to measure and control the obligations between an individual and the rest of society.

The Ganymeans confirmed that their system had functioned without the motivational forces of profit and a need to maintain any kind of financial solvency. This was another area in which the radically different psychology and conditioning of the Ganymeans made a smooth dialogue impossible, mainly because they had no comprehension of many of the facts of living that were accepted as self-evident on Earth. That some means of control was desirable to insure that everybody put into society at least as much as he took out was strange to them; so was the concept that any measure of a "normal" input-output ratio could be specified since, they maintained, every individual had his own preferred ratio at which he functioned optimally, and which it was his basic right to choose. The concept of financial necessity or any other means of coercing somebody to live a life that he would not otherwise follow was, to them, a grotesque infringement of freedom and dignity. Besides that, they seemed unable to understand why it should be necessary to base any society on such principles.

What then, they were asked, was there to prevent everybody becoming purely a taker, with no obligation to give anything in return? That being the case, how could a society survive at all? Again the Ganymeans seemed unable to understand the problem. Surely, they pointed out, individuals possessed an instinct to contribute and one of the essential needs of living was the satisfaction of that instinct; why would anybody deliberately deprive himself of the feeling of being needed? Apparently that was what motivated the Ganymean in place of monetary incentives—he simply could not live with the thought of not being of any use to anybody. He was just made that way. The worst situation he could find himself in was that of having to depend on society for his wants without being able to reciprocate, and anybody who sought such an existence deliberately was regarded as a social anomaly in need of psychiatric help and an object of sympathy—rather like a mentally retarded child. The observation that this was regarded by many on Earth as the ultimate fulfillment of ambition reinforced the Ganymean conviction that *Homo sapiens* had inherited some awful defects from the Lunarians. On a more encouraging note they expressed the view, based on what they knew of the last few decades of Man's history, that Nature was slowly but surely repairing the damage.

By the time the conference had finished Hunt found that all the talking had made him thirsty. He asked ZORAC if there was anywhere nearby where he might get a drink and was informed that if he went out through the main door of the room he was in, turned right and followed the corridor for a short distance, he would come to an open seating area where refreshments were available. Hunt ordered a GTB and Coke—the latest product of the fusion of the two cultures and an instant hit with both—and left the mêlée of producers and technicians to follow the directions and pick up the drink at the dispensing unit.

As he turned and cast an eye around the area to look for a suitable seat, he noted absently that he was the only Earthman present. A few Ganymeans were scattered around singly or in small groups, but most of the places were empty. He picked out a small table with a few unoccupied chairs around it, sauntered across and sat down. Apart from one or two slight nods of acknowledgment, none of the Ganymeans took any notice of him; anyone would have thought it an everyday occurrence for unaccompanied aliens to wander around their ship. The sight of the ashtray on the table prompted him to reach into his pocket for his cigarette pack. Then he stopped, momentarily puzzled; the Ganymeans didn't smoke. He peered more closely at the ashtray and realized that it was standard

UNSA issue. He looked around. Most of the tables had UNSA ashtrays. As usual the Ganymeans had thought of everything; naturally there would be Earthmen around with the conference that day. He sighed, shook his head in admiration and settled back into the huge expanse of upholstered luxury to relax with his thoughts.

He didn't realize Shilohin was standing nearby until ZORAC spoke in his ear with the voice that it reserved for her. "Dr. Hunt, isn't it? Good afternoon."

Hunt looked up with a start and then recognized her. He grinned at the standard salutation and gestured toward one of the empty seats. Shilohin sat down and placed her own drink on the table.

"I see we seem to have had the same idea," she said. "It's thirsty work."

"You can say that again."

"Well . . . how do you think it went?"

"It was great. I think they were all fascinated. . . . I bet it'll cause some pretty lively arguments back home."

Shilohin seemed to hesitate for a second before going on. "You don't think Monchar was too direct . . . too openly critical of your way of life and your values? Those things he said about the Lunarians for example . . ."

Hunt reflected for a moment while he drew on his cigarette.

"No, I don't think so. If that's the way Ganymeans see it, it's much better if it's said straight. . . . If you ask me, something like that has needed saying for a long time. I can't think of anybody better to say it; more people might start taking notice now . . . good thing too."

"That's nice to know anyway," she said, sounding suddenly more at ease. "I was beginning to feel a little worried about it."

"I don't think anybody's very worried about that side of it," Hunt commented. "Certainly the scientists aren't. They're more worried about having the laws of physics collapse around their ears. I don't think you've realized yet what a stir you've started. Some of our most basic convictions are going to have to be re-thought—right from square one. We thought we had just a few more pages to add to the story; now it looks as if we might have to rewrite the whole book."

"That's true I suppose," she conceded. "But at least you won't have to go all the way back as far as the Ganymean scientists did." She noted his look of interest. "Oh yes, believe me, Dr. Hunt, we went through the same process ourselves. The discovery of relativity and quantum mechanics turned all of our classical ideas upside down just as happened in your own science in the early twentieth century. And then when the things we were talking about earlier began fitting together, we had another major scientific upheaval; all the concepts that had survived the first time and were regarded as absolute turned out to be wrong—all the ingrained beliefs had to be changed."

She turned to look at him and made a Ganymean gesture of resignation. "Your science would have reached the same point eventually even if we hadn't arrived, and not all that far in the future either if my judgment is anything to go by. As things are, you'll dodge the worst since we can show you most of what's involved anyway. Fifty years from now you'll be flying ships like this one."

"I wonder." Hunt's voice was far away. It sounded incredible, but then he thought of the history of aviation; how many of the colonial territories of the 1920s would have believed that fifty years later they would be independent states running their own jet fleets? How many Americans would have believed that the same time span would take them from wooden bi-planes to Apollo?

"And what happens after that?" he murmured, half to himself. "Will there be more scientific upheavals waiting . . . things that even you people don't know about yet either?"

"Who knows?" she replied. "I did outline where research had got to when we left Minerva; anything could have happened afterward. But don't make the mistake of thinking that we know everything, even within our existing framework of knowledge. We've had our surprises too, you know—since we came to Ganymede. The Earthmen have taught us some things we didn't know."

This was news to Hunt.

"How do you mean?" he asked, naturally intrigued. "What kind of things?"

She sipped her drink slowly to collect her thoughts. "Well, let's take this question of carnivorism, for example. As you know, it was unknown on Minerva, apart from in certain deep-sea species that only scientists were interested in and most other Ganymeans preferred to forget."

"Yes, I know that."

"Well, Ganymean biologists had, of course, studied the workings of evolution and reconstructed the story of how their own race originated. Although layman's thinking was largely governed by the concept of some divinely ordained natural order, as I mentioned earlier, many scientists recognized the chance aspect of the scheme that had established itself on our world. Purely from the scientific viewpoint, they could see no reason why things *had* to be the way they were. So, being scientists, they began to ask what might have happened if things had been different . . . for example, if carnivorous fish had not migrated to midocean depths, but had remained in coastal waters."

"You mean if amphibian and land-dwelling carnivores had evolved," Hunt supplied.

"Exactly. Some scientists maintained that it was just a quirk of fate that led to Minerva being the way it was—nothing to do with any divine laws at all. So they began constructing hypothetical models of ecological systems that included carnivores . . . more as intellectual exercise, I suppose."

"Mmm . . . interesting. How did they turn out?"

"They were hopelessly wrong," Shilohin told him. She made a gesture of emphasis. "Most of the models predicted the whole evolutionary system slowing down and degenerating into a stagnant dead end, much as happened in our own oceans. They hadn't managed to separate out the limitations imposed by an aquatic environment, and attributed the result to the fundamentally destructive nature of the way of life there. You can imagine their surprise when the first Ganymean expedition reached Earth and found just such a land-based ecology in action. They were amazed at how advanced and how specialized the animals had become . . . and the birds! That was something none of them had dreamed of. Now you can see why many of us were stunned by the sight of the animals that you showed us at Pithead. We had heard of such creatures, but none of us had actually seen one."

Hunt nodded slowly and began to comprehend fully at last. To a race that had grown up surrounded by Danchekker's cartoons, the sight of *Trilophodon,* the four-tusked walking tank, or of the saber-toothed killing machine *Smilodon,* must have been awesome. What kind of picture had the Ganymeans formed of the ferocious arena that had molded and shaped such gladiators, he wondered.

"So, they had to change their ideas on that subject in a hurry as well," he said.

"They did. . . . They revised all their theories on the strength of the evidence from Earth, and they worked out a completely new model. But, I'm afraid, they got it all wrong again."

Hunt couldn't suppress a short laugh.

"Really? What went wrong this time?"

"Your level of civilization and your technology," she told him. "All our scientists were convinced that an advanced race could never emerge from the pattern of life that they saw on Earth twenty-five million years ago. They argued that intelligence could never appear in any stable form in such an environment, and even if it did it would destroy itself as soon as it had the power to do so. Certainly any kind of sociable living or communal society was out of the question and, since the acquisition of knowledge depends on communication and cooperation, the sciences could never be developed."

"But we proved that was all baloney, eh?"

"It's incredible!" Shilohin indicated bewilderment. "All our models showed that any progression from the life forms of your Miocene period toward greater intelligence would depend on selection for greater cunning and more sophisticated methods of violence; no coherent civilization could possibly develop from a background like that. And yet . . . we have returned and found not only a civilized and technologically advanced culture, but one that is accelerating all the time. It seemed impossible. That was why we took so much convincing that you came from the third planet from the sun—the Nightmare Planet."

These remarks made Hunt feel flattered, but at the same time he remembered how close the Ganymean prophecies had come to being true.

"But you were so nearly right, weren't you," he said soberly. "Don't forget the Lunarians. They did destroy themselves in just the way that your model predicted, although it looks as if they too advanced further than you thought they would. It was only the fact that a handful of them survived it that we're here at all, and they only made it on a million-to-one shot." He shook his head and exhaled a cloud of smoke sharply. "I wouldn't feel too bad about what your models said; they came far too near the truth for comfort as far as I'm concerned . . . far too near. If whatever it was that made the Lunarians the way they were hadn't modified itself somehow and become diluted in the course of time, we'd be going the same way and your model would be proved right again. With luck though, we're over that hump now."

"And that's the most incredible thing of all," Shilohin said, picking up the point immediately. "The very thing that we believed would prove an insurmountable barrier to progress has turned out to be your biggest advantage."

"How do you mean?"

"The aggressiveness, the determination—the refusal to let anything defeat you. All that is built deep into the basic Earthman character. It's a relic from your origins, modified, refined, and adapted. But that's where it comes from. You maybe don't see it that way, but we can. We're astounded by it. Try to understand, we've never seen or imagined anything like it before."

"Danchekker said something like that," Hunt mumbled, but Shilohin continued, apparently not having heard him.

"Our instincts are to avoid any form of danger, because of the way we originated . . . certainly not to seek it deliberately. We are a cautious people. But Earthmen . . . ! They climb mountains, sail tiny boats around a planet alone, jump out of aircraft for fun! All their games are simulated combat; this thing you call 'business' reenacts the survival struggle of your evolutionary system and the power-lust of your wars; your 'politics' is based on the principle of meeting force with force and matching strength with strength." She paused for a moment, and then went on. "These are completely new to Ganymeans. The idea of a race that will actually rise up and answer threats with defiance is . . . unbelievable. We have studied large portions of your planet's history. Much of it is horrifying to us, but also, beneath the superficial story of events, some of us see something deeper—something stirring. The difficulties that Man has faced are appalling, but the way in which he has always fought back at them and always won in the end—I must confess there is something about it that is strangely magnificent."

"But why should that be?" Hunt asked. "Why should the Ganymeans feel that we have some unique advantage, especially with their different background? They achieved the same things . . . and more."

"Because of the time it's taken you to do it," she said.

"Time?"

"Your rate of advancement. It's stupendous! Haven't Earthmen realized? No, I don't suppose there's any reason why they should." She looked at him again, seemingly at a loss for a second. "How long ago did Man harness steam? It took you less than seventy years from learning to fly to reach your Moon. Twenty years after you invented transistors half your world was being run by computers. . . ."

"That's good, compared to Minerva?"

"Good! It's miraculous! It makes our own development pale into insignificance. And it's getting faster all the time! It's because you attack Nature with the same innate aggressiveness that you hurl at anything that stands in your way. You don't hack each other to pieces or bomb whole cities anymore, but the same instinct is still there in your scientists, engineers . . . your businessmen, your politicians. They all love a good fight. They thrive on it. That's the difference between us. The Ganymean learns for knowledge and finds that he solves problems as a by-product; the Earthman takes on a problem and finds that he's learned something when he's solved it, but it's the kick he gets out of fighting and winning that matters. Garuth summed it up fairly well when I was talking to him yesterday. I asked him if he thought that any of the Earthmen really believed in this God they talk about. Know what he said?"

"What'd he say?"

" 'They will once they've made Him.' "

Hunt couldn't help grinning at Garuth's bemusement that was at the same time a compliment. He was about to reply when ZORAC spoke into his ear in its own voice:

"Excuse me, Dr. Hunt."

"Yes?"

"A Sergeant Brukhov wants to talk for a second. Are you accepting calls?"

"Excuse me a minute," he said to Shilohin. "Okay. Put him on."

"Dr. Hunt?" The voice of one of the UNSA pilots came through clearly.

"Here."

"Sorry to bother you, but we're sorting out the arrangements for getting everybody back to Pithead. I'm taking a transporter back half an hour from now and I've got a couple of empty seats. Also there's a Ganymean ship leaving about an hour later and some of the guys are hitching a ride on it. You're on the list to go; it's your choice which way."

"Any idea who's going on the Ganymean ship?"

"Don't know who they are, but they're standing

right in front of me. I'm in the big room that the conference was held in."

"Give me a shot, would you?" Hunt asked.

He activated his wrist unit and observed the view being picked up by Brukhov's headband. It showed a group of faces that Hunt recognized at once, all of them from the labs at Pithead. Carizan was there . . . so was Frank Towers.

"Thanks for the offer," Hunt said. "I'll go with them though."

"Okay . . . oh . . . hang on a sec . . ." Indistinct background noises, then Brukhov again. "One of them wants to know where the hell you've got to."

"Tell him I've found the bar."

More noises.

"He wants to know where the hell that is."

"Okay, look over at the wall," Hunt replied. "Now follow it along to your left . . . a bit farther . . ." He watched the image move across the screen. "Hold it there. You're looking at the main door."

"Check."

"Through there, turn right and follow the passage. They can't miss it. Drinks are on the house; order through ZORAC."

"Okay, I got it. They say they'll see you there in a coupla minutes. Over and out."

"Channel cleared down," ZORAC informed him.

"Sorry about that," Hunt said to Shilohin. "We've got company on the way."

"Earthmen?"

"Bunch of drunks from up north. I made the mistake of telling them where we are."

She laughed—he could recognize the sound now —and then, slowly, her mood became serious again. "You strike me as a very rational and level-headed Earthman. There is something that we have never mentioned before because we were unsure of the reactions it might produce, but I feel it is something that we can talk about here."

"Go on." Hunt sensed that she had been giving some thought to whatever the matter was while he had been talking to the pilot. He detected a subtle change in her manner; she was not quite conveying that the topic was one of strict confidence, but that how he chose to use the information would be left to his own discretion. He knew his own kind better than she did.

"There was an occasion when the Ganymeans resorted to the use of willful violence . . . deliberate destruction of life."

Hunt waited in silence, unsure of what kind of response would be appropriate.

"You know," she went on, "about the problem that Minerva was experiencing—with the carbon-dioxide level rising. Well, one possible solution presented itself immediately—simply migrate to another planet. But this was at a time before there were any ships like the *Shapieron* . . . before we could travel to other stars. Therefore we could contemplate only the planets of the Solar System. Apart from Minerva itself, only one of them could have supported life."

Hunt looked at her blankly; the message had not quite registered.

"Earth," he said with a slight shrug.

"Yes, Earth. We could move our whole civilization to Earth. As you know, we sent expeditions to explore it, but when they sent back details of the environment that they found there, we knew that there could be no simple answer to Minerva's problems. Ganymeans could never have survived amid such savagery."

"So the idea was abandoned then?" Hunt suggested.

"No . . . not quite. You see, the whole terrestrial ecology and the creatures that formed part of it were thought by many Ganymeans to be so unnatural as to constitute a perversion of life itself—a smear upon an otherwise perfect universe that the universe would be a better place without." Hunt gaped at her as what she was saying began to sink in. "A suggestion was put forward that the whole planet be wiped clean of the disease that infested it. Terrestrial life would be exterminated, and then Minervan forms would be substituted. After all, the supporters of the scheme argued, it would be simply playing the game by Earth's own rules."

Hunt was stunned. After everything that had been said, the Ganymeans could actually have been capable of conceiving a scheme like that? She watched and seemed to read the thought in his mind.

"Most Ganymeans opposed the idea, instinctively, totally and without compromise. It was completely against their basic nature. The public protest that it provoked was probably the most vigorous in our whole history.

"Nevertheless, our own world was in danger of becoming uninhabitable, and some members of the government took the view that they had an obligation to investigate every possible alternative. So, in secret, they set up a small colony on Earth to experiment on a local scale." She saw the questions forming on Hunt's lips and held up a hand to forestall them. "Don't ask me where on Earth this colony was or what methods they employed to do the things they were sent there to do; I have great difficulty in speaking about this at all. Let us just say that the results were catastrophic. In some regions the ecology collapsed completely as a consequence of the things that were done and many terrestrial species became extinct during what you call the Oligocene period for this reason. Some of the areas affected remain deserts on Earth to this day."

Hunt didn't know what to say, so said nothing. The things he had just been told were shocking not because of the means or ends that they implied, which were all too familiar to humans, but because they were so unexpected. For him the conversation was a revelation and a staggering one at that, but no more. For the Ganymean, he realized, it was traumatic.

Shilohin seemed somewhat reassured by the absence of any violent emotional response on his part, and so continued. "Not surprisingly, the psychological effects on the colonists were equally disastrous. The whole sorry affair was quietly ended and filed away as one of the shabbier episodes of our history. We prefer to try and forget about it."

A babble of human voices interspersed with laughter came from further along the corridor. As Hunt looked up expectantly Shilohin touched his arm to retain his attention for a moment longer.

"That, Dr. Hunt, is the real reason why we feel too ashamed to talk about the Oligocene Earth and its animals," she said.

chapter thirteen

The *Shapieron* was pronounced fully functional once more and the Ganymeans announced their intention to take the ship for a test flight to the outermost fringe of the Solar System. The trip was expected to take about a week.

A mixed gathering of scientists, engineers and UNSA personnel had congregated in the messroom at Pithead to watch the takeoff, the view of which was being relayed from Main Base and shown on the wall screen. Hunt, Carizan and Towers were sharing a table at the back of the room and drinking coffee. As the countdown neared zero, the hubbub of conversation quieted and an air of expectancy descended.

"All UNSA vessels have cleared the area. You're okay to go on schedule." The voice of the controller at Main sounded from the audio grille.

"Acknowledged," the familiar voice of ZORAC replied. "All our prelaunch checks are positive. We're lifting off now. *Au revoir* until about a week from now, Earthmen."

"Sure. See ya around."

For a few seconds longer the huge, majestic shape, its tail end now retracted and its outer bays closed, remained motionless, towering skyward to dominate the untidy sprawl of the base in the foreground. Then the ship began to lift, slowly and smoothly, sliding up into an unbroken background of stars as the camera followed it and the last ice crest disappeared off the bottom of the picture. Almost at once it started to contract rapidly as the foreshortening increased with the angle at a rate that hinted of the fearsome buildup of speed.

"Man, look at her go!" came the voice from Main. "Do you have radar contact yet, *J5?*"

"It's going like greased lightning out of hell," another voice answered. "We're starting to lose it. The image is breaking up. They must be on main drive already—their stress field's starting to scramble the echoes. Image on the optical scanners is losing coherence too . . ." And then: "That's it. It's gone . . . like it was never there at all. Fantastic!"

That was that. A few low whistles of surprise broke the silence in the messroom at Pithead, followed by muttered exclamations and murmurings. Gradually the fragments of conversation flowed together and merged into a steady continuum of noise that rose and found its own level. The picture on the screen reverted to the view of Main, now looking somehow empty and incomplete without the ship standing in the background. Even after so short a time, life on Ganymede without the Giants around didn't feel quite right.

"Well, I've got to go," Hunt said, rising from his chair. "Chris wants to talk about something. See you both later." The other two looked up.

"Sure. See you later."

"See you, Vic."

As he moved toward the door, Hunt realized that Pithead didn't seem right either without a single Ganymean in sight. It was strange, he thought, that every one of them should need to go on a test flight; but . . . that was not really something for Earthmen to reason why. He realized also that not having ZORAC around would also take some getting used to. He had come unconsciously to accept the ability to communicate directly with others and to consult with the machine, whatever time of day it was or wherever he happened to be. ZORAC had come to be a guide, mentor, tutor and advisor all rolled into one—an omniscient and omnipresent companion. Hunt suddenly felt very alone and isolated without it. The Ganymeans could have left specialized relay equipment at Ganymede that would have sustained a link to ZORAC, but the mutual slowing down of clocks that the

Shapieron's velocity would produce, together with the large distance that its flight would entail, would soon have made any form of meaningful communication impossible. It was, he admitted privately to himself, going to be a long week.

Hunt found Danchekker in his lab fussing over his Minervan plants, which by this time were proliferating in every corner of the room and seemed set to embark on an invasion of the corridor outside. The subject that the professor wanted to discuss was the theory that he and Hunt had formulated jointly, before the arrival of the Ganymeans, concerning the low inherent tolerance of all Minervan land-dwelling species to atmospheric carbon dioxide. This theory held that the trait had been inherited, along with the basic system of chemical metabolism, from some very early, common, marine ancestor. After discussing the matter at some length with various Ganymean scientists through ZORAC, Danchekker now knew that this theory was wrong.

"In fact, when land dwellers eventually appeared on Minerva, they evolved a very efficient method of coping with the planet's high carbon-dioxide level. The way in which they did it was one which, with the benefit of hindsight, was very obvious and very simple." Danchekker stopped rummaging around among the mass of leaves for a moment and half turned his head to allow Hunt time to reflect on the statement. Hunt, perched casually on one of the stools with an elbow resting on the edge of the bench beside him, said nothing and waited.

"They adaped their secondary circulation systems to absorb the excess," Danchekker told him. "Systems that had evolved specifically to remove toxins in the first place. They provided a ready-made mechanism ideal for the job."

Hunt turned the proposition over in his mind and rubbed his chin thoughtfully.

"So . . ." he said after a while. "This idea we had that they all inherited a low tolerance was way off the rails . . . all baloney."

"Baloney."

"And this characteristic stayed, did it? I mean, all the species that came later inherited the mechanism . . . they were all well-adapted to their environment?"

"Yes. Perfectly adequately."

"But there's still something I don't see yet," Hunt said, frowning. "If what you've just said was true, the Ganymeans should have inherited an adequate resistance too. If they did, they wouldn't have had a CO_2 problem. But they themselves said they did have a CO_2 problem. So how come?"

Danchekker turned to face him and wiped his palms on the front of his lab coat. He beamed through his spectacles and showed his teeth.

"They did inherit it . . . the resistance mechanism. They did have a problem too. But, you see, the problem wasn't natural; it was artificial. They brought it upon themselves, far later in their history."

"Chris, you're talking in riddles. Why not start at the beginning?"

"Very well." Danchekker began wiping dry the tools he had been using and replaced them in one of the drawers as he spoke. "As I said a moment ago, when land-dwelling life appeared on Minerva, the secondary circulation systems that all species already possessed—which caused them to be poisonous—adapted to absorb the excess carbon dioxide. Thus although Minervan air was high in carbon dioxide compared to that of Earth, all the forms of life that emerged there flourished quite happily since they had evolved a perfectly good means of adapting to their surroundings . . . which is the way one would expect Nature to work. When, after hundreds of millions of years, intelligence emerged in the form of primitive Ganymeans, they too possessed the same basic architecture, which had remained essentially unchanged. So far so good?"

"They were still poisonous and they were well adapted," Hunt said.

"Quite so."

"What happened then?"

"Then a very interesting thing must have happened.

The Ganymean race appeared and went through all the stages you would expect of a primitive culture beginning to grope its way toward civilization—making tools, growing food, building houses and so on. Well, by this time, as you might imagine, the ancient self-defense that they had inherited from their remote marine ancestors for protecting them against carnivores was turning out to be more of a damned nuisance than a help. There were no carnivores to be protected from and it was soon obvious that none were likely to appear. On the other hand, the acute accident-proneness that resulted from self-poisoning was proving to be a severe handicap." Danchekker held up a finger to show a small band of adhesive plaster around the second joint. "I nicked myself with a scalpel yesterday," he commented. "Had I been one of those early Ganymeans, I would most probably have been dead within the hour."

"Okay, point taken," Hunt conceded. "But what could they do about it?"

"Somewhere around the time that I was describing —the early beginnings of civilization—the ancients discovered that the poisons in the secondary system could be neutralized by including certain plants and molds in their diet. They discovered this by observing the habits of some animals whose immunity to damage that should have meant certain death was well known. That simple step was probably their biggest single leap forward. Coupled with their intelligence it virtually insured dominance over all forms of Minervan life. It opened up the whole of medical science, for example. With their self-poisoning mechanism defused, surgery became possible. At a later stage in their history they developed a simple surgical method of neutralizing the secondary system permanently without having to rely on drugs. It became standard practice for every Ganymean to be treated in this way soon after birth. Even later still, when they had progressed to a level beyond ours, they isolated the gene that caused the secondary system to develop in the fetus in the first place and eradicated it completely. They literally bred this trait out of themselves. None of the Ganymeans we've met was born with a secondary system at all, and neither were quite a few generations before them. Rather an elegant solution, don't you think?"

"Incredible," Hunt agreed. "I've never had a chance to talk about that kind of thing with them . . . not yet anyway."

"Oh, yes." Danchekker nodded. "They were extremely proficient genetic engineers, were our Ganymean friends . . . very proficient."

Hunt thought for a second and then snapped his fingers in sudden comprehension.

"But of course," he said. "In doing that they buggered their CO_2 tolerance too."

"Precisely, Vic. All the other animals on Minerva retained the high natural tolerance. Only the Ganymeans were different; they sacrificed it in exchange for accident-resistance."

"But I don't see how they could," Hunt said, frowning again. "I mean, I can see how they did it, but I don't see how they could get away with it. They must have needed the CO_2 tolerance, otherwise they wouldn't have evolved it in the first place. They must have known that too. Surely they weren't stupid."

Danchekker nodded as if he already knew what Hunt was going to say.

"That probably wasn't so obvious at the time," he said. "You see, the composition of the Minervan atmosphere fluctuated through the ages much the same as that of Earth has. From various researches the Ganymeans established that at the time land life first emerged, volcanic activity was at a peak and the level of CO_2 was very high; naturally, therefore, the earliest species developed a high resistance. But as time went on the level decreased progressively and appeared to have stabilized itself by the time of the Ganymeans. They came to regard their tolerance mechanism as an ancient relic of conditions that no longer existed and their experiences showed that they could get by without it. The margin was small—the CO_2 level was still high by our standards—but they could manage. So, they decided to do away with it permanently."

"Ah, but then the level started going up again," Hunt guessed.

"Suddenly and catastrophically," Danchekker confirmed. "On a geological time scale anyway. They were in no immediate danger, but all their measurements and calculations indicated that if the rate of increase went on, they—or their descendants one day anyway—would be in trouble. They would be unable to survive without their ancient tolerance mechanism, but they had eliminated that mechanism from their race. All the other animals would have no difficulty in adapting, but the Ganymeans were somewhat stuck."

The full magnitude of the problem that had confronted the Ganymeans dawned on Hunt at last. They had bought a one-way ticket out of the hard-labor camp only to find that it led to the death cell.

"What could they do?" Danchekker asked, and then went on to answer the question for himself. "First— use their technology to hold the CO_2 level down by artificial means. They thought of that but their models couldn't guarantee them a tight enough measure of control over the process. There was a high risk that they'd end up freezing the whole planet solid and, being the cautious breed that they were, they elected not to try it—at least not until it was a last-resort measure.

"Second—they could reduce the CO_2 as before, but have ready at hand a method for warming up the sun to compensate for the loss of the greenhouse effect if the atmospheric engineering got out of control. They tried that on Iscaris but it went wrong, as the scientists on Minerva learned when they received a message from the *Shapieron* that was sent just before the ship itself got away."

Hunt made no move to interrupt, so Danchekker continued. "Third—they could migrate to Earth. They tried doing so on a pilot scale, but that went wrong too." Danchekker shrugged and held the posture, his arms extended to indicate that he had run out of possibilities. Hunt waited for a moment longer, but the professor evidently had nothing more to say.

"So what the devil did they do?" Hunt asked.

"I don't know. The Ganymeans don't know either, since whatever else may have been thought of was thought of after they had left Minerva. They are as curious as we are—more so I would imagine. It was their world."

"But the animals from Earth," Hunt insisted. "They were all imported later on. Couldn't they have had something to do with the solution?"

"They could have, certainly, but what exactly, I've no idea. Neither have the Ganymeans. We're satisfied, though, that it would not have been anything to do with using a terrestrial type of ecology to absorb the CO_2. That simply wouldn't have worked."

"That idea's gone right out the window, eh?"

"Right out," Danchekker said decisively. "Why they brought the animals there and whether or not it had anything to do with their atmospheric problem is still all a mystery. . . ." The professor paused and peered intently over the top of his spectacles. "There's another mystery too now—a new one—from what we've just been talking about."

"Another one?" Hunt returned his stare curiously. "What?"

"All the other Minervan animals," Danchekker replied slowly. "You see, if they all possessed a perfectly adequate mechanism for dealing with CO_2, it couldn't have been the changing atmosphere of Minerva that wiped them all out after all. If that didn't, then what did?"

chapter fourteen

The landscape was a featureless, undulating sheet of ice that extended in every direction to merge into the gloom of a perpetual night. Overhead a diminutive Sun, barely more than just a bright star among millions, sent down its feeble rays to paint an eerie and foreboding twilight on the scene.

The huge shadowy shape of the ship soared upward to lose itself in the blackness above; arc lights set high on its side cast down a brilliant cone of whiteness, etching out an enormous circle on the ice next to where the ship stood. Around the inside of the periphery of the pool of light, several hundred spacesuited, eight-foot-tall figures stood four deep in unmoving ranks, their heads bowed and their hands clasped loosely before them. The area within the circle was divided into a series of concentric rings and at regular intervals around each ring rectangular pits had been cut into the ice, each one aligned with the center. By the side of each of the pits lay a metallic, box-shaped container roughly nine feet long and four feet wide.

A small group of figures walked slowly to the center and began moving around the innermost ring, stopping at each pit in turn and watching in silence while the container was lowered before moving on to the next. A second small group followed, filling each of the pits with water from a heated hose; the water froze solid in seconds. When they had finished the first ring they moved out to begin on the second, and continued until they were back at the edge of the circle.

They stood gazing for a long time at the simple memorial that they had erected in the center of the circle—a golden obelisk with an inscription on each face, surmounted by a light that would burn for a hundred years. And as they gazed, their thoughts went back in time to friends and faces that they once had known, and who could never again be more than memories.

Then, when the time had come, they turned away and began filing slowly back toward their ship. When the arc lights were turned out, only the tiny glow of light around the obelisk remained to hold the night at bay.

They had honored the pledge that they had made and carried with them through all the years that had brought them here, from another place, from another time.

Beneath the ice field of Pluto lay the soil of Minerva.

The Giants had come home to lay their dead to rest.

chapter fifteen

The *Shapieron* reappeared out of space as suddenly as it had gone. The surveillance radars of *Jupiter Five* picked up an indistinct echo hurtling in from the void and rapidly consolidating itself as it shed speed at a phenomenal rate. By the time the optical scanners had been brought to bear, there it was, coasting into orbit over Ganymede just like the first time. This time, however, the emotions that greeted its arrival were very different.

The exchange of messages recorded in *Jupiter Five*'s Communications Center Day Log was enthusiastic and friendly.

Shapieron	Good afternoon.
J5	Hi. How was the trip?
Shap.	Excellent. How has the weather been?
J5	Pretty much the same as ever. How were the engines?
Shap.	Never better. Did you save our rooms?
J5	Same ones as before. You wanna go on down?
Shap.	Thanks. We know the way.

Within five hours of the *Shapieron* touching down at Ganymede Main Base, familiar eight-foot-tall figures were clumping up and down the corridors at Pithead once again.

Hunt's conversation with Danchekker had stimulated his curiosity about biological mechanisms for combating the effects of toxins and contaminants in the body, and he spent the next few days accessing

153

the data banks of *Jupiter Five* to study up on the subject. Shilohin had mentioned that terrestrial life had evolved from early marine species that hadn't developed a secondary circulation system because they hadn't needed one; the warmer environment of Earth had imposed less strenuous demands for oxygen with the result that load-sharing had not been necessary. But it was this same mechanism that had later enabled the emerging Minervan land dwellers to adapt to a CO_2-rich atmosphere. The terrestrial animals imported to Minerva had obviously possessed no similar mechanism, and yet they had adapted readily enough to their new home. Hunt was curious to find out how they did it.

His researches failed, however, to throw up anything startling. Each world had evolved its own family of life, and the two systems of fundamental chemistry on which the two families were based were not the same. Minervan chemistry was rather delicate, as Danchekker had deduced long ago from his study of the preserved Minervan fish discovered in the ruins of a wrecked Lunarian base; land animals inheriting such chemistry would be inherently sensitive to certain toxins, including carbon dioxide, and would require an extra line of defense to give them a reasonable tolerance if atmospheric conditions were extreme—hence the adaptation of the secondary system in the earliest land dwellers. Terrestrial chemistry was more rugged and flexible and could survive a far wider range of changes, even without any assistance. And that was really all there was to it.

One afternoon, Hunt found himself sitting in front of the viewscreen in one of the computer console rooms at Pithead at the end of another unsuccessful attempt to uncover a new slant on the subject. Having nobody else to talk to, he activated his channel into the Ganymean computer network and discussed the problem with ZORAC. The machine listened solemnly without offering much in the way of comment while Hunt spoke. Afterward it had one comment. "I really don't see much to add, Vic. You seem to have got it pretty wrapped up."

"There's nothing you can think of that I might have left out?" Hunt queried. It seemed a funny question for a scientist to put to a machine, but Hunt had come to know well ZORAC's uncanny ability to spot a missing detail or a small flaw in what appeared to be a watertight line of reasoning.

"No. The evidence adds up to what you've already concluded: Minervan life needed the help of a secondary system to adapt and terrestrial life didn't. That is an observed fact, not a deduction. Therefore there's not a lot I can say."

"No, I guess not," Hunt conceded with a sigh. He flipped a switch to cut off the terminal, lit a cigarette and slumped back in a chair. "It wasn't really that important, I suppose," he commented absently after a while. "I was just curious to see if the differences in biochemistry between our life forms and Minervan ones pointed to anything significant. Looks as if they don't."

"What were you hoping to find?" ZORAC asked. Hunt shrugged automatically.

"Oh, I don't know . . . something that might shed light on the kinds of things we've been asking . . . what happened to all the Minervan land dwellers, what was it that they couldn't survive that the animals from Earth could—we know it wasn't the CO_2 concentration now. . . . Things like that."

"Anything unusual, in fact," ZORAC suggested.

"Mmm . . . guess so."

A few seconds passed before ZORAC spoke again. Hunt had the uncanny impression that the machine was turning the proposition over in its mind. Then it said in a matter-of-fact voice: "Maybe you've been asking the wrong question."

It took a moment for the implication to sink in. Then Hunt snatched the cigarette from his lips and sat forward in his chair with a start.

"What d'you mean?" he asked. "What's wrong with the question?"

"You're asking why Minervan life and terrestrial

life were different and succeeding only in proving that the answer is, 'because they were.' It's undeniably true, but singularly ineffective in telling you anything new. It's like asking, 'Why does salt dissolve in water when sand doesn't?' and coming up with the answer, 'because salt's soluble and sand isn't.' Very true, but it doesn't tell you much. That's what you're doing."

"You mean I've simply been working around a circular argument?" Hunt said, but even as he spoke he could see it was true.

"An elaborate one, but when you analyze the logic of it—yes," ZORAC confirmed.

Hunt nodded to himself and flicked his cigarette to the ashtray.

"Okay. What question should I be asking?"

"Forget about Minervan life and terrestrial life for a moment, and just concentrate on the terrestrial," ZORAC replied. "Now ask why Man is so different from any other species."

"I thought we knew all that." Hunt said. "Bigger brains, opposable thumbs, high-quality vision all in one species together—all the tools you need to stimulate curiosity and learning. What's new?"

"I know *what* the differences are," ZORAC stated. "My question was *why* are they?"

Hunt rubbed his chin with his knuckle for a while as he reflected on the question. "Do you think that's significant?"

"Very."

"Okay. I'll buy it. Why is Man so different from any other species?"

"I don't know."

"Great!" Hunt exhaled a long stream of smoke with a sigh. "And how exactly is that supposed to tell us more than my answers did?"

"It doesn't," ZORAC conceded. "But it's a question that needs answering. If you're looking for something unusual, that's a good place to start. There's something very unusual about Man."

"Oh, how come?"

"Because by rights Man shouldn't exist. It shouldn't have been possible for him to evolve. Man simply can't happen, but he did. That seems very unusual to me."

Hunt shook his head, puzzled. The machine was speaking in riddles.

"I don't understand. Why shouldn't Man have happened?"

"I have computed the interaction matrix functions that describe the responses of neuron trigger potentials in the nervous systems of higher terrestrial vertebrates. Some of the reaction coefficients are highly dependent on the concentrations and distributions of certain microchemical agencies. Coherent response patterns in key areas of the cerebral cortex could not stabilize with the levels that are usual in all species except Man."

Pause.

"ZORAC, what are you talking about?"

"I'm not making sense?"

"To put it mildly—no."

"Okay." ZORAC paused for a second as if getting its thoughts organized. "Are you familiar with Kaufmann and Randall's recent work at the University of Utrecht, Holland? It is fully recorded in *Jupiter Five*'s data bank."

"Yes, I did come across some references to it," Hunt replied. "Refresh my memory on it."

"Kaufmann and Randall conducted extensive research on the way in which terrestrial vertebrates protect themselves against toxic agents and harmful microorganisms that enter their systems," ZORAC said. "The details vary somewhat from species to species, but essentially the basic mechanism is the same —presumably handed down and modified from common remote ancestral forms."

"Ah yes, I remember," Hunt said. "A kind of natural self-immunization process, wasn't it."

He was referring to the discovery by the scientists at Utrecht that the animals of Earth manufactured a whole mixture of contaminants and toxins on a small scale, which were injected into the bloodstream in quantities just high enough to stimulate the production of specific antitoxins. The "blueprint" for manufacturing these antitoxins was thus permanently impressed into the body's chemical system in such a way that production would multiply prodigiously in the event of the body being invaded on a dangerous scale.

"Correct," ZORAC answered. "It explains why animals are far less bothered by unwholesome environments, polluted diets and so on than Man is."

"Because Man is different; he doesn't work that way—right?"

"Right."

"Which brings us back to your question."

"Right."

Hunt regarded the blank screen of the console for a while, frowning to himself in an effort to follow what the machine was getting at. Whatever it was, it failed to register.

"I still don't see where it gets us," Hunt said at last. "Man's different because he's different. It's just as much a pointless question as before."

"Not quite," ZORAC said. "The point is that it shouldn't have been possible for Man to become different. That's what's interesting."

"How come? I'm not with you."

"Permit me to show you some equations that I have solved," ZORAC suggested.

"Go ahead."

"If you key in a channel-activate command I'll put them on the large screen via the UNSA comnet."

Hunt obliged by tapping a quick sequence of characters into the keyboard in front of him. A second later the screen above kaleidoscoped into a blaze of colors which immediately stabilized into a mass of densely packaged mathematical expressions. Hunt stared at the display for a few seconds and then shook his head.

"What's it all supposed to be?" he asked.

ZORAC was happy to explain. "Those expressions describe quantitatively certain aspects of behavior of the generalized central nervous system of the terrestrial vertebrate. Specifically they define how the basic nervous system will respond to the presence of given concentrations and mixes of various chemical agents in the bloodstream. The coefficients indicated in red are modifiers that would be fixed for a given species, but the dominant factors are the general ones shown in green."

"So?"

"It reveals a fundamental drawback in the method that was adopted by terrestrial animals to protect themselves from their chemical environment. The drawback is that the substances introduced into the bloodstream by the self-immunization process will interfere with the functions of the nervous system. In particular, they will inhibit the development of higher brain functions."

Suddenly Hunt realized what ZORAC was driving at. Before he could voice his thoughts, however, the machine went on.

"In particular, intelligence shouldn't be capable of emerging at all. Larger and more complex brains demand a greater supply of blood; a greater supply of blood carries more contaminants and concentrates them in the brain cells; contaminated brain cells can't coordinate sufficiently to exhibit higher levels of activity, that is, intelligence.

"In other words, intelligence should never have been able to evolve from the terrestrial line of vertebrate evolution. All the figures there say that terrestrial life should have got itself truly stuck up a dead end."

Hunt gazed for a long time at the symbols frozen on the screen while he pondered the meaning of all this. The ancient architecture evolved by the remote ancestors of the vertebrates hundreds of millions of years before had met a short-term need but failed to anticipate the longer-term consequences. But Man, somewhere along his evolutionary line, had abandoned the self-immunization mechanism. In doing this he had increased his vulnerability to his surroundings, but at the same time he had opened up the way to evolving the superior intelligence that would, in time, more than make up for the initial disadvantage.

The intriguing question of course was: How and when had Man done it? The theory offered by the

Utrecht researchers was: during the forced exodus of
his ancestors to Minerva, during the period that lasted
from twenty-five million to fifty thousand years ago.
Twenty-five million years before, many species of ordinary terrestrial life had been shipped there; nearly
that long later, only one had come back—one that
had been very far from ordinary. *Homo sapiens,* in
the shape of the Lunarians, had returned—the most
ferocious adversary that the survival arena of either
world had ever witnessed. He had dominated Minerva
while contemporaneous anthropoids on Earth groped
around in the dim twilight zone on the fringes of self-
awareness, and then, having destroyed that world, had
returned to Earth to claim his place of origin, completely and ruthlessly extinguishing his remote cousins
in the process.

Danchekker had reasoned that a violent mutation
had taken place along the line of human descent isolated on Minerva. This latest piece of information
pointed out the area in which the mutation had occurred; it didn't attempt to explain why it had happened. But then, mutations are random events; there
was nothing to suggest that there had been any specific
cause to look for.

The evident fact of the emergence of Ganymean intelligence fitted in nicely with this body of theory too.
The architecture of Minervan land dwellers had isolated the system that carried the toxins from the
system that carried blood. Thus, when larger brains
became in order, the way was clear to evolve a brain
that could draw more blood without more toxins—
the density of one network simply increased while
that of the other didn't. Higher brain functions could
develop without hindrance. The intelligence of the
Ganymeans was the natural and logical outcome of
Minervan evolution. Terrestrial evolution, however,
pointed to no such natural and logical outcome; Man
had somehow cheated the system.

"Well," Hunt declared finally. "It's interesting, sure.
But what makes you say it shouldn't have happened?
Mutations are random events. The change came about
as a mutation that took place on Minerva, somewhere

along the line that led to the Lunarians and from there to Man. It looks straightforward. What's wrong with that?"

"I thought you'd say that," ZORAC commented, somehow managing to give the impression of sounding quite pleased with itself. "That's the obvious first reaction."

"So—what's wrong with it?"

"It couldn't work. What you're saying is that somewhere early on in the primate line on Minerva, a mutation must have occurred that deactivated the self-immunization system."

"Yes," Hunt agreed.

"But there's a problem in that," ZORAC advised him. "You see, I have performed extensive computations on further data available from J5—data that describe the genetic coding contained in vertebrate chromosomes. In all species, the coding that controls the development of the self-immunization process in the growing embryo contains the coding that enables the animal specifically to absorb excess carbon dioxide. In other words, if you deactivated the self-immunization mechanism, you'd also lose the ability to tolerate a CO_2-rich environment. . . ."

"And Minerva was becoming CO_2-rich," Hunt supplied, seeing the point.

"Exactly. If a mutation of the kind you're suggesting occurred, then the species in which it had occurred could not have survived on Minerva. Hence, the ancestors of the Lunarians could not have mutated like that. If they did, they'd have died out. The Lunarians would never have existed and you wouldn't exist."

"But I do," Hunt pointed out needlessly, but with a certain sense of satisfaction.

"I know, and you shouldn't, and that's my question," ZORAC concluded.

Hunt stubbed out his cigarette and lapsed into thought again. "What about the funny enzyme that Chris Danchekker is always talking about? He found it in all the preserved Oligocene animals in the ship here, didn't he? There were traces of a variant of it in Charlie too. D'you reckon that could have something to do with it? Maybe something in the environment on Minerva reacted in some complicated way and got around the problem and the enzyme appeared somehow in the process. That would explain why today's terrestrial animals haven't got it; the ancestors they're descended from never went there. Perhaps that's why modern Man doesn't have it either—he's been back on Earth for a long time now and away from the environment that stimulated it. How about that?"

"Impossible to confirm," ZORAC pronounced. "Inadequate data available on the enzyme at present. Very speculative. Also, there's another point it doesn't explain."

"Oh, what?"

"The radioactive decay residues. Why should the enzymes found in the Oligocene animals appear to have been formed from radioisotopes while the ones found in Charlie didn't?"

"I don't know," Hunt admitted. "That doesn't make sense. Anyhow, I'm not a biologist. I'll talk about all this to Chris later." Then he changed the subject. "ZORAC—about all those equations you computed."

"Yes?"

"Why did you compute them? I mean . . . do you just do things like that spontaneously . . . on your own initiative?"

"No. Shilohin and some of the other Ganymean scientists asked me to."

"Any idea why?"

"Routine. The computations were relevant to certain researches that they are conducting."

"What kind of researches?" Hunt asked.

"On the things we have been discussing. The question that I suggested a few minutes ago was not something that I originated myself; it was a question that they have been asking. They are very interested in the whole subject. They're curious to find out how Man came to exist at all when all available data says he shouldn't and all their models predicted that he would destroy himself if he did."

Hunt was intrigued to learn that the Ganymeans

were studying his kind with such intensity, especially since they appeared to have progressed so much further in their deductions than the UNSA team had. He was surprised also that ZORAC would so readily divulge something that could be considered sensitive information.

"I'm amazed that there aren't any restrictions on you talking about things like that," he said.

"Why?"

The question caught Hunt unprepared.

"Oh, I don't know really," he said. "On Earth I suppose things like that would only be accessible to people authorized . . . certainly not freely available to anyone who cared to ask for it. I suppose I . . . just assumed it would be the same."

"The fact that Earthmen are neurotic is no reason for Ganymeans to be furtive," ZORAC told him bluntly.

Hunt grinned and shook his head slowly.

"I guess I asked for that," he sighed.

chapter sixteen

The first and most important task that the Ganymeans had faced—that of getting their ship in order again—had now been successfully accomplished. So the focal point of their activities shifted to Pithead, where they commenced working intensively toward their second objective—coming to grips with the computer system of the wrecked ship. Whether the Ganymean race had migrated to another star, and if so which star, had still not been answered. A strong probability remained that this information was sitting waiting to be found, buried somewhere in the intricate molecular circuits and storage banks that went to make up the data-processing complex of a ship that had been built after the answers to these questions were known. The ship might even have been involved in that very migration.

The task turned out to be nowhere near as straightforward as the first one. Although the Pithead ship was of a later and more advanced design than the *Shapieron,* its main drives worked on similar principles and used components which, although showing certain modifications and refinements in some instances, performed functions that were essentially the same as those of their earlier counterparts. The drive system thus exemplified a mature technology that had not changed radically between the times of the two ships' construction, and the repair of the *Shapieron* had been possible as a consequence.

The same was not true for the computer systems. After a week of intensive analysis and probing, the Ganymean scientists admitted they were making little headway. The problem was that the system components that they found themselves trying to comprehend were, in most cases, unlike anything they had seen before. The processors themselves consisted of solid crystal blocks inside which millions of separate circuit elements of molecular dimensions were interconnected in three dimensions with complexities that defied the imagination. Only somebody who had been trained and educated in the design and physics of such devices could hope to unravel the coding locked inside them.

Some of the larger processors were completely revolutionary in concept, even to the Ganymeans, and seemed to represent a merging of electronic and gravitic technologies; characteristics of both were inextricably mingled together to form devices in which the physical interconnections between cells holding electronic data could be changed through variable gravitic-bonding links. The hardware configuration itself was programable and could be switched from nanosecond to nanosecond to yield an array in which any and every cell could function as a storage element at one instant or as a processing site the next; processing could, in the ultimate, be performed everywhere in the complex, all at the same time—surely the last word in parallelism. One interested but bemused UNSA engineer described it as "soft hardware. A brain with a billion times the speed . . ."

And every subsystem of the ship—communications, navigation, computation, propulsion control, flight control, and a hundred others—consisted of a network of interconnected processing nodes like that, with all the networks integrated into an impossible web that covered the length and breadth of the vessel.

Without detailed documentation and technical design information there was no way of tackling the problem. But no documentation was available. All the information was locked away inside the same system that they needed the information to get into; it was like having a can with the can opener inside it.

So, at the next progress meeting aboard the *Shapieron,* the senior Ganymean computer scientist declared himself ready to quit. When somebody commented that the Earthmen wouldn't have given up so easily he thought about it, agreed with the evaluation and went back to Pithead to try again. After another week he came back again and stated, emphatically and finally, that if anybody thought the Earthmen could do better they'd be welcome to try. He'd quit.

And that, it seemed, was that.

There was nothing further to be achieved on Ganymede. Therefore the aliens at last announced their long-awaited decision to accept the invitation that had been extended to them by the world's governments, and come to Earth. This did not mean that they had also accepted the invitation to settle there. Admittedly there was nowhere else within many light-years for them to go, but many of them still harbored misgivings at what might await them on the Nightmare Planet. But they were rational beings and the rational thing to do was obviously to go and see the place before prejudging it. Any decision as to what to do about the longer-term future would wait until they were in possession of more concrete information on which to base it.

A number of UNSA personnel from the Jupiter missions were at the end of their duty tours and already scheduled to return to Earth as the comings and goings of ships permitted. The Ganymeans offered a ride in the *Shapieron* to anybody planning on going their way and were almost overwhelmed by the rush to accept.

Fortuitously, Hunt's latest communication from Gregg Caldwell, executive director of UNSA's Navcomms Division and Hunt's immediate chief, had indicated that Hunt's assignment on Ganymede was considered fulfilled and there was other work to be done back at Houston. Arrangements were being put in hand to ship him back. He had no difficulty in getting his name deleted from the UNSA schedule and added to the list of passengers due to go with the *Shapieron*.

Danchekker's main reason for coming to Ganymede had been to investigate the terrestrial Oligocene animals found in the Pithead ship. The professor persuaded Monchar, second in command of the Ganymean expedition, that there was plenty of room in the *Shapieron* to carry all the specimens of interest; after that he persuaded his director, at the Westwood Biological Institute, Houston, that the investigations would be carried out more thoroughly back on Earth, where all the facilities needed were available for the asking. The outcome was exactly as he had intended: Danchekker was going too.

And so the time came for Hunt to pack his belongings and take one last look around the tiny room that had been home for so long. Then he made the familiar walk along the well-worn corridor that led to the Domestic Dome to join the handful of others who were shipping out. There they stood a last round of drinks for their friends staying on and made their farewells. After promises to keep in touch and assertions that everybody's paths would cross again one day, they trooped through into the Site Operations Control building where the base commander and some of his staff were waiting in the airlock anteroom to bid them an official adieu. The access tube beyond the airlock took them through into the cabin of the tracked ice crawler that would carry them across to the landing pads, where a transporter ship was waiting.

Hunt's feelings were mixed as he gazed out of one of the crawler's viewing ports at the shadowy snatches of buildings and constructions that came and went among Pithead's swirling, eternal methane–ammonia mist. Going home after a long time away was always a nice feeling of course, but he would miss many aspects of the life he had grown used to in the tightly knit UNSA community here, where everybody shared in everybody else's problems and strangers were unknown. The spirit of comradeship that he had found here, the feeling of belonging, the sense of a common purpose . . . all these things gave a special intimacy to this tiny, manmade haven of survival that had been carved out of the hostile Ganymedian wilderness. The feelings he was experiencing so intensely at that moment would soon be diluted and forgotten when he returned to Earth and again rubbed shoulders every day with faceless millions, all busily living out their different lives in their different ways and with their different aims and values. There, custom and synthetic social barriers served to mark out the lines of demarcation that men needed in order to satisfy their psychological need to identify with definable cultural groups. The colony on Ganymede had not needed to build any artificial walls around itself to set it apart from the rest of the human race; Nature and several hundred million miles of empty space provided all the isolation necessary.

Perhaps, he thought to himself, that was why men pitched camps on the South Col of Everest, sailed ships across the seven seas, and held reunion dinners year after year to share nostalgic memories of school or army days. The challenges and the hardships that they faced together forged bonds between them that the protective cocoon of normal society could never emulate and awakened an awareness of qualities in themselves and in each other that could never be erased. He knew then that, like the sailor or the mountaineer, he would return time after time to know again the things that he had found on Ganymede.

Danchekker, however, was less of a romantic.

"I don't care if they discover seven-headed monsters on Saturn," the professor said as they boarded the transporter. "Once I get home again I'm staying there. I've lived quite enough of my life already surrounded by these wretched contraptions."

"I bet you find you've developed agoraphobia when you get there," Hunt told him.

At Main there was another round of farewells to go through before they were driven out, now wearing spacesuits, to the *Shapieron*'s lowered entrance section; they could not be flown directly up into the ship's outer bays because the telescopic access tubes that projected from the buildings of the base—affording direct entry to UNSA ships and vehicles—were not designed to mate with the airlocks of Ganymean daughter vessels. Members of the Ganymean crew received them at the foot of the entrance ramp and conducted them up into the stern section, where an elevator was waiting to carry them up into the main body of the ship.

Three hours later loading was complete and the final departure preparations had been made. Garuth and a small Ganymean rearguard exchanged formal words of parting with the base commander and some of his officers, who had driven out to the ramp for the ceremony. Then the Earthmen boarded their vehicle and returned to the base while the Ganymeans withdrew into the *Shapieron* and the stern section retracted upward into its flight position.

Hunt was alone in the cabin that had been allocated to him, taking in his last view of Main from a mural videoscreen, when ZORAC announced that takeoff was imminent. There was no sensation of motion at all; the view just started to diminish in size and flatten out as the ground fell away beneath. The Ganymedian landscape flowed inward from the edges of the picture and the surface details rapidly dissolved into a uniform sea of frosty whiteness as the ship gained altitude. Soon even the pinpoint of reflected light that was Main faded into the background, and an arc of blackness began advancing upward across the view as Ganymede's dark side moved into the picture. At the top, the curvature of the moon's sunlit side appeared, ushering in a gaggle of attendant background stars. The bright strip left in the center of the screen continued to narrow steadily, and at last its ends slipped in from beyond the edges of the frame to reveal it as a brilliant crescent hanging in the heavens, and already shrinking as he watched. Then the crescent and the stars seemed to dissolve into diffuse smudges of light that flowed into one another until the whole screen was reduced to a uniform expanse of featureless, iridescent fog. The ship was now under main drive, he realized, and temporarily shut off from information coming in from the rest of the universe —information carried as electromagnetic waves anyway. He wondered what the Ganymeans used instead

—to navigate by, for instance. Here was something he would raise with ZORAC.

But that could wait for now. For the moment he just wanted to relax and prepare his mind for other things. Unlike his voyage out aboard *Jupiter Five*, the journey to Earth would be measured in days.

chapter seventeen

And so the Ganymeans came at last to Earth.

After the failure of the various governments to reach agreement among themselves as to where the aliens should be received in the event of their accepting the invitation to visit, the Parliament of the United States of Europe had voted to go it alone and make their own preparations anyway—just in case. The place they selected was an area of pleasant open country on the Swiss shore of Lake Geneva, where, it was hoped, the climate would prove agreeable to the Ganymean constitution and the historical tradition of nonbelligerence would add a singularly appropriate note.

About halfway between the city of Geneva and Lausanne, they fenced off an area just over a mile square on the edge of the lake, and inside it erected a village of chalets that had been designed for Ganymean occupation; the ceilings were high, the doorways big, the beds strong, and the windows slightly tinted. Communal cooking and dining facilities were provided, along with leisure rooms, terminals linked into the World's integrated entertainments/data/news grid, an outsize swimming pool, a recreation area, and just about anything else which seemed likely to contribute to making life comfortable and could be included in the time available. A huge concrete pad was laid to support the *Shapieron* and afford parking for vehicles and daughter ships, and accommodation inside the perimeter was provided for delegations of visiting Earthmen, together with conference and social facilities.

When the news came in from Jupiter that the aliens

were planning on departing for Earth in just a couple of weeks' time and—even more startling—the journey would take only a few days, it was obvious that the issue of where to receive them had already been decided. By the time the *Shapieron* appeared from the depths of space and went into Earth orbit, a fleet of suborbital aircraft was converging on Geneva with officials and Heads of State from every corner of the globe, all hurrying to participate in the hastily worked out welcoming formalities. Swarms of buzzing VTOL jets shuttled back and forth between Geneva International Airport and what was now being called Ganyville to convey them to their final destination while traffic on the Geneva/Lausanne highway below deteriorated to a bumper-to-bumper jam, private aircars having been banned from the area. A peppering of colors, becoming denser as the hours went by, appeared on the green inland slopes that overlooked Ganyville, as the first spectators arrived and set up camp with tents, sleeping bags, blankets and picnic stoves, determined to secure and hold a grandstand view. A continuous cordon of jovial but overworked policemen, including some from Italy, France and Germany since the numbers of the tiny Swiss force were simply not up to the task, maintained a clear zone two hundred meters wide between the rapidly growing crowd and the perimeter fence, while on the lakeward side a flotilla of police launches scurried to and fro to keep at bay an armada of boats, yachts and craft of every description. Along the roadsides an instant market came into being as the more entrepreneurial members of the shopkeeping fraternity from the nearby towns loaded their stocks into trucks and brought the business to where the customers were. A lot of small fortunes were made that day, from selling everything from instant meals and woolly sweaters to hiking boots and high-power telescopes.

Several thousand miles above, the *Shapieron* was not quite away from it all. An assortment of UNSA craft had formed themselves into a ragged escort around the ship, sweeping with it round the Earth every hour and a half. Many of them carried newsmen and camera crews broadcasting live to an enthralled audience via the World News Grid. They had exchanged messages with ZORAC and the Earthmen aboard who had come with the *Shapieron* from Jupiter, thrilled the viewers below by beaming down views from inside an alien spacecraft, and mixed in constantly updated reports of the latest developments at Lake Geneva. In between, the commentators had described *ad nauseam* how the ship had first appeared over Ganymede, what had transpired since, where their race had originated in the first place, why the expedition had gone to Iscaris and what had happened there, and anything else they could think of to fill in time before the big event. Half the factories and offices on Earth were estimated to have given it up as a bad job and closed down until after the big event was all over, since the employees who weren't glued to a screen somewhere else were glued to one being paid out of the firm's money. As one president of a New York company commented to an NBC street interviewer: "I'm not gonna spend thousands to find out all over again what King Canute proved centuries ago—you can't stop the tide once it's made its mind up. I've sent 'em all home to get it outa their systems. I guess this year we've got an extra day's public holiday." On being asked what he himself intended doing, he replied with surprise: "Me? I'm going home to watch the landing, of course."

Inside the *Shapieron,* Hunt and Danchekker were among the mixed group of Ganymeans and Earthmen gathered in the ship's command center—the place to which Hunt had been conducted with Storrel and the others at the time of their momentous first visit from *Jupiter Five.* A number of eggs had been dispatched from the *Shapieron* to descend to lower altitudes and obtain, for the aliens' benefit, a bird's-eye preview of different parts of Earth. The Earthmen were explaining the significance of some of the pictures that the eggs were sending back. Already the Ganymeans had gazed incredulously at the teeming density of life in cities such as New York, Tokyo and London, gasped at the spectacles of the Arabian desert and the Amazon jungle—terrain unlike any that had existed on Minerva—and stared in mute, horrified fascination at a telescopic presentation of lions stalking zebra in the African grasslands.

To Hunt, the familiar sights of green continents, sun-drenched plains and blue oceans, after what felt like an eternity of nothing but rock, ice and the blackness of space, were overpowering. As different parts of the mosaic of Earth came and went across the main screen, he detected a steady change in the moods of the Ganymeans too. The earlier misgivings and apprehensions that some of them had felt were being swept away by an almost intoxicating enthusiasm that became contagious as time went by. They were becoming restless and excited—keen to see more, firsthand, of the incredible world where chance had brought them.

One of the eggs was hovering three miles up over Lake Geneva and relaying up to the *Shapieron* its telescopic view of the throngs that were still building up on the hills overlooking Ganyville and all over the meadows surrounding it. The Ganymeans were pleasantly surprised, and at the same time astounded, that they should be the objects of such widespread interest and such a display of mass emotion. Hunt had tried to explain that the arrival of alien spacecraft was not something that happened very often, let alone one from twenty-five million years in the past, but the Ganymeans appeared unable to comprehend how anything could give rise to a spontaneous demonstration of emotion on so vast a scale. Monchar had wondered if the Earthmen that they had so far met represented "the more stable and rational end to the human spectrum rather than a typical cross section." Hunt had decided to say nothing and leave it at that. Monchar would no doubt be able to answer that for himself in good time.

A lull in the conversation had occurred and everybody was watching the screen as one of the Ganymeans muttered commands to ZORAC to take the egg a little lower and zoom in closer. The view expanded and closed in on the side of a small, grassy hill, by this time thick with people of all ages, sizes, manners and garbs. There were people cooking, people drinking, people playing and people just sitting; it could have been a day at the races, a pop festival, a flying display, or all of them rolled into one.

"Are they all safe out in the open there?" one of the Ganymeans asked dubiously after a while.

"Safe?" Hunt looked puzzled. "How do you mean?"

"I'm surprised that none of them seem to be carrying guns. I'd have thought they would have guns."

"Guns? What for?" Hunt asked, somewhat bewildered.

"The carnivores," the Ganymean replied, as if it was obvious. "What will they do if they are attacked by carnivores?"

Danchekker explained that few animals existed that were dangerous to Man, and that those that did lived only in a few restricted areas, all of them many thousands of miles from Switzerland.

"Oh, I assumed that was why they have built a defensive system around the place," the Ganymean said.

Hunt laughed. "That's not to keep carnivores out," he said. "It's to keep humans out."

"You mean they might attack us?" There was a sudden note of alarm in the question.

"Not at all. It's simply to insure your privacy and to make sure that nobody makes a nuisance of himself. The government assumed that you wouldn't want crowds of sightseers and tourists wandering around you all the time and getting in the way."

"Couldn't the government just make a law ordering them to stay away?" Shilohin asked from across the room. "That sounds much simpler."

Hunt laughed again, probably because the feeling of seeing home again was affecting him a little. "You haven't met many Earth-people yet," he said. "I don't think they'd take very much notice. They're not what you might call . . . easily disciplined."

Shilohin was evidently surprised by the statement. "Really?" she said. "I had always imagined them to be precisely the opposite. I mean . . . I've watched some of the old newsreels from Earth—from the archives of your J5 computers, newsreels from the times when there were wars on Earth. Thousands of Earthmen all dressed the same walked backward and forward in straight lines while others shouted commands which they obeyed instantly. And the wars . . . when they were ordered to fight the wars and kill other Earthmen, they obeyed. Is that not being disciplined?"

"Yes . . . it is," Hunt admitted uncomfortably, hoping he wasn't about to be asked for an explanation; there wasn't one.

But the Ganymean who had been worried about carnivores was persistent.

"You mean that if they are ordered to do something that is clearly irrational, they will do it unhesitatingly," he said. "But if they are ordered to do something that is not only eminently sensible but also polite, they will take no notice?"

"Er . . . I guess that's about it," Hunt said weakly. "Very often anyway."

Another Ganymean crewman half turned from the console that he was watching.

"They're all mad," he declared firmly. "I've always said so. It's the biggest madhouse in the Galaxy."

"They are also our hosts," Garuth broke in sharply. "And they have saved our lives and offered us their home as our home. I will not have them spoken of in that manner."

"Sorry, sir," the crewman mumbled and returned his attention to his console.

"Please forgive the remark, Dr. Hunt," Garuth said.

"Think nothing of it," Hunt replied with a shrug. "I couldn't have put it better myself. . . . It's what keeps us sane, you see," he added for no particular reason, causing more bewildered looks to be exchanged between his alien companions.

At that moment ZORAC interrupted with an announcement.

"Ground Control is calling from Geneva. Shall I put the call through for Dr. Hunt again?"

Hunt walked over to the communications console from which he had acted as intermediary during previous dialogues. He perched himself up on the huge Ganymean chair and instructed ZORAC to connect him. The face of the controller at Geneva, by now familiar, appeared on the screen.

" 'Allo again, Dr. 'unt. 'Ow are zings going up zere?"

"Well, we're still waiting," Hunt told him. "What's the news?"

"Ze Prime Meenister of Australia and ze Chinese Premier 'ave now arrived at Geneva. Zey weel be at Ganyville eenside ze 'alf ower. I am now auzorized to clear you for touchdown een seexty meenutes from now. Okay?"

"We're going down one hour from now," Hunt announced to the expectant room. He looked at Garuth. "Do I have your approval to confirm that?"

"Please do," Garuth replied.

Hunt turned back toward the screen. "Okay," he informed the controller. "Sixty minutes from now. We're coming down."

Within minutes the news had flashed around the globe and the world's excitement rose to fever pitch.

chapter eighteen

Hunt stood inside one of the central elevators of the *Shapieron,* gazing at the blank expanse of the door panel in front of him while the seemingly interminable length of the vessel sped by outside. Behind him, the rest of the UNSA contingent from Ganymede were packed tightly together, every one of them silently absorbed in his own thoughts as the moment of home-coming drew nearer. The *Shapieron* was now descending stern-first on its final approach. A number of Ganymeans were present in the elevator too, on their way to join the main body of Ganymeans that had been selected to make the first exit out onto the surface of Earth, most of whom were already assembled in the stern section of the ship.

The symbols appearing and disappearing on the face of the indicator panel by the door suddenly stopped changing and became stable. A second later the wide doors slid aside and the company began spilling out of the elevator to find themselves in a vast, circular space that extended all the way around the cylindrical wall of the ship's inner core. Entrances to six huge airlocks were equally spaced around the outer walls and the floor in between was filled with a dense throng of Ganymeans, most of them strangely silent. Hunt spotted Garuth, surrounded by a small group of Ganymeans, standing near one of the airlocks. Shilohin was on one side of him and Monchar on the other; Jassilane was nearby. Like all of the Ganymeans present, they were staring up at an enormous display screen set high on the wall of the central core, dominating the floor from above the elevator doorways. Hunt made his way through the throng of giant figures toward where Garuth's group was standing. He stopped next to Garuth and turned to look back at the screen.

The view being shown was one looking vertically down on the shore of the lake. The picture was bisected into two roughly equal halves, one showing the greens and browns of the hills, the other the reflected blues of the sky. The colors were vivid and obscured in places by scattered puffs of small white clouds. The shadows of the clouds made sharp blotches on the land beneath, indicating the day was bright and sunny. The features in the terrain slowly revealed themselves and began flowing outward toward the edges of the screen as the ship descended.

The clouds blossomed up from flat daubs of paint to become islands of billowing whiteness floating on the landscape; then they were gone from the steadily narrowing and enlarging view.

Dots that were houses were visible now, some standing isolated among the hills and others clustered together along the twisting threads of the roads that were becoming discernible. And precisely in the center of the screen, vertically below the *Shapieron's* central axis, a speck of whiteness right on the shoreline marked the concrete landing area of Ganyville, with the rows of neatly aligned chalets inside the perimeter now beginning to take shape. A narrow strip of green emphasized the perimeter line, denoting the zone outside the fence that had been kept clear of people. Beyond the cleared zone the land was visibly lighter in hue with the additive effect from thousands upon thousands of upturned faces.

Hunt noticed that Garuth was speaking quietly into his throat microphone and pausing at intervals as if to listen to replies. He assumed that Garuth was updating himself with reports from the flight crew back in the command center, and elected not to interrupt. Instead he activated his own channel via his wrist unit. "ZORAC, how's it going?"

"Altitude nine thousand six hundred feet, descent speed two hundred feet per second, reducing," the familiar voice replied. "We've locked on to the approach radars. Everything's under control and looking good."

"Looks like we're in for a hell of a welcome," Hunt commented.

"You should see the pictures coming in from the probes. The hills are packed for miles around and there are hundreds of small boats on the lake all packed together about a quarter-mile offshore. The air space above and around the landing zone is clear, but the sky's thick with aircars all around. Half your planet must have turned out."

"How are the Ganymeans taking it?" Hunt asked.

"A bit overawed, I think."

At that moment Shilohin noticed Hunt and moved across to join him.

"This is incredible," she said, gesturing upward toward the screen. "Are we really important enough for all this?"

"They don't get many aliens dropping in from other stars," Hunt told her cheerfully. "So they're making the most of the occasion." He paused as another thought struck him, then said: "You know, it's a funny thing . . . people on Earth have been claiming that they've seen UFOs and flying saucers and things like that for hundreds of years, and all the time there's been all kinds of arguing about whether they really existed or not. You'd think they'd have guessed that when it really happened, it'd be unmistakable. Well, they sure know all about it today."

"Touchdown in twenty seconds," ZORAC announced. Hunt could sense a wave of emotion rippling through the ranks of Giants all around him.

All that was visible on the screen now was the waffle-iron pattern of the chalets of Ganyville and the white expanse of the concrete landing area. The ship was descending toward the lakeward side of the landing area, which was clear; on the landward side, between the landing area and the edge of the chalets, rows of dots arranged into ordered geometric groups became visible, and resolved themselves rapidly into human figures.

"Ten seconds," ZORAC recited. The murmuring

that had been building up as a vague background subsided abruptly. The only sound was the distant rush of air around the ship and the muted surging of power from its engines.

"*Touchown*. We have landed on the planet Earth. Awaiting further instructions."

"Deploy ship for surface access," Garuth ordered. "Proceed with routing shutdown of flight systems and prepare Engineers' Report."

Although there was no sensation of motion, Hunt knew that the whole section of the ship in which they were all standing was now moving smoothly toward the ground as the three elevator tubes telescoped downward from the main body of the vessel. While this was taking place, the main screen high above their heads presented a full-circle scan of the ground in the immediate vicinity of the ship.

Beyond the area bridged by the *Shapieron's* tail fins, arrayed in a vast arc between the ship and the rows of chalets in the background, several hundred people were standing stiffly at attention in a series of boxed groups, as if lined up for inspection at a military parade. In front of every group was a flag bearer carrying the standard of one of the nations of Earth; in front of the flag bearers the Heads of State and their aides, all attired in dark business suits and standing rigidly erect, were waiting. Hunt picked out the Stars and Stripes of the USA, the Union Jack and several more of the emblems of US Europe, the Hammer and Sickle of the USSR and the Red Star of China. There were scores more that he could not identify readily. Behind and to the sides he caught snatches of brightly colored ceremonial military uniforms and the glint of sunlight reflected from brass. He tried to put himself in the position of those people standing outside. None of them had yet seen an alien face to face. He tried to capture their feelings and emotions as they stood there gazing up at the huge tower of silver metal that they had just watched slide down out of the sky. The moment was unique; never before in history had anything like this happened, and it could never happen for the first time again.

Then ZORAC's voice sounded once more.

"Tailgate is down. Pressures are balanced, outer lock-doors open and surface-access ramps extended. Ready to open up."

Hunt sensed the expectation building up around him. All heads were now turning to gaze toward Garuth. The Ganymean leader cast his eyes slowly around the assembly, allowed them to rest for a moment on the party of Earthmen still grouped together by the elevator door, and then shifted them toward Hunt.

"We will go out in the order already agreed. However, we are strangers on this world. There are others among us who are coming home. This is their world and they should lead us out onto it."

The Ganymeans needed no further prompting. Even as Garuth finished speaking, their ranks parted to form a long, straight aisle leading from the group of Earthmen by the elevators to where Garuth and Hunt were standing. After a few seconds, the Earthmen began walking slowly forward. Danchekker was in front. As they approached the airlock near which Hunt was waiting, the Ganymeans moved aside to make room for them in front of the inner door.

"All set then, Chris?" Hunt asked as the two drew face to face. "A few more seconds and you'll be home again."

"I must say all this publicity is something I could have done without," the professor replied. "I feel rather like some kind of Moses leading the tribes in. However, let us get on with it."

Hunt turned to stand beside Danchekker, facing the inner door. He glanced at Garuth and nodded.

"ZORAC, open inner door, lock five," Garuth ordered.

The ribbed metal panels slid noiselessly out of Hunt's field of vision. He stepped forward into the lock chamber and began moving forward toward the outer door, vaguely aware through the torrent of emotions rising inside him of Danchekker to one side and the rest of the UNSA contingent following behind. Beyond the outer door a broad, shallow ramp sloped down to the concrete. They stepped out onto the top of the ramp to find themselves in what appeared to be a vast cathedral of arched metal vaulting ribs, formed by the sweeping curves of the undersides of the *Shapieron*'s tail fins, soaring upward and inward to meet the body of the ship high above their heads. The ramp and the area straddled by the ship were in the shadow of the bulk of the vessel and its mighty fins. But beyond the ship the day was a blaze of sunlight, painting the scene around them in a riot of color—the green of the overlooking hills and the purple, white and blue of the mountains and the sky behind; the rainbow speckling of the crowds packed on the hillsides; the pastel pinks, greens, reds, blues and oranges of the chalets; the whiteness of the concrete apron below them and even the snowy shirtfronts of the delegates standing there in their precise, unmoving ranks.

And then came the cheering. It was like a slow tide of noise that seemed to begin far away on the tops of the hills and roll downward gathering strength and momentum as it went, until it broke over them in a roaring ocean of sound that flooded their senses. The hills themselves suddenly seemed to become alive as a pattern of spontaneous movement erupted as far as the eye could see. People in the tens of thousands were on their feet, shouting out the tension and the anticipation that had been building up inside them for days, and as they shouted, they waved—arms, hats, shirts, coats— anything that came to hand. And behind it all, rising and falling and rising again as if striving to be heard above the din came sporadic strains of massed bands.

The Earthmen halted a few feet down the ramp, momentarily overcome by the combined assault on their senses from all sides. Then they began moving again, down the ramp and onto the solid ground of Earth beneath the towering columns of the *Shapieron*'s fins. They marched forward into the sunlight toward a spot where a small party of Earth's representatives were standing ahead of the main body. They walked as if in a trance, their heads turning to take in the scenes around them, the multitudes on the hills, the lake behind . . . to gaze up at the ship stretching toward the sky above, now quiet and motionless. A few of them raised their arms and began waving back at the crowds on the surrounding hills. The noise redoubled as the crowds roared their approval. Soon they were all waving.

Hunt drew closer to the party ahead and recognized the features of Samuel K. Wilby, Secretary General to the UN. Beside him were Irwin Frenshaw, Director General of UNSA from Washington, D.C., and General Bradley Cummings, Supreme Commander of the uniformed arm of the UNSA. Wilby greeted him with an extended hand and a broad smile.

"Dr. Hunt, I believe," he said. "Welcome home. I believe you've brought some friends with you." He shifted his eyes. "Ah—and you are Professor Danchekker. Welcome."

Danchekker had no sooner completed shaking hands when the noise around them rose to an unprecedented crescendo. They looked up and back at the ship.

The Ganymeans were coming out.

With Garuth in the lead, the first group of Giants had emerged at the top of the ramp. There they had stopped, and were staring around them in a way that hinted at their complete bewilderment.

"ZORAC," Hunt said. "They look a bit lost up there. Tell 'em to come on down and meet the folks."

"They will," the machine replied in his ear. "They need a minute to get used to it. Remember they have not breathed natural air for twenty years. This is the first time they've been out in the open for all that time."

At the tops of other ramps around the ship's stern section more airlocks had opened and more Ganymeans were appearing. Garuth's carefully planned order of emergence was already forgotten. Some of the Giants were milling around in the airlock doors, while others were already partway down the ramps; some were just standing motionless and staring.

"They're a bit lost," Hunt said to Wilby. "We ought to go over and straighten them out." Wilby nodded and motioned his group to follow. Some UN aides conducted the main party of Earthmen from Ganymede toward the national delegations while Hunt, Danchekker and a couple of others turned back to escort Wilby's group to the ramps.

"ZORAC, connect me to Garuth," Hunt muttered as they walked.

"You're through."

"This is Vic Hunt. Well, how d'you like it?"

"My people are temporarily overwhelmed," the familiar voice answered. "Come to that, so am I. I had expected that the sensation of coming out under an open sky after so long would be traumatic, but never anything like this. And all these people . . . the shouting . . . I can find no words."

"I'm with the group that's approaching the ramp you're on now," Hunt advised. "Get your act together and come on down. There's people here you have to say hello to."

As they neared the base of the ramp, Hunt looked up and saw Garuth, Shilohin, Monchar, Jassilane and a few others moving down toward them. To the left and right, other Ganymeans who had already reached the ground via the other ramps began converging on the spot where Wilby's group was waiting.

Garuth stepped off the ramp, his companions following close behind, and halted to look down at the Secretary General. Slowly and solemnly they shook hands.

Hunt acted as an interpreter via ZORAC and concluded introductions between the two groups.

"This is one of the guys who runs the whole of the UNSA show," he said to Garuth when they came to Irwin Frenshaw. "Without it we'd never have been there for you to find."

And then the two groups turned and, now mingled together, began walking away from the ramp. From above and behind them, scores of eight-foot-tall figures flowed downward along the ramps to join the lead group from behind. They came out into the sunlight and halted for a moment to survey the delegations from the nations of Earth arrayed before them. A sudden hush descended upon the hills behind.

And then Garuth slowly raised his right arm in a gesture of salutation. One by one the rest of the

Ganymeans copied him. They stood there silent and unmoving, a hundred arms extended and raised to convey a common message of greeting and friendship to all of the peoples of Earth.

At once the roar swept down from the hillsides again. If what had come before had been a flood, then this was a tidal wave. It seemed to echo back and forth across the valleys as if the mountains of Switzerland themselves were reverberating and joining in their welcome.

Wilby turned toward Hunt and leaned forward to speak close to his ear.

"I think your friends have made something of a hit," he said.

"I expected some fuss," Hunt told him, "but never this in a million years. Shall we carry on?"

"Let's go."

Hunt turned toward Garuth and tuned in.

"Come on, Garuth," he said. "It's time to pay our respects. Some of these people out there have come a long way to meet you."

Slowly, with the small mixed party of Earthmen and Ganymean leaders in front, the Giants began moving forward *en masse* toward the waiting heads of the governments of Earth's nations.

chapter nineteen

For the next hour or so, the Ganymean leaders went from one group of national representatives to the next, exchanging brief formal speeches of goodwill. As the Ganymeans moved on, the groups broke up and dispersed to join the growing mass of Earthmen and aliens mingling on the concrete apron below the *Shapieron*. It was a very different reception from the one that had greeted the first hesitant emergence of the Ganymeans out onto the ice at Ganymede Main Base.

"I still don't quite understand it," Jassilane said to Hunt as the party moved toward the delegation from Malaysia. "So far you've told us that everyone we've met was from a government. But what I want to know is who is *the* government?"

"*The* government?" Hunt asked, not quite following. "Which one?" The Giant made motions of exasperation in the air.

"The one that runs the planet. Which one is it?"

"None of them," Hunt told him.

"That's what I thought. So where are they?"

"There isn't one," Hunt said. "It's run by all of them and none of them."

"I should have guessed," Jassilane replied. In translating, ZORAC managed to inject a good simulation of a weary sigh.

For the rest of the day the formalities continued amid an almost carnival atmosphere. Garuth and the Ganymean leaders spent some time with each group of government representatives, establishing relationships and arranging a timetable of projected official visits to the various nations represented. It was a busy day for Hunt and the other Earthmen from Ganymede, whose familiarity with the aliens put them in great demand for performing introductions and made them the obvious choice for acting as general mediators in the dialogues. By invitation of the European Government, a liaison bureau—a representative international body operating under UN sponsorship—had been established as a permanent institution within the Earthman sector of Ganyville. By evening the program of affairs to be discussed between the two races was being handled in a more-or-less orderly and coordinated fashion.

That night there was a grand welcoming banquet in Ganyville, vegetarian of course, in which words, and wine flowed freely. After the meal and still more speeches were over and the two races had begun mixing and socializing, Hunt found himself, glass in hand, standing to one side of the room with three Ganymeans —Valio and Kralom, two of the crew officers from the *Shapieron,* and Strelsya, a female administrator. Valio was explaining his confusion over some of the things he had learned that day.

"Emmanuel Crow, I think he said his name was," Valio told them. "He was with the delegation from the place you live in, Vic—USA. Said he was from Washington . . . State Department or something. The thing that puzzled me was when he said he was a Red Indian."

Hunt propped himself casually against the table behind him and sipped his scotch.

"Why, what's the problem?" he asked.

"Well, we met the Indian government spokesman later on, and he said India isn't anywhere near the USA," Valio explained. "So how could Crow be an Indian?"

"That's a different Indian," Hunt replied, fearing as he spoke that the conversation was about to get itself into a tangle. Sure enough, Kralom had something to add.

"I met someone who was a West Indian, but he said he came from the east."

"There is an East Indies . . ." Strelsya began.

"I know, but that's way over in the west," Kralom said.

Hunt groaned inwardly and reached in his pocket for his cigarette pack while he collected his thoughts. Before he could inject a word of explanation, Valio resumed.

"I thought that maybe when he said he was a *Red* Indian he might be really from China because they're supposed to be red and they're not far from India, but it turns out they're yellow."

"Perhaps he was Russian," Kralom suggested. "Somebody told me they're red too."

"No, they're pink," Strelsya declared firmly. She motioned her head in the direction of a short, heavily built man in a black suit with his back toward them, talking to another mixed group. "There—he's one if I remember rightly. See for yourself."

"I've met him," Kralom said. "He's a White Russian. He said so, but he doesn't look white."

The three aliens looked imploringly toward Hunt for some words of wisdom to make sense of it all.

"Not to worry—it's all hangovers from a long time ago. The whole world's getting so mixed up together now that I really don't suppose it'll matter much longer," he said lamely.

By the early hours of the morning, while a thousand lights still twinkled on the shadows of the surrounding hills, all was quiet, except for occasional scuffling noises and every now and again an ominous crash of bulk against timber, as gigantic frames tottered unsteadily but contentedly to bed through the narrow alleys between the chalets.

The next morning, the august visitors from every corner of the globe began departing to give Ganyville a week of undisturbed rest and relaxation. A light schedule of discussions with visiting groups of Earthmen, mainly scientists, had been arranged for the week and some news features were laid on for the benefit of the public; for the most part, however, the Giants were left free to enjoy the feeling of having a world under their feet again.

Many simply spent their time stretched out on the

grass, basking in a splendor that was, to them, tropical. Others walked for hours along the perimeter, stopping all the time to savor the air as if making sure they were not dreaming it all and standing and staring in unconcealed delight at the lake, the hills, and the snow-capped peaks of the distant Alps. Others became addicted to the Earthnet terminals in the chalets, and displayed an insatiable appetite for information on every facet of Earth, its people, its history, its geography, and everything else there was to know about it. To facilitate this, ZORAC had been connected into the Earthnet system, enabling an enormous interchange of the accumulated knowledge of two civilizations.

But best of all to watch was the reaction of the Ganymean children. Born aboard the *Shapieron* during its epic voyage from Iscaris, they had never seen a blue sky, a landscape or a mountain, never breathed natural air, and had never before conceived the notion of leaving their ship without requiring any kind of protection. To them, the lifeless void between the stars was the only environment that existed.

At first, many of them shrank from coming out of the ship at all, fearful of consequences that had been instilled into them all their lives and which they accepted unquestioningly as fundamental truths. When at last a few of the more trusting and adventurous ones crept warily to the doors at the tops of the access ramps and peered outside, they froze in utter disbelief and confusion. From the things both their elders and ZORAC had told them, they had a vague idea of planets and worlds—places bigger than the *Shapieron* that you could live *on* instead of *in,* they gathered, though what this could possibly mean had never been clear. And then they had come to Ganymede; obviously that was a planet, they'd thought.

But now this! Hundreds of people outside the ship clad only in their shirtsleeves; how could that be possible? How could they breathe and why did they not explode with decompression? Space was supposed to be everywhere, but it wasn't here; what had happened to it? How did the universe suddenly divide itself into two parts, half "up" and half "down"—words that could only mean anything inside a ship? Why was down all green; who could have made anything so large and why had they made it in strange shapes that stretched away as far as one could see? Why was up all blue and why weren't there any stars? Where did all the light come from?

Eventually, with much coaxing, they ventured down the ramps and onto the ground. Nothing awful happened to them. Soon they became reassured and began to explore their new and wondrous surroundings. The concrete at the bottom of the ramps, the grass beyond, the wooden walls of the chalets—all were new and each held its own particular fascination. But the most astounding sight of all was that stretching away, seemingly forever, on the other side of the ship—more water than they had ever believed existed in the whole of the universe.

Before long they were romping and reveling in an ecstasy of freedom greater than anything they had ever known. The crowning glory came when the Swiss police launches started running joy rides for them, up along the shore, out into the middle of Lake Geneva, and back again. It soon became obvious that only the grownups and their hang-ups stood in the way of the question of settling on Earth; the kids had made *their* minds up in no uncertain manner.

Two days after the landing, Hunt was enjoying a coffee break in the resident's cafeteria at Ganyville when a low buzz from his Ganymean wrist unit signaled an incoming call. He touched a button to activate the unit and ZORAC's voice promptly informed him: "The coordination office in the Bureau Block is trying to contact you. Are you accepting?"

"Okay."

"Dr. Hunt?" The voice sounded young and, somehow, pretty.

"That's me," he acknowledged.

"Coordination office here. Sorry to trouble you but could you come over? We could use your help on something."

"Not until you promise to marry me." He was in

that kind of mood. Maybe it was coming home after being away for so long.

"What? . . ." The voice rose in surprise and confusion. "I don't . . . that is, I'm serious . . ."

"What makes you think I'm not?"

"You're crazy. Now how about coming over? . . . on business." At least, he thought, she recovered her balance nice and quickly.

"Who are you?" he asked lightly.

"I told you—the coordination office."

"Not them—*you*."

"Yvonne . . . why?"

"Well, I'll make a deal. You need me to help you out. I need someone to show me around Geneva before I go back to the States. Interested?"

"That's different," the voice retorted, though not without a hint of a smile. "I'm doing a UN job. You're conducting private enterprise. Now are you coming over?"

"Deal?"

"Oh . . . maybe. We'll see later. For the moment what about our problem?"

"What's the problem?"

"Some of your Ganymean pals are here and want to go outside. Somebody thought it would be a good idea if you went too."

Hunt sighed and shook his head to himself. "Okay," he said finally. "Tell 'em I'm on my way."

"Will do," the voice replied, then in a suddenly lowered and more confidential tone added: "I'm off on Sundays, Mondays and Tuesdays." Then it cut itself off with a click. Hunt grinned to himself, finished his coffee and rose to leave the table. A sudden thought struck him.

"ZORAC," he muttered.

"Yes, Vic?"

"Are you coupled into the Earthnet local comms grid?"

"Yes. That's how I routed the call through."

"Yes I know . . . What I meant was, was she talking through a standard two-way vi-terminal?"

"Yes."

"With a visual pickup?"

"Yes."

Hunt rubbed his chin for a moment.

"You didn't record the visual by any chance, did you?"

"I did," ZORAC informed him. "Want a playback?"

Without waiting for an answer, the machine reran a portion of the conversation on the screen of the wrist unit. Hunt nodded and whistled his silent approval. Yvonne was blond, blue-eyed, and attractive, her appearance somehow enhanced by the trim cut of her light-gray UN uniform jacket and white blouse.

"Do you record everything you handle?" Hunt inquired as he sauntered toward the door.

"No, not everything."

"What made you record that then?"

"I knew you'd ask for it," ZORAC told him.

"I don't think I like eavesdroppers in on my calls," Hunt said. "Consider yourself reprimanded."

ZORAC ignored the remark. "I logged her extension number too," it said. "Seeing as you didn't think to ask for it."

"D'you know if she's married?"

"How could I know that?"

"Oh, I don't know . . . Knowing you, you could probably crack the access codes and get into UN's personnel records through the Earthnet or something like that."

"I could, but I won't," ZORAC said. "There are things that a good computer will do for you and things that it won't. From here on in, you're on your own."

Hunt cut off the channel. Shaking his head, he emerged from the cafeteria and turned in the direction of the Bureau Block.

He appeared a few minutes later inside the coordination office on the first floor, where Garuth and some other Ganymeans were waiting with a number of UN officials.

"We feel we want to return the welcome that the people of Earth have given us," Garuth said. "So, we'd like to go for a walk outside the perimeter to meet them."

"That okay?" Hunt asked, directing his words at the portly, silver-haired man who appeared to be the most senior of the officials present.

"Sure. They're guests here, not prisoners. We thought it would be a good idea if someone they knew went with them though."

"Fine by me," Hunt said, nodding. "Let's go." As he turned toward the door, he caught a glimpse of Yvonne operating a vi-console at the back of the office and winked mischievously. She colored slightly and looked down at the keyboard below the screen. Then she glanced up, winked back with a quick smile and busied herself at the keyboard again.

Outside the building they were joined by more Ganymeans and a contingent of Swiss police headed by an apprehensive chief. The party walked down a path to the roadway and turned left to proceed between the rows of chalets toward a steel-mesh gate that formed part of the perimeter fence. As they walked clear of the chalets and continued up along the gently sloping gravel road toward the gate, a stir ran through the crowds sitting on the grassy mounds beyond the fence on the far side of the clear zone. People began jumping to their feet and looking down toward the fence. The excitement grew as the Ganymeans halted while Swiss constables unlocked the gate and swung it aside.

With Garuth on one side of him and the Swiss police chief on the other. Hunt led the party through the gate as the clamor of voices ahead of them rose and became cheering. People began running down the slopes to press together just short of the police cordon, waving and calling as the party continued along the roadway across the clear zone.

The cordon opened to let them through, and suddenly the people massed together across the roadway found themselves staring up into the awesome faces from another world. While the noise from all around continued unabated, the ranks immediately in front of the Giants grew strangely hushed, and fell back as if to maintain a respectful distance. Garuth stopped and looked slowly around the semicircle of faces. As his gaze traveled from one to another the eyes averted. Hunt could understand their uncertainty, but at the same time he was anxious that the gesture the Giants had wanted to make should not go unreciprocated.

"I'm Vic Hunt," he called to the crowd in a loud voice. "I have traveled with these people all the way from Jupiter. This is Garuth, commander of the Ganymean ship. He and his companions have come to meet you all personally and at their own request. Let's make them feel at home."

Still the people seemed to shrink back. Some seemed to want to make a welcoming gesture, but everybody was waiting for somebody else to take the first step. And then a boy at the front of the crowd wrenched his hand free from his mother's, marched forward and confronted Garuth's towering frame boldly. Wearing stout mountain boots below a pair of alpine-style leather shorts, he was about twelve years old with a tangle of fair hair and a face covered with freckles. His mother started forward instinctively, but the man standing next to her restrained her with his arm.

"I don't care about them, Mr. Garuth," the boy declared loudly. "I wanna shake your hand." With that he confidently extended his arm upward. The Giant stooped, his face contorting into an expression that could only be a smile, grasped the hand and shook it warmly. The tension in the crowd evaporated and they began surging forward jubilantly.

Hunt looked around and saw that the scene had suddenly transformed itself. In one place a Ganymean was posing with an arm around the shoulders of a laughing middle-aged woman while her husband took a photograph; in another, a Giant was accepting a proffered cup of coffee while behind him a third was looking down dubiously at a persistent, tail-wagging Alsatian dog that one family had brought along. After patting it experimentally a few times, the Giant squatted down and began ruffling its fur, to be rewarded by a frenzy of licks on the tip of his long, tapering face.

Hunt lit a cigarette and sauntered across to join the

Swiss police chief, who was mopping copious perspiration from his brow with a pocket handkerchief.

"There—it didn't go badly at all, Heinrich," he said. "Told you there was nothing to worry about."

"Maybe, Dr. 'unt," Heinrich answered, still not sounding too happy. "All ze same, I will be much ze 'appier when we can, 'ow you say in ze America . . . 'get ze 'ell out of 'ere.' "

Hunt spent a couple more days in the Earthmen sector of Ganyville helping the liaison bureau get organized and taking his own share of rest and relaxation. Then, having voted himself a spell of special leave for conduct which, he was sure, was well beyond the call of duty, he collected Yvonne, hitched them both a ride into Geneva on one of the still-shuttling VTOL jets, and embarked on a spree in the city. Three days later they tumbled out of an eastbound groundcar that stopped on the main highway running along the perimeter, slightly disheveled, distinctly unsteady on their feet and deliriously happy.

By that time—over a full week since the day the *Shapieron* had landed—the liaison bureau had got things fully under control and parties of Ganymeans were already beginning to leave to make visits and attend conferences all over the world. Some groups, in fact, had been gone for some time and news reports were already coming in on how they were faring.

Small parties of eight-foot-tall aliens, together with their ever-vigilant police escorts, had become accepted, if not yet commonplace, sights in Times Square, Red Square, Trafalgar Square and the Champs-Elysées. They had listened appreciatively to a Beethoven concert in Boston, toured the London Zoo with a mixture of awe and horror, attended lavish receptions in Buenos Aires, Canberra, Cape Town and Washington, D.C., and paid their respects at the Vatican. In Peking their culture had been complimented as the ultimate exemplification of the communist ideal, in New York as that of the democratic ideal, and in Stockholm as that of the liberal ideal. And everywhere the crowds thronged to greet them.

The reports from around the globe told of the aliens' total amazement at the variety of life, color, vitality and exuberance that they saw all around them wherever they went. Everybody on Earth, they said, seemed to be in a hurry to live a whole lifetime each day, as if they feared there might not be sufficient hours in a mortal span to accommodate all the things to be seen and done. The Minervan cities had been bigger in terms of engineering constructions and architecture, but had offered nothing that compared even remotely with the variety, energy and sheer zest for living that teemed day and night in the metropolises of Earth. The Minervan technology had been further advanced, but its rate of advancement was paltry compared to the stupendous mushrooming of human civilization that resulted from the hustling, bustling, restlessness exploding outward from this incredible planet.

Speaking at a scientific conference in Berlin, a Ganymean told his audience: "The Ganymean theory of the origin of the universe describes a steady equilibrium in which matter appears, quietly acts out its appointed role, and then quietly vanishes—a slow, easy-going, evolutionary situation that goes well with our temperament and our history. Only Man could have conceived the catastrophic discontinuity of the Big Bang. I believe that when you have had an opportunity to examine our theories more closely, you will discard your Big Bang ideas. And yet I feel it singularly appropriate that Man should have formulated such a theory. You see, ladies and gentlemen, when Man visualized the cataclysmic expansion of the Big Bang Model, he was not seeing the universe at all; he was seeing himself."

After he had been back on Earth for ten days, Hunt was contacted again by UNSA, who conveyed their hopes that he had enjoyed his leave. But some people at Houston knew him better than he thought and suggested that it might be a good idea if he began thinking about coming back.

More to the point, UNSA had made arrangements through the bureau for a Ganymean scientific delegation to visit Navcomms Headquarters at Houston, primarily to learn more about the Lunarians. The Ganymeans had been expressing a lot of interest in Man's immediate ancestral race for some reason and, since the Lunarian investigations had been controlled from Houston and much of the work had been done there, it was the obvious place to bring them. UNSA suggested that since Hunt was due to return to Houston anyway, he could act as organizer and courier for the delegation and insure their safe arrival in Texas. Danchekker, who was also due to return to Houston to resume his duties at the Westwood Biological Institute, decided to fly with them.

And so, at the end of his second week home, Hunt found himself in a familiar environment: the inside of a Boeing 1017 skyliner, fifty miles up over the North Atlantic and westward bound.

chapter twenty

"When I sent you off to Ganymede, I just wanted you to find out a little bit more about the guys. I didn't expect you to come back with a whole shipful of them." Gregg Caldwell chewed on his cigar and looked out across his desk with an expression that was half amusement and half feigned exasperation. Hunt, sprawled in the chair opposite, grinned and took another sip of his scotch. It was good to be back among the familiar surroundings of Navcomms HQ again. The inside of Caldwell's luxurious office with its murals and one wall completely dedicated to a battery of viewscreens; the panoramic view down over the rainbow towers of Houston—nothing had changed.

"So you've got more than your money's worth, Gregg," he replied. "Not complaining, are you?"

"Hell no. I'm not complaining. You've done another good job by the way things are shaping up. It's just that whenever I set you an assignment, things seem to have this tendency to kinda . . . get outa hand. I always end up with more than I bargained for." Caldwell removed his cigar from his teeth and inclined his head briefly. "But as you say, I'm not complaining."

The executive director studied Hunt thoughtfully for a few seconds. "So . . . what was it like to be away from Earth for the first time?"

"Oh, it was . . . an experience," Hunt answered automatically, but when he looked up he saw from the mischievous twinkle that danced in the eyes below the craggy brows that the question had been more than casual. He should have known. Caldwell never said or did anything without a reason.

" 'Know thyself,' " Caldwell quoted softly. "And

others too, maybe, huh?" He shrugged as if making light of the matter, but the twinkle still remained in his eyes.

Hunt's brows knitted for a split second, and then his eyes slowly widened as the cryptic message behind this turn in the conversation became clear. It took perhaps two seconds for the details to click into place in his brain. In the early days of the Lunarian investigations, just after Hunt had moved to Houston from England, his relationship with Danchekker had been caustic. Progress toward unraveling the mystery was more often than not hampered because the two scientists dissipated their energies fruitlessly in personal conflicts. But later on, in the wilderness of Luna and out in the void between Earth and Jupiter, all that had somehow been forgotten. It was then that the two scientists had begun to work in harmony, and the difficulties had crumbled before the powerful assault of their combined talents, which was what had been needed to solve the Lunarian problem. Hunt could see that clearly now. Suddenly, he also realized that this state of affairs had not come about through mere accident. He stared at Caldwell with new respect, and slowly nodded ungrudging approval.

"Gregg," he said, in a tone of mock reproach. "You've been pulling strings again. You set us up."

"I did?" Caldwell's voice was suitably innocent.

"Chris and me. It was out there we began to see each other as people and learned to pool our marbles. That's what cracked the Lunarian riddle. You knew it would happen . . ." Hunt pointed an accusing finger across the desk. "That's why you did it."

Caldwell compressed his heavy jowls momentarily into a tight-lipped grin of satisfaction. "So, you got more than your money's worth," he threw back. "Not complaining, are you?"

"Smooth operator," Hunt complimented, raising his glass. "Okay, we've both had a good deal. That's how I think business ought to be. But now to the present and the future—what have you got lined up next?"

Caldwell sat forward and rested his elbows on the desk. He exhaled a long stream of blue smoke. "What about this bunch of alien guys you brought back from Europe; are you still tied up most of the time with looking after them?"

"They've been introduced over at Westwood now," Hunt told him. "They're interested in the Lunarians and particularly want to have a look at Charlie over there. Chris Danchekker is handling that side of things, which leaves me fairly free for a while."

"Fine. What I'd like you to start giving some thought to is a preliminary overview of Ganymean science," Caldwell said. "What with this ZORAC machine of theirs and all the conferences and discussions they're having all over the place, there's more information coming across than we can handle. When all the excitement dies down there's going to be one hell of a lotta work to get through with all that. When you were coordinating the Charlie business you operated a pretty good network of channels to most of the leading scientific institutions and establishments around the world. I'd like you to use those channels again to make a start at cataloging and evaluating everything that's new, especially things that could be of particular use to UNSA—like their gravitics. We may find we want to revise a lot of our own research programs in light of what these big guys have got to tell us. Now seems as good a time as any to begin."

"The group stays intact for a while then?" Hunt guessed, referring to the team that he had headed during the Lunarian investigations and which had continued working under the supervision of his deputy, mainly to tidy up the unresolved details, during his time on Ganymede.

"Yep," Caldwell nodded. "The way they work seems set up for the job. Have you said hello to them yet?"

Hunt shook his head. "Only got back this morning. I came straight on here."

"Do that then," Caldwell said. "There are probably a lot of old friends around here that you want to see. Take the rest of this week to settle in again. Then make a start on what we just talked about on Monday. Okay?"

"Okay. The first thing I'll do is go see the group and

give them an idea of what our next job's going to be. I think they'll like it. Who knows . . . they might even have half of it organized for me by Monday if they start thinking about it." He cocked an inquiring eye at Caldwell. "Or is that what you figure you pay me to do?"

"I pay you to think smart," Caldwell grunted. "That's called delegation. If you wanna delegate too, that's what I call thinking smart. Do it."

Hunt spent the rest of that day with his own staff, familiarizing himself with some of the fine points of how they had been getting on—he had kept in touch with them almost daily for the general things—and outlining for them his recent directive from Caldwell. After that there was no getting away; they quizzed him for hours about every scrap of information that he had managed to absorb on Ganymean scientific theory and technology, kept him talking all through lunch, and succeeded in extracting a commitment from him to arrange for a Ganymean scientist or two to come and give them an intensive teach-in. At least, he reflected as he finally left for home at nine o'clock that night, he was not going to have any problems with motivation there.

Next morning he made a point of avoiding that part of Navcomms HQ building that contained his own offices and started his day by paying a call on another old friend of his—Don Maddson, head of the linguistics section. It was Don's team, working in cooperation with several universities and research institutes all over the world, that had played one of the most important roles in the Lunarian saga by untangling the riddle of the Lunarian language, using documents found on Charlie's person and, later, a library of microdot texts from the remains of a Lunarian base that had come to light near Tycho. Without the translations, it would never have been possible even to prove conclusively that the Lunarians and the Ganymeans had come from the same planet.

Hunt stopped outside the door of Maddson's office, knocked lightly and entered without waiting for a reply. Maddson was sitting behind his desk studying a sheet from a stack of the innumerable pieces of paper without which his office would never have seemed complete. He glanced up, stared incredulously for a second, and then his face split into a broad ear-to-ear smile.

"Vic! What the . . ." He half rose from his chair and began pumping Hunt's proffered hand vigorously. "It's great to see ya . . . great. I knew you were back on Earth but nobody told me you were Stateside yet . . ." He beckoned Hunt toward an easy chair on the other side of the desk. "Sit down, sit down . . . When did you get in?"

"Yesterday morning," Hunt replied, settling himself comfortably. "I had to see Gregg and then I got tied up completely with the *Group L* bunch. Gregg wants us to start thinking about writing a compendium of Ganymean science. They're all dead keen to go on it . . . kept me talking till heavens knows what time last night in the Ocean Bar."

"Ganymeans, eh?" Maddson grinned. "I thought maybe you'd have brought us one back."

"There's a load of 'em over at Westwood with Chris Danchekker right now."

"Yeah. I know about that. They're due to pay us a call here later. Everybody around here's getting keyed up with the suspense. They can't wait." Maddson sat back in his chair and regarded Hunt over interlaced fingers for a few seconds. At last he shook his head. "Well, I dunno where to start Vic. It's been all this time . . . there are so many questions . . . I guess there's enough to keep us talking all day, huh? Or maybe you're getting tired of people asking all the same things all the time, over and over?"

"Not at all," Hunt said. "But why don't we save all that for lunch? Maybe some of the others might like to join us and then I'll only need to say it all to everybody once; otherwise I *might* end up getting tired of it, and that wouldn't do."

"Great idea," Maddson agreed. "We'll reserve the topic for lunch. In the meantime, have a guess what we're into now?"

"Who?"

"Us . . . the section . . . Linguistics."

"What?"

Maddson took a deep breath, stared Hunt straight in the eye and proceeded to deliver a string of utterly meaningless syllables in a deep, guttural voice. Then he sat back and beamed proudly, his expression inviting Hunt to accept the implied challenge.

"What the hell was that all about?" Hunt asked, as if doubting his own ears.

"Even *you* don't know?"

"Why should I?"

Maddson was evidently enjoying himself. "That, my friend, was Ganymean," he said.

"Ganymean?"

"Ganymean!"

Hunt stared at him in astonishment. "How in God's name did you learn that?"

Maddson waited a moment longer to make the most of Hunt's surprise, then gestured toward the display unit standing on one side of his desk.

"We've got ourselves a channel through to ZORAC," he said. "There's been a pretty fantastic demand for access into it ever since it was hooked into the Earthnet, just as you'd imagine. But being UNSA we qualify for high priority. That sure is one hell of a machine."

Hunt was duly impressed. "So, ZORAC's been teaching you Ganymean, eh," he said. "It fits. I should have guessed you wouldn't let a chance like that slip by."

"It's an interesting language," Maddson commented. "It's obviously matured over a long period of time and been rationalized extensively—hardly any irregular forms or ambiguities at all. Actually, it's pretty straightforward to learn structurewise, but the pitch and vocal inflections don't come naturally to a human. That's the most difficult part." He made a throwing-away motion in the air. "It's only of academic interest I guess . . . but as you say, a chance we couldn't resist."

"How about the Lunarian texts from Tycho," Hunt

asked. "Been making progress on the rest of those too?"

"You bet." Maddson waved toward the piles of papers covering the desk and the table standing against the wall on one side of his office. "We've been pretty busy here all around."

Maddson proceeded to describe some of the details his team of linguists had been able to fill in during Hunt's absence, concerning the Lunarian culture and the way in which it had been organized on the Minerva of fifty thousand years before. There was a thumbnail sketch of the war-torn history of the Lunarian civilization; some detailed maps of parts of the planet's surface with accounts of geographic, climatic, agricultural and industrial characteristics; a treatise on the citizen's obligations and duties toward the State in the totalitarian fortress-factory that was Minerva; a description of native Minervan life forms as reconstructed from fossil remains and some speculations on the possible causes of their abrupt extinction twenty-five million years before. There were numerous references to the earlier race that had inhabited the planet before the Lunarians themselves had emerged; obviously, a civilization such as that of the Ganymeans could never have passed away without leaving ample traces of itself behind for posterity. The Lunarians had marveled at the ruins of Ganymean cities, examined their awesome machines without growing much the wiser, and reconstructed a fairly comprehensive picture of how their world had once looked. In most of their writings, the Lunarians had referred to the Ganymeans simply as the Giants.

Then, more than an hour after they had begun talking, Maddson drew out a set of charts from below some other papers and spread them out for Hunt's inspection. They were views of the heavens at night, showing the stars in groupings that were not immediately recognizable. Captions, which Hunt identified as being written in Lunarian, were scattered across the charts and below each caption, in smaller print, a translation appeared in English.

"These might interest you, Vic," Maddson said, still

bubbling with enthusiasm. "Star charts drawn by Lunarian astronomers fifty thousand years ago. When you've looked at them for a little while, you'll pick out all the familiar constellations. They're a bit distorted from the ones we see today because the relative displacements have altered a little with time, of course. In fact, we passed these on to some astronomers at Hale who were able to calculate from the distortions exactly how long ago these charts were drawn. It doesn't come out at too far off fifty thousand years at all."

Hunt said nothing but leaned forward to peer closely at the charts. This was fascinating—a record of the skies as they had appeared when the Lunarian civilization had been at its peak, immediately prior to its catastrophic fall. As Maddson had said, all the familiar constellations were there, but changed subtly from those seen in modern times. The other thing that made them difficult to identify were the sets of lines drawn all over the charts to interconnect groups of the more prominent stars into patterns and shapes that bore no resemblance to the familiar constellations; the lines tended to draw the eye along unfamiliar paths and obscure the better-known patterns. Orion, for example, was there, but not connected up as a single, intact configuration; part of it was grouped independently into a subset, while the other part was separated from the rest of Orion and linked to the normally distinct parallelogram of Lepus to form something else instead. The result was that it took time to identify the two parts of Orion and mentally fuse them back together again to reveal that Orion was there at all.

"I see," Hunt observed thoughtfully at last. "They saw pictures in the stars just like we do, only they saw different ones. Takes a while to get used to, doesn't it?"

"Yeah—interesting, huh?" Maddson agreed. "They not only saw different shapes; they grouped the stars differently too. That doesn't really come as a surprise though; I've always said there was more dog in the mind of the beholder than there ever was in Canis Major. Still, it's interesting to see that their minds seemed to work the same way . . . even if they were every bit as susceptible to autosuggestion."

"What's this?" Hunt inquired after a few more seconds. He indicated a pattern that lay over toward the left-hand side of the chart he had been studying. The Lunarians had formed a large constellation by connecting together Hercules, Serpens, Corona Borealis and part of Boötes to produce a starfish-shaped pattern. The English translation of its name read simply *The Giant*.

"I wondered if you'd spot that one," Maddson said, nodding in approval. "Well, as we know, the Lunarians knew all about the Ganymeans having been there before them. I guess they musta kinda named one of their constellations . . . sort of in honor of them, or something like that." He swept a hand over the chart to take in the whole extent of it. "As you can see, they named their constellations after all kinds of things, but mainly after animals just like we did. I suppose it must be a natural tendency in some kind of way." He pointed back at the one Hunt had picked out. "If you're the imaginative kind, you can see something in that which vaguely suggests the Ganymean form . . . it does to me anyhow. I mean . . . in Hercules you can see the head and the two arms raised up . . . Serpens forms a slightly flexed leg trailing back . . . and then the lines through Corona Borealis and then down to Arcturus give you the other leg. See what I mean? It sorta looks like a figure running or leaping."

"It does, doesn't it," Hunt agreed. His eyes held a faraway look for a moment, then he went on: "I'll tell you something else this tells us. Don: The Lunarians knew about the Giants very early in their history too—not just later on after they discovered the sciences."

"How d'you figure that?"

"Well, look at the names that they've given to all their constellations. As you said, they're all simple, everyday things—animals and so on. Those are the kinds of names that a simple and primitive people would think up . . . names that come from the things they see in the world around them. We got our names for our constellations in exactly the same way."

"You mean that these names were handed down from way back," Maddson said. "Through the generations . . . from the early times when the Lunarians were just starting to think about getting civilized. Yeah, I suppose you could be right." He paused to think for a second. "I see what you mean now. . . . The one they called *The Giant* was probably named at about the same time as the rest. The rest were named while the Lunarians were still primitive, so *The Giant* was named while they were still primitive. Conclusion: The Lunarians knew about the Ganymeans right from the early days. Yeah—I'll buy that . . . I suppose it's not all that surprising, though. I mean, from the pictures that the Ganymeans have shown us of their civilization, there must have been all kinds of evidence left lying around all over the planet. The early Lunarians could hardly have missed it, primitive or not. All they had to do was have eyes."

"No wonder their writings and legends were full of references to the Giants then," Hunt said. "That knowledge must have had a terrific influence on how their civilization and thinking developed. Imagine what a difference it might have made if the Sumerians had seen evidence of a long-lost, technically advanced race all around them. They might—hey, what's this?" Hunt had been scanning idly over the remaining star charts while he was talking. Suddenly he stopped and peered closely at one of them, at the same time pointing to one of the inscriptions with his finger. The inscription did not refer to a constellation of stars this time, but to a single star, standing alone and shown relatively faintly. The inscription, however, stood out in bold Lunarian characters. Its English equivalent read: *The Giants' Star.*

"Something wrong?" Maddson asked.

"Not wrong . . . just a bit odd." Hunt was frowning thoughtfully. "This star—it's nowhere near that other constellation. It's in another hemisphere completely, out near Taurus . . . yet it's got a name like that. I wonder why they gave it a name like that."

"Why not?" Maddson shrugged. "Why shouldn't they give it a name like that? It's as good as any other. Maybe they were kinda running outa names."

Hunt was still looking perturbed.

"But it's so faint," he said slowly. "Don, are the different brightnesses of the stars shown on these charts significant? I mean, did they tend to show the brighter stars larger, same as we do?"

"As a matter of fact, yes they did," Maddson answered. "But what of it? Does it really . . ."

"Which star is this?" Hunt asked, now evidently intrigued and apparently not hearing.

"Search me." Maddson spread his hands wide. "I'm no astronomer. Is it so important?"

"I think it is." Hunt's voice was curiously soft, and still held a faraway note.

"How come?"

"Look at it this way. That looks like a very faint star to me—magnitude four, five or less at a guess. Something makes me wonder if that star would be visible at all from the Solar System to the naked eye. Now if that were the case, it could only have been discovered after the Lunarians invented telescopes. Right?"

"That figures," Maddson agreed. "So what?"

"Well, now we get back to the name. You see, that kind of name—*The Giants' Star*—is in keeping with all the rest. It's the kind of name that you'd expect the ancients of the Lunarian race to come up with. But what if the ancients of the Lunarian race never knew about it . . . because they'd never seen it? That means that it had to have been given its name later, after the science of astronomy had been refined to a high level, by the advanced civilization that came later. But why would an advanced civilization give it a name like that?"

A look of growing comprehension spread slowly across Maddson's face. He looked back at Hunt but was too astounded by the implication to say anything. Hunt read the expression and nodded to confirm what Maddson was thinking.

"Exactly. We have to grope around in the dark to find out anything about what kind of evidence of their existence the Ganymeans left behind them. The Lunarian scientists had no such problem because they had the one thing available to them that we don't have —the planet Minerva, intact, right under their feet, no doubt with enough evidence and clues buried all over it to keep them busy for generations." He nodded again in response to Maddson's incredulous stare. "They must have built up a very complete record of what the Ganymeans had done, all right. But all the evidence they used to do it was lost with them."

Hunt paused and drew his cigarette case slowly from his inside jacket pocket while he quickly checked over the line of reasoning in his mind.

"I wonder what they knew about that star that we don't know," he said at last, his voice now become very quiet. "I wonder what they knew about that star that caused them to choose a name like that. We've suspected for a long time that the Giants might have migrated to another star, but we've never been able to prove it for sure or been able to say what star it might have been. And now this turns up . . ."

Hunt stopped with his lighter poised halfway toward his mouth. "Don," he said. "In your life, do you find that fate steps in and lends a hand every now and again?"

"Never really thought about it," Maddson admitted. "But now you come to mention it, I guess I have to agree."

chapter twenty-one

As time went by, the Ganymean scientists grew to know better and work more closely with the scientific community of Earth. In several areas, information supplied by the aliens contributed significantly to advances in human knowledge.

Maps reproduced from ZORAC's data banks showed the surface of the Earth as it had appeared at the time of the early Minervan expeditions to the planet, during its late Oligocene period. These same maps showed the Atlantic Ocean little more than half as wide as was shown on twenty-first-century maps, indicating that the time represented was that much nearer to the breaking adrift of the American continent. The Mediterranean Sea was much wider with Italy half rotated prior to being driven into Europe by Africa's relentless northward drive to create the Alps; India had just made contact with Asia and begun throwing up the Himalayas; Australia was much closer to Africa. Measurements of these maps enabled current theories of plate techtonics to be thoroughly checked and brought a whole new light to bear on many aspects of the Earth sciences.

Throughout all this the Ganymeans declined to say exactly where their experimental colonies on Earth had been located, or what areas had been affected by the ecological catastrophes that they had induced. These matters, they said, were best left in the past where they belonged.

At institutes of physics and universities all over the world, the Ganymeans unveiled the rudiments and fundamental concepts of the theoretical basis of the extended science that had led to the emergence of their

211

technology of gravitics. In this they did not provide blueprints for constructing gadgets and devices whose principles would not be comprehended and whose introduction would have been premature; they offered only general guidance, declaring that Man would fill in the details in his own way, and would do so when the time was right.

The Ganymeans also painted bright and promising pictures of the future by describing the unlimited abundance of resources that the universe had to offer. All substances, they pointed out, were built from the same atoms and, given the right knowledge and sufficient energy, anything required—metals, crystals, organic polymers, oils, sugars and proteins—could be synthesized from plentiful and freely available materials. Energy, as Man was beginning to discover, was waiting to be trapped in undreamed of quantities. Of the total amount of energy radiated out into space by the sun, less than one thousandth part of one billionth was actually intercepted by the disk of the Earth. Nearly half of that was reflected away back into space, and of the remainder that actually penetrated through to the surface, only a minute fraction was harnessed to any useful purpose. Borrowing from the commercial jargon of Earth, the Ganymeans described the tiny pockets of energy that happened to be trapped in one form or another about the surface of his planet as representing Man's starting capital. Future generations, they predicted, would look back at Apollo as just the down payment on the best long-term investment Man ever made.

As the months passed by, the two cultures interlocked more closely and adjusted to accommodate one another so well that it seemed to many that the Giants had always been there. The *Shapieron* toured the globe and spent a day or two at most of the world's major airports, attracting visitors by the tens of thousands; on several occasions it took selected parties on one-hour rides around the Moon and back! Anybody who had access to an Earthnet terminal and who could get through the permanently jammed public exchange could speak to ZORAC, and a number of high-priority channels were permanently reserved for allocation to schools. Despite their ancestry, many of the young Ganymeans developed a passion for baseball, soccer, and other such sports—pastimes the likes of which had been unknown to them in their previous ship-bound existence. Before long they had formed their own leagues to challenge their terrestrial counterparts. At first their elders were a little disturbed by this turn of events, but later they reasoned that the notion of competition seemed to have brought Man a long way in a short time; perhaps the grafting, in small doses, of the Earthman's will to win onto the Ganymean's analytical ability to see just how to go about doing it, wouldn't be so bad after all.

For six months the Ganymeans toured every nation of Earth learning its ways, absorbing its culture, meeting its peoples—the high, the low, the rich, the poor, the ordinary and the famous. After a while they were no longer the "aliens." They became simply a new factor in an environment that the people of Earth were by now accustomed to accept as constantly changing. Hunt noticed again, this time on a global scale, the same thing he had noticed at Pithead in the week that the Ganymeans had gone to Pluto—they seemed to belong on Earth. Without them being constantly around or featured in the headlines, Earth would not, somehow, have seemed normal.

Then, one day, the news flashed around the globe that Garuth would shortly appear on the Earthnet to make an important announcement to all the people of Earth. No hint was given as to what this announcement would contain, but there was something about the mood of the moment that forewarned of some significant development. When the evening arrived on which Garuth was due to speak, the world was watching and waiting at a billion viewscreens.

Garuth spoke for a long time on the events that had taken place since the time of the Ganymeans' arrival. He touched upon most of the sights that he and his companions had seen, the places they had been to and the things that they had learned. He expressed again the amazement that the Ganymeans had experienced at the restlessness, vivacity and impatient frenzy for living that they had found on every side in what he described as "this fantastic, undreamed-of world of yours." And, speaking on behalf of all his kind, he repeated their gratitude to the governments and people of the planet that had shown them friendship, hospitality and generosity without limit, and offered their home to share.

But then his mood, which had been slightly solemn throughout, took on a distinctly somber note. "As most of you, my friends, know, for a long time now there has been speculation that long ago, sometime after our ship departed from Minerva, our race abandoned that planet forever to seek a new home elsewhere. There have been suggestions that the new home they found was a planet of a distant star—the one that has become known as *The Giants' Star*.

"Both these notions must remain mere speculation. Our scientists and yours have been working together for many months now, studying the Lunarian records and following up every clue that might possibly add further credence to these notions. I have to tell you that these efforts have thus far proved fruitless. We cannot say for certain that *The Giants' Star* is indeed the new home of our race. We cannot even say for certain that our race did in fact migrate to a new home at all.

"There is a chance, nevertheless, that these things could be true."

The long face paused and stared hard at the camera for what seemed a long time, almost as if it knew that the watchers at the screens all over the world could sense suddenly what was coming next.

"I must now inform you that I and my senior officers have discussed and examined these questions at great length. We have decided that, slim though the chances of success appear to be, we must make the attempt to find these answers. The Solar System was once our home, but it is no longer our home. We must take to the void again and seek our own kind."

He paused again to allow time for his meaning to sink in.

"This decision did not come easily. My people have spent a large part of their natural lives wandering in depths of space. Our children have never known a home. A journey to *The Giants' Star* will, we know, take many years. In many ways we are sad, naturally, but, like you, we must in the end obey our instincts. Deep down we could never rest until the question of *The Giants' Star* has been finally answered.

"And so, my friends, I am bidding you farewell. We will carry with us pleasant memories of the time that we knew here on the sunny blue and green world of Earth. We will never forget the warmth and hospitality of the people of this world, nor will we forget what they did for us. But, sadly, it must end.

"One week from today we will depart. Should we fail in our quest, we, or our descendants, will return. This I promise."

The Giant raised his arm in a final salute, and inclined his head slightly.

"Thank you—all of you. And good-bye."

He held the posture for a few more seconds. Then the broadcast cut out.

A half-hour after the broadcast, Garuth emerged from the main door of the conference center at Ganyville. He stopped for a while, savoring the first hint of winter being carried down from the mountains on the night air. Around him all was still apart from an occasional figure flitting through the pools of warm orange light that flooded out of the windows into the alley between the wooden walls of the chalets. The night was clear as crystal. He stood for a long time staring up at the stars. Then he began walking slowly along the path in front of him and turned into the broad throughway that led down, between the rows of chalets, toward the immense floodlit tower of the *Shapieron*.

He passed by one of the ship's supporting legs and moved on into the space spanned by its four enormous fin surfaces, suddenly dwarfed by the sweeping lines of metal soaring high above him. As he approached the foot of one of the ramps that led up into the lowered stern and stepped into the surrounding circle of light, a half-dozen or so eight-foot figures straightened up out of the shadows at the bottom of the ramp. He recognized them immediately as members of his crew, no doubt relaxing and enjoying the calm of the night. As he drew nearer, he sensed from the way they stood and the way they looked at him that something had changed. Normally they would have called out some jovial remark or made some enthusiastic sign of greeting, but they did not. They just stood there, silent and withdrawn. As he reached the ramps they stood aside to make way and raised their hands in acknowledgment of his rank. Garuth returned the salutes and passed between them. He found that he could not meet their eyes. No one spoke. He knew that they had seen the broadcast, and he knew how they felt. There was nothing he could say.

He reached the top of the ramp, passed through the open airlock and crossed the wide space beyond to enter the elevator that ZORAC had waiting. A few seconds later he was being carried swiftly upward into the main body of the *Shapieron*.

He came out of the elevator over five hundred feet above ground level, and followed a short corridor to a door which brought him into his private quarters. Shilohin, Monchar and Jassilane were waiting there, sitting in a variety of poses around the room. He sensed the same attitude that he had felt a minute before at the ramp. He stood for a moment looking down at them while the door slid silently shut behind him. Monchar and Jassilane were looking at one another uneasily. Only Shilohin was holding his gaze, but she said nothing. Garuth emitted a long-drawn-out sigh then moved slowly between them to stand for a while contemplating a metallic tapestry that adorned the far wall. Then he turned about to face them once more. Shilohin was still watching him.

"You're still not convinced that we have to go," he said at last.

The remark was unnecessary, but somebody had to say something. No reply was necessary either.

The scientist shifted her eyes away and said, as if addressing the low table standing between her and the other two. "It's the way in which we're going about it. They've trusted you unquestioningly all this time. All the way from Iscaris . . . all those years . . . You . . ."

"One second." Garuth moved across to a small control panel set into the wall near the door. "I don't think this conversation should go on record." He flipped a switch to cut off the room from all channels to ZORAC, and hence to the ship's archived records.

"You know that there's no Ganymean civilization waiting at *The Giants' Star* or anywhere else," Shilohin resumed. Her voice was about as near an accusation as a Ganymean could get. "We've been through the Lunarian records time and again. It adds up to nothing. You are taking your people away to die somewhere out there between the stars. There will be no coming back. But you allow them to believe in fantasies so that they will follow where you lead them. Surely those are the ways of Earthmen, not Ganymeans."

"They offered us their world as home," Jassilane murmured, shaking his head. "For twenty years your people have dreamed of nothing but coming home. And now that they have found one, you would take them back out into the void again. Minerva is gone; nothing we can do will change that. But by a quirk of fate we have found a new home—here. It will never happen a second time."

Suddenly Garuth was very weary. He sank down into the reclining chair by the door and regarded the three solemn faces staring back at him. There was nothing that he could add to the things that had already been said. Yes, it was true; the Earthmen had greeted his people as if they were long-lost brothers. They had offered all they had. But in the six months that had gone by, Garuth had looked deep below the surface. He had looked; he had listened; he had watched; he had seen.

"Today the Earthmen welcome us with open arms," he said. "But in many ways, they are still children. They show us their world as a child would open its toy cupboard to a new play-friend. But a play-friend who visits once in a while is one thing; one who moves in to stay, with equal rights to ownership to the toy cupboard, is another."

Garuth could see that his listeners wanted to be convinced, to feel the reassurance of thinking the way he thought, but could not—no more than they had been able to a dozen times before. Nevertheless he had no choice but to go through it yet again.

"The human race is still struggling to learn to live with itself. Today we are just a handful of aliens— a novelty; but one day we would grow to a sizable population. Earth does not yet possess the stability and the maturity to adapt to coexistence on that scale; they are just managing to coexist with one another. Look at their history. One day, I'm sure, they will be capable, but the time is not ripe yet.

"You forget their pride and their innate instincts to compete in all things. They could never accept passively a situation in which their instincts would compel them, one day, to see themselves as inferiors and us as dominant rivals. When that time came, we would be forced to go anyway, since we would never impose ourselves or our ways on unwilling or resentful hosts, but that would happeen only after a lot of problems and eventual unpleasantness. It is better this way."

Shilohin heard his words, but still everything inside her recoiled from the verdict that they spelled out.

"So, for this you would deceive your own people," she whispered. "Just to insure the stable evolution of this alien planet, you would sacrifice your own kind —the last few pathetic remnants of our civilization. What kind of judgment is this?"

"It is not my judgment, but the judgment of time and fate," Garuth replied. "The Solar System was once the undisputed domain of our race, but that time ended long ago. We are the intruders now—an anachronism; a scrap flotsam thrown up out of the ocean of time. Now the Solar System has become rightly the inheritance of Man. We do not belong here any longer. That is not a judgment for us to make, but one that has already been made for us by circumstances. It is merely ours to accept."

"But your people . . ." Shilohin protested. "Shouldn't they know? Haven't they the right. . . . ?" She threw her arms in the air in a gesture of helplessness. Garuth remained silent for a moment, then shook his head slowly.

"I will not reveal to them that the new home at *The Giants' Star* is a myth," he declared firmly. "That is a burden that need be carried only by us, who command and lead. They do not have to know . . . yet. It was their hope and their belief in a purpose that nurtured them from Iscaris to Sol. So it can be again for a while. If we are taking them away to their doom to perish unsung and unmourned somewhere in the cold, uncharted depths of space, they deserve at least that before the final truth has to become known. That is precious little to ask."

A grim silence reigned for a long time. A faraway look came over Shilohin as she turned over again in her mind the things that Garuth had said. And then the look changed gradually into a frown. Her eyes cleared and swung slowly upward to meet Garuth's.

"Garuth," she said. Her voice was curiously calm and composed. All traces of the emotions she had felt previously were gone. "I've never said this to you ever before, but . . . I don't believe you." Jassilane and Monchar looked up abruptly. Garuth seemed strangely unsurprised, almost as if he had been expecting her to say that. He leaned back in his chair and contemplated the tapestry on the wall. Then he swung his eyes slowly back toward her.

"What don't you believe, Shilohin?"

"Your reasons . . . everything you've been saying for the last few weeks. It's just not . . . you. It's a rationalization of something else . . . something deeper." Garuth said nothing, but continued to regard her steadfastly. "Earth *is* maturing rapidly," she continued. "We've mixed with them and been accepted by them in ways that far exceeded our wildest hopes.

There's no evidence to support the predictions you made. There's no evidence that we could never co-exist, even if our numbers did grow. You would never sacrifice your people just on the off-chance that things might not work out. You'd try it first . . . for a while at least. There has to be another reason. I won't be able to support your decision until I know what that reason is. You talked about the burden of us who command and lead. If we carry that burden, then surely we've a right to know why."

Garuth continued staring at her thoughtfully for a long time after she had finished speaking. Then he transferred his gaze, still with the same thoughtful expression, to Jassilane and Monchar. The look in their eyes echoed Shilohin's words. Then, abruptly, he seemed to make up his mind.

Without speaking, he rose from the chair, walked over to the control panel, and operated the switch to restore normal communications facilities to the room.

"ZORAC," he called.

"Yes, Commander?"

"You recall the discussion that we had about a month ago concerning the data that the human scientists have collected on the genetics of the Oligocene species discovered in the ship at Pithead?"

"Yes."

"I'd like you to present the results of your analysis of that data to us. This information is not to be made accessible to anyone other than myself and the three people who are in this room at present."

chapter twenty-two

The crowds that came to Ganyville to see the *Shapieron* depart were as large as those that had greeted its arrival, but their mood was a very different one. This time there was no jubilation or wild excitement. The people of Earth would miss the gentle Giants that they had come to know so well, and it showed.

The governments of Earth had again sent their ambassadors and, on the concrete apron below the towering ship, two groups of Earthmen and aliens faced each other for the last time. After the final formalities had been exchanged and the last farewell speeches had been uttered, the spokesman for each of the two races presented his parting gift.

The Chairman of the United Nations, acting on behalf of all of the peoples and nations of Earth, handed over two ornamental metal caskets, heavily inscribed on their outside faces and decorated with precious stones. The first contained a selection of seeds of many terrestrial trees, shrubs and flowering plants. The second, somewhat larger, contained the national flag of every one of the world's states. The seeds, he said, were to be planted at a selected place when the Giants arrived at their new home; the plants that grew from them would symbolize all of terrestrial life and provide a lasting reminder that henceforth both worlds would always be a home to Man and Ganymean equally. The flags were to be flown above that place on some as yet unknown future day when the first ship from Earth reached *The Giants' Star*. Thus, when Man came at last to launch himself into the void between the stars, he would find a small part of Earth waiting to greet him on the other side.

Garuth's gift to Earth was knowledge. He presented a large chest filled with books, tables, charts and diagrams which, he stated, provided a comprehensive introduction to the Ganymean genetic sciences. In presenting this knowledge to Earth, the Ganymeans were attempting to atone in the only way that they could for the species of Oligocene animals that had been made extinct during the ugly extermination experiments of long ago. By techniques that were explained in these texts, Garuth said, the DNA codes that existed in any preserved cell from any part of an animal organism could be extracted and used to control the artificially induced growth of a duplicate, living organism. Given a sliver of bone, a trace of tissue or a clipping of horn, a new embryo could be synthesized and from it the complete animal would grow. Thus, provided that some remnant remained, all of the extinct species that had once roamed the surface of the Earth could be resurrected. In this way, the Ganymeans hoped, the species that had met with sudden and untimely ends as a result of their actions would be allowed to live and run free again.

And then the last group of Ganymeans stood for a while to return the silent wavings of the multitudes on the surrounding hills before filing slowly up into the ship. With them went a small party of Earthmen destined for Ganymede, where the *Shapieron* was scheduled to make a short call to allow the Ganymeans to bid farewell to their UNSA friends there.

ZORAC spoke over the communications network of Earth to deliver a final message from the Ganymeans and then the link was broken. The *Shapieron* retracted its stern section into its flight position and for a while the huge ship stood alone while the world watched. And then it began to rise, slowly and majestically, before soaring up and away to rejoin its element. Only the sea of upturned faces, the lines of tiny figures arrayed around the empty space in the center of the concrete apron, and the rows of outsize deserted wooden chalets remained to show that it had ever been.

The mood inside the *Shapieron* was solemn too. In the command center, Garuth stood in the area of open floor below the dais surrounded by a group of senior officers and watched in silence as the mottled pattern of blue and white on the main screen shrank and became the globe of Earth. Shilohin was standing beside him, also silent and absorbed in thoughts of her own.

Then ZORAC spoke, his voice seemingly issuing from the surrounding walls. "Launch characteristics normal. All systems checked and normal. Request confirmation of orders."

"Existing orders confirmed," Garuth replied quietly. "Destination Ganymede."

"Setting course for Ganymede," the machine reported. "Arrival will be as scheduled."

"Hold off main drives for a while," Garuth said suddenly. "I'd like to see Earth for a little longer."

"Maintaining auxiliaries," came the response. "Main drives being held on standby pending further orders."

As the minutes ticked by the globe on the screen contracted slowly. The Ganymeans continued to watch in silence.

At last Shilohin turned to Garuth. "And to think, we called it the Nightmare Planet."

Garuth smiled faintly. His thoughts were still far away.

"They've woken up from the nightmare now," he said. "What an extraordinary race they are. Surely they must be unique in the Galaxy."

"I still can't bring myself to believe that everything we have seen can have evolved from such origins," she replied. "Don't forget I was brought up in a school that taught me to believe that this could never happen. All our theories and our models predicted that intelligence was unlikely to develop at all in any ecology like that, and that any form of civilization would be absolutely impossible. And yet . . ." she made a gesture of helplessness, "look at them. They've barely learned to fly and already they talk about the stars. Two hundred years ago they knew nothing of electricity; today they generate it by fusion power. Where will they stop?"

"I don't think they ever will," Garuth said slowly. "They can't. They must fight all the time, just as their ancestors did. Their ancestors fought each other; they fight the challenges that the universe throws at them instead. Take away their challenges and they would waste away."

Shilohin thought again about the incredible race that had struggled to claw its way upward through every difficulty and obstacle imaginable, not the least of which was its own perversity, and which now reigned unchallenged and triumphant in the Solar System that the Ganymeans had once owned.

"Their history is still abhorrent in many ways," she said. "But at the same time there is something strangely magnificent and proud about them. They can live with danger where we could not, because they know that they can conquer danger. They have proved things to themselves that we will never know, and it is that knowledge that will carry them onward where we would hesitate. If Earthmen had inhabited the Minerva of twenty-five million years ago, I'm sure that things would have turned out differently. They wouldn't have given up after Iscaris; they would have found a way to win."

"Yes," Garuth agreed. "Things would certainly have turned out very differently. But before long, I feel, we will see what would have happened if that had been true. Very soon now the Earthmen will explode outward all over the Galaxy. Somehow, I don't think it will ever be quite the same again after that happens."

The conversation lapsed once more as the two Ganymeans shifted their eyes again to take in a last view of the planet that had defied all their theories, laws, principles and expectations. In the years to come they would no doubt gaze many times at this image, retrieved from the ship's data banks, but it would never again have the impact of this moment.

After a long time, Garuth called out aloud, "ZORAC."

"Commander?"

"It's time we were on our way. Activate main drives."

"Switching over from standby. Commencing run-up to full power now."

The disk of Earth dissolved into a wash of colors that ran across the screen and began to fade. After a few minutes the colors had merged into a sheet of drab, uniform, grayish fog. The screen would show nothing more until they reached Ganymede.

"Monchar," Garuth called. "I have things to attend to. Will you take over here for a while?"

"Aye-aye, sir."

"Very good. I will be in my room if I am needed for anything."

Garuth excused himself from the company, acknowledged the salutations around him, and left the command center. He walked slowly through the corridors that led to his private quarters, fully preoccupied with the thoughts inside his head and largely oblivious to his surroundings. When he had closed the door behind him, he stared at himself in the wall mirror in his stateroom for a long time, as if looking for visible changes in his appearance that might have been brought about by what he had done. Then he sank into one of the reclining armchairs and stared unseeingly at the ceiling until he lost track of time.

Eventually he activated the wall screen in the stateroom and called up a star chart that showed the part of the sky that included the constellation of Taurus. For a long time he sat staring at the faint point that would grow progressively brighter in the course of the long voyage ahead. There was a hope that they could all be wrong. There was always a chance. If the Ganymeans *had* migrated there, what kind of civilization would they have developed over the millions of years that had passed by since the *Shapieron* departed from Minerva? What kind of science would they possess? What wonders would they accept as commonplace that even he could never conceive? As his mind went out toward the faint spot on the star chart, he felt a sudden surge of hope welling up inside him. He began to picture the world that was there waiting to greet them and he grew restless and impatient at the thought of the years that would have to pass by before they could know.

He knew that the optimism of the human scientists knew no bounds. Already the huge disks of the radio-observatory situated on Lunar Farside were beaming a high-power transmission in Ganymean communications code out toward *The Giants' Star* to forewarn of the *Shapieron*'s coming—a message that would take years to cover the distance, but which would still arrive well ahead of the ship.

Then he slumped back in the chair, despairing and dispirited. He knew, as his few trusted companions knew, that there would be nobody there to receive it. Nothing in the Lunarian records had proved anything. It was all Earthmen's wishful thinking.

His thoughts went back to the incredible Earthmen —the race that had struggled and fought for millennia to overcome such horrendous difficulties, and who now, at last, were emerging from their past to a prospect of lasting prosperity and wisdom . . . if they could only be left alone for a little longer to complete the things they had so valiantly strived to achieve. They had built their world out of chaos, against all the theories and predictions of all the sages and scientists of Minerva. They deserved to be left alone to enjoy their world without interference.

For Garuth knew, as now only Shilohin, Jassilane and Monchar knew, that the Ganymeans had created the human race.

The Ganymeans had been the direct cause of all the defects, handicaps and problems that should by rights have left Man with all the odds piled hopelessly against him. But Man had triumphed over all of them. Justice demanded now that Man be left alone to perfect his world in his own way and without further interference from the Ganymeans.

The Ganymeans had already interfered enough.

chapter twenty-three

In Danchekker's office, high in the main building of the Westwood Biological Institute on the outskirts of Houston, the professor and Hunt were watching the view of the *Shapieron* being sent down from a telescopic camera tracking from a satellite high above the Earth. The image grew gradually smaller and then suddenly enlarged again as the magnification was stepped up. Then it began to shrink once more.

"It's just coasting," Hunt commented from an armchair set over to one side of the room. "Seems as if they want to get one last look at us." Danchekker said nothing but just nodded absently as he watched from behind his desk. The commentary coming over on audio confirmed Hunt's observation.

"Radar indicates that the ship is still traveling quite slowly compared to the performance that we have seen before. It doesn't seem to be going into orbit . . . just continuing to move steadily away from Earth. This is the last time you'll have a chance to see this fantastic vessel live, so make the most of the moment. We are looking at the closing page of what has surely been the most astounding chapter ever written in the history of the human race. How can things ever be the same again?" A short pause. "Hello, something's happening I'm told. . . . The ship's starting to accelerate now. It's really streaking away from us now, building up speed fast all the time. . . ." The image on the screen began to perform a crazy dance of growing and shrinking again at a bewildering rate.

"They're on main drive," Hunt said, as the commentator continued.

"The image is starting to break up. . . . The stress-

227

field's becoming noticeable now. . . . It's going . . . getting fainter . . . That's it. Well I guess that just about—" The voice and picture died together as Danchekker flipped a switch behind his desk to cut off the display.

"So, there they go to meet whatever destiny awaits them," he said. "I wish them well." A short silence ensued while Hunt fished in his pockets for his lighter and cigarette case. As he leaned back in his chair again he said, "You know, Chris, when you think about it, these last couple of years have been pretty remarkable."

"To say the least."

"Charlie, the Lunarians, the ship at Pithead, the Ganymeans . . . and now this." He gestured toward the blank screen. "What better time could we have picked to be alive? It makes every other period of history seem a bit dull, doesn't it?"

"It does indeed . . . very dull indeed." Danchekker seemed to be answering automatically, as if part of his mind were still hurtling out into space with the *Shapieron*.

"It's a bit of a pity, though, in some ways," Hunt said after a while.

"What is?"

"The Ganymeans. We never really got to the bottom of some of the interesting questions, did we? It's a pity they couldn't have stayed around just a little longer—until we'd managed to figure out a few more of the answers. Actually I'm a bit surprised they didn't. At one stage they seemed even more curious about some things than we were."

Danchekker seemed to turn the proposition over in his mind for a long time. Then he looked up and across to where Hunt was sitting and eyed him in a strange way. When he spoke his voice was curiously challenging.

"Oh really? Answers to questions such as what, might I ask?"

Hunt frowned at him for a second, then shrugged as he exhaled a stream of smoke.

"You know what questions. What happened on Minerva after the *Shapieron* left? Why did they ship all those terrestrial animals there? What bumped off all the Minervan animals? That kind of thing . . . It would be nice to know, even if it is a bit academic now, if only to tidy all the loose ends up."

"Oh, those." Danchekker's air of studied nonchalance was masterly. "I think I can supply you with whatever answers you require to those questions." The matter-of-factness in Danchekker's voice left Hunt at a loss for words. The professor cocked his head to one side and regarded him quizzically but could not contain a slight admission of the amusement that he felt.

"Well . . . Good God, what are they then?" Hunt managed at last. He realized that in his astonishment he had let his cigarette slip from his fingers and made hasty efforts to retrieve it from the side of his chair.

Danchekker watched the pantomime in silence, then replied. "Let me see now, to answer directly the questions that you have just asked would not really convey very much, since they all interrelate. Most of them follow from the work I have been doing here ever since we got back from Ganymede, which covers quite a lot of ground. Perhaps it would be simpler if I just start at the beginning and follow it through from there." Hunt waited while Danchekker leaned back and interlaced his fingers in front of his chin and contemplated the far wall to collect his thoughts.

At last Danchekker resumed. "Do you recall the piece of research from Utrecht that you brought to my attention soon after we got back—concerning the way in which animals manufacture small amounts of toxins and contaminants to exercise their defensive systems?"

"The self-immunization process. Yes, I remember. ZORAC picked that one up. Animals possess it but human beings don't. What about it?"

"I found the subject rather intriguing and spent some time after our discussion following it up, which included holding some very long and detailed conversations with a Professor Tatham from Cambridge, an old friend of mine who specializes in that kind of thing. In particular, I wanted to know more about the genetic codes that are responsible for this self-immunization mechanism forming in the developing embryo. It seemed to me that if we were going to try to pinpoint the causes for this radical difference between us and the beasts, this was the level at which we should look for it."

"And . . . ?"

"And, the results were extremely interesting . . . in fact, remarkable." Danchekker's voice fell almost to a whisper that seemed to accentuate every syllable. "As ZORAC discovered, in virtually all of today's terrestrial animals, the genetic coding that determines their self-immunization mechanism is closely related to the coding responsible for another process; you might say that both processes are subsets of the same program. The other process regulates carbon-dioxide absorption and rejection."

"I see . . ." Hunt nodded slowly. He didn't yet see exactly where Danchekker was leading, but he was beginning to sense something important.

"You're always telling me you don't like coincidences," Danchekker went on. "I don't either. There was far too much of a coincidence about this, so Tatham and I started delving a bit deeper. When we investigated the experiments performed at Pithead and on board *Jupiter Five*, we came across a second rather remarkable thing, that tied in with what I have just been talking about—concerning the Oligocene animals found in the ship there. The Oligocene animals all contain the same genetic coding elements, but in their case there is a difference. The subprograms that control the two processes I mentioned have somehow been separated out; they exist as discrete groupings that lie side by side on the same DNA chain. Now that is very remarkable, wouldn't you say?"

Hunt considered the question for a few seconds.

"You mean that in today's animals both processes are there, but all scrambled up together, but in the Oligocene species they're separated out."

"Yes."

"*All* the Oligocene species?" Hunt asked after a moment's further reflection. Danchekker nodded in satisfaction at seeing that Hunt was on the right track.

"Precisely, Vic. *All* of them."

"That doesn't really make sense. I mean, the first thing you'd think would be that some kind of mutation had occurred to change one form into the other —the scrambled-up form and the separated-out form. That could have happened either way around. In one case the scrambled form could be the 'natural' terrestrial pattern that became mutated on Minerva; that would explain why the animals from there have it and the descendants of the ones that were left here don't. Alternatively, you could suppose that twenty-five million years ago the scparated-out form was standard, which explains of course why the animals from that time exhibit it, but that in subsequent evolution here on Earth it changed itself into the scrambled form." He looked across at Danchekker and threw his arms out wide. "But there's one basic flaw in both those arguments—it happened in lots of different species, all at the same time."

"Quite," Danchekker nodded. "And, by all the principles of selection and evolution that we accept, that would appear to rule out the possibility of any kind of mutation—*natural* mutation, anyway. It would be inconceivable for the same chance event to occur spontaneously and simultaneously in many distinct and unrelated lines . . . utterly inconceivable."

"*Natural* mutation?" Hunt looked puzzled. "What are you saying then?"

"It's perfectly simple. We've just agreed that the difference couldn't be due to ordinary natural mutation, but nevertheless it's there. The only other explanation possible then is that it was *not* natural."

Impossible thoughts flashed through Hunt's mind. Danchekker read the expression on his face and voiced them for him.

"In other words they didn't just happen; they were made to happen. The genetic codings were *deliberately* rearranged. We are talking about an *artificial* mutation."

For a moment Hunt was stunned. The word deliberate denoted conscious volition, which in turn implied an intelligence.

Danchekker nodded again to confirm his thoughts. "If I may rephrase your question of a minute ago, what we are really asking is, did the animals that were shipped to Minerva change, or did the animals that were left on Earth change after the others were shipped? Now add to the equation the further fact that we have established—that *somebody* deliberately caused the change to happen—and we are left with only one choice."

Hunt completed the argument for him. "There hasn't been anybody around on Earth during the last twenty-five million years that could have done it, so it must have been done on Minerva. That can only mean . . ." His voice trailed off as the full implication became clear.

"The Ganymeans!" Danchekker said. He allowed some time for this to sink in and then continued. "The Ganymeans altered the genetic coding of the terrestrial animals that they took back to their own planet. I am fairly certain that the samples that were recovered from the ship at Pithead were descendants of a strain that had been mutated in this way and had faithfully carried on the mutation in themselves. This is the only logical conclusion that can be drawn from the evidence we have reviewed. Also, it is strongly supported by another interesting piece of evidence."

By now Hunt was ready for anything.

"Oh?" he replied. "What?"

"That strange enzyme that turned up in all of the Oligocene species," Danchekker said. "We know now what it did." The look on Hunt's face asked all the questions for him. Danchekker continued: "That enzyme was constructed for one specific task. It cleaved the DNA chain at precisely the point where those two coding groups were joined—in species where they were separated out, of course. In other words, it isolated the genetic code that defined the CO_2-tolerance characteristics."

"Okay," Hunt said slowly, but still not following the argument fully. "I'll take your word for that. . . .

But how does that support what you just said about the Ganymeans? I'm not quite—"

"That enzyme was not a result of any *natural* process! It was something that had been manufactured and introduced artificially. That was where the radioactive decay products came from; the enzyme was manufactured artificially and included radioactive tracer elements to allow its progress through the body to be tracked and measured. We use the same technique widely in medical and physiological research ourselves."

Hunt held up a hand to stop Danchekker going any further for the time being. He sat forward in his chair and closed his eyes for a second as he mentally stepped through the reasoning that the professor had summarized.

"Yes . . . okay . . . You've pointed out all along that chemical processes can't distinguish a radioisotope from a normal one. So, how could the enzyme have selected radioisotopes to build into itself? Answer: It couldn't; somebody must have selected them and therefore the enzyme must have been manufactured artificially. Why use radioisotopes? Answer: Tracers." Hunt again looked across at the professor, who was following and nodding encouragement. "But the enzyme does a specialized job on the modified DNA chain, and you've already established that the DNA was modified artificially in the animals that were shipped to Minerva. . . . Ah, I see . . . I can see how the two tie in together. What you're saying is that the Ganymeans altered the DNA coding of the terrestrial animals, and then manufactured a specific enzyme to operate on the altered DNA."

"Exactly."

"And what was the purpose of it all?" Hunt was becoming visibly excited. "Any ideas on that?"

"Yes," Danchekker replied. "I think we have. In fact the things that we have just considered tell us all that we need to know to guess at what they were up to." He sat back and interlaced his fingers again. "With the enzyme performing in the way that I have just described, the object of the exercise becomes clear. At least I think it does. . . . If the animals that possessed the already altered DNA were implanted with the enzymes, the chromosomes in their reproductive cells would have been modified. This would have made it possible for a strain of offspring to be bred from them who possessed the CO_2 coding in the form of an isolated, compact unit that could be manipulated and 'got at' with comparative ease. If you like, it enabled this particular characteristic to be separated out, perhaps with a view to its becoming the focal point of further experiments with later generations. . . ." Danchekker's voice took on a curious note as he uttered the last few words, as if he were hinting that the main implication of his dissertation was about to emerge.

"I can see what you're saying," Hunt told him. "But not quite why. What *were* they up to then?"

"*That* was how they sought to solve their environmental problem after all else had failed," Danchekker said. "It must have been something that was thought of during the later period of Ganymean history on Minerva—sometime after the *Shapieron* went to Iscaris, otherwise Shilohin and the others would have known about it."

"What was how they sought to solve it? Sorry, Chris, I'm afraid I'm not with you all the way yet."

"Let us recapitulate for a moment on their situation," Danchekker suggested. "They knew that the CO_2 level on Minerva had begun to rise, and that one day it would reach a point that they would be unable to withstand; the other Minervan native species would be unaffected, but the Ganymeans would be vulnerable as a consequence of their breeding their original tolerance out of themselves as part of the trade-off for better accident-resistance. They lost it when they took the decision to dispense permanently with their secondary circulation systems. They declined climatic engineering as a solution and tried migration to Earth and the Iscaris experiment but both failed. Later on, it appears, they must have tried something else."

Hunt was all ears. He made a gesture of total capitulation and said simply, "Go on."

"One thing that they did discover on Earth, however, was a family of life that had evolved from origins in a warmer environment than that of Minerva, and which had not had to contend with the load-sharing problem that had caused the double-circulatory-system architecture to become standard on their own planet. Of particular interest, terrestrial life had evolved a completely different mechanism for dealing with carbon dioxide—one that did not depend on any secondary circulation system."

Hunt looked incredulous. He stared at Danchekker for a second while the professor waited for the response.

"You're not trying to say . . . they didn't try and pinch it?"

Danchekker nodded. "If my suspicions are anything to go by, that is exactly what they tried to do. The animals from Earth were transported back to Minerva for the purpose of large-scale genetic experiments. The object of those experiments, I believe, was threefold: first, to modify the DNA coding in such a way that the CO_2-tolerance portion became separated out from the scrambled form—as you put it—that had evolved naturally on Earth; second, to perfect a means —the enzyme—of isolating that block of code and passing it on in an intact and workable unit to later strains; third, but this is a guess, to implant those codes into *Minervan* animals in an attempt to find out if a Minervan life form could be modified into developing a mechanism for dealing with carbon dioxide that did not depend on its secondary system. We have evidence that they achieved the first two of these objectives; the third must necessarily remain speculative, at least for the time being."

"And if they did succeed in the third, then the next stop would be . . ." Hunt's voice trailed off again. The sheer ingenuity of the Ganymean scheme made it difficult for him to accept it unquestioningly.

"If it worked, and if there were no undesirable side effects, the intention was no doubt to engineer the same codes into themselves," Danchekker confirmed. "Thus they would enjoy an in-built tolerance that would happily continue to perpetuate itself through succeeding generations, while at the same time preserving all the advantages that they had already gained by doing away with their secondary systems. A fascinating example of what intelligence can do to improve on Nature when natural evolution throws up a solution that leaves much to be desired, don't you think?"

Hunt rose from his chair and began pacing slowly from one side of the office to the other as he marveled at the sheer audacity of even conceiving such a scheme. The Ganymeans had expressed wonder at Man's readiness to meet Nature head-on in every challenge, but here was something, surely, that Man would have balked at. The basic instincts of the Ganymeans steered them away from physical danger, conflict and the like, but their thirst for intellectual adventure and combat, it appeared, was unquenchable; that was the spur that had driven them to the stars. Danchekker watched in silence, waiting for the question that he knew would come next. At length Hunt stopped and wheeled to face the desk.

"Yes, it was neat, all right," he agreed. "But it didn't work, did it, Chris?"

"Regrettably, no," Danchekker conceded. "But not for reasons for which, I feel, they were really to blame. We might have some catching up to do with them technically, but nevertheless I believe that we are in a position to see where they went wrong." He didn't wait for the obvious question at that point but went on. "We have the advantage of knowing far more than they possibly could have about life on our own planet. We have access to the work of thousands of scientists who have studied the subject for centuries, but the Ganymeans who came here twenty-five million years ago did not. In particular, they could not have known what Professor Tatham and his team at Cambridge have only just discovered."

"The scrambling together of the self-immunization and the CO_2-tolerance codings?"

"Yes, exactly that. The thing that the Ganymean genetic engineers would never have realized was that in isolating the latter, in order to make their proposed later experiments simpler, they were losing the former. Because of the method they adopted, the descendant strains that they bred would have been ideal subjects for further CO_2-tolerance research, but they would also have lost their self-immunization capabilities. In other words the Ganymeans created and raised a whole range of mixed terrestrial animal species that possessed no trace of the age-old mechanism for stimulating their own defensive processes by flooding the body with mild doses of pollutants—a mechanism which we still see today in the descendants of the animals that remained on Earth to continue evolving naturally, of course."

Hunt had stopped pacing and was now looking down at Danchekker with a slow frown spreading across his face, as if another thought had just struck him.

"But there's something else, isn't there?" he said. "The self-immunization process has something to do with higher brain functions. . . . Are you saying what I think you're saying?"

"I suspect so. As you know, the toxins introduced into the body by the self-immunization process in today's animals has the effect of inhibiting the development of the higher brain centers. And another thing— Tatham's latest work indicates that, because of the way terrestrial life happens to have evolved, the capacity for violence and aggression is closely related to the development of those centers too. Thus, the Ganymeans would have found themselves unable to produce variants of the type they wanted without also removing the inhibition on the development of higher brain functions, and in addition producing an enhanced tendency toward aggression. That being the case and the Ganymeans being the way they were, I can't really see them taking the experiment any further. They would never have risked introducing anything like that into themselves, whatever the urgency of the situation. Never."

"So they gave the whole thing up as a bad job in

the end and went off to pastures new," Hunt completed.

"Maybe, and again maybe not. We have no way of telling for sure. I certainly hope so for the sake of Garuth and his friends." Danchekker leaned forward on the desk and at once his mood became more serious. "But whatever the answer to that is, at least we have a definite answer to another of the questions that you asked at the beginning."

"Which one?"

"Well, consider the situation that must have existed on Minerva when the Ganymeans came to the point of accepting that their ambitious genetic engineering solution was running into trouble. They could go away to another star or stay on their own world and perish. Either way, the days of the Ganymean presence on Minerva were numbered. Now take them out of the equation, and what is left? Answer—two populations of animals both of which are well adapted to handling the environmental conditions. First there are the native Minervan types, and second the artificially mutated descendants of the imported terrestrial types, free to roam the planet after the departure of the Ganymeans. Now return to the equation one further factor that I have established through long interrogation of ZORAC's archives—the native Minervan species would *not* have been poisonous to terrestrial carnivores—and what do you conclude?"

Hunt gazed back with eyes that were suddenly aghast.

"Christ!" he breathed. "It would have been a bloody slaughter."

"Yes, indeed. Consider a planet inhabited only by those ridiculous Techicolored cartoon animals that we found drawn on the walls of that ship at Pithead—animals that had never evolved any specializations for defense, concealment or escape, and which had no need for fight-or-flight instincts at all. Now throw in among them a typical mix of predators from Earth—every one a selected product of millions of years of improvement of the arts of ferocity, stealth and cunning . . . added to which they were evolving higher levels of intelligence that had previously been inhibited and their already fearsome aggressiveness was being further reinforced. Now what picture do you see?"

Hunt just continued to stare in horrified silence as the picture unfolded before his mind's eye.

"*That's* what wiped them all out," he said at last. "That poor bloody Minervan zoo wouldn't have had a chance. No wonder it didn't last for more than a few generations after the Ganymeans disappeared from the scene."

"With another consequence as well," Danchekker came in. "The terrestrial carnivores concentrated on the most readily available prey—the native species—and so gave the terrestrial herbivores a breathing space to increase their numbers and become firmly established. By the time the Minervan natives had been wiped out the carnivores would have been forced to revert to their old habits, but by that time the situation would have stabilized. A mixed and balanced terrestrial animal ecology had been given time to establish itself across Minerva. . . ." The professor's voice took on a soft and curious tone. "And that is the way things must have remained . . . right on through until the time of the Lunarians."

"Charlie . . ." Hunt sensed that Danchekker was at last hinting at something he had been building up to all along. "Charlie," Hunt repeated. "You found that same enzyme in him too, didn't you?"

"We did, but in a somewhat degenerate form . . . as if it were in the last phases of fading away completely. It did fade away of course, since Man no longer possesses it. . . . But the interesting point, as you say, is that Charlie had it and so, presumably, did the rest of the Lunarians."

"And there was only one place for it to come from . . ."

"Precisely."

Hunt raised a hand to his brow as the full import of these revelations hit him. He turned slowly to meet Danchekker's solemn gaze and then slowly, his features knotted into a mask of disbelief that strove to reject the things that reason now stripped bare, sank weakly down onto an arm of the nearest chair. Danchekker said nothing, waiting for Hunt to put the pieces together for himself.

"The population on Minerva included samples of the latest Oligocene primates," Hunt said after a while. "They were almost certainly as advanced as anything that Earth had produced at the time, and with the greatest potential for advancing further. The Ganymeans had unwittingly removed the inhibition on further brain development. . . ." He looked up and met Danchekker's imperturbable stare again. "They'd have raced ahead from there. There was nothing to stop them. And with their aggressive streak unleashed as well . . . a whole race of runaway mutants . . . psychological Frankenstein monsters . . "

"Which is, of course, where the Lunarians came from," Danchekker said. His voice was grave. "By rights they shouldn't have survived. All the theories and models of the Ganymean scientists said that they would inevitably destroy themselves. They almost did. They turned a whole planet into one vast fortress and by the time they had developed technology their lives revolved around unceasing warfare and the ruthless, uncompromising determination to exterminate all other rival states. They were capable of conceiving no other formula to solve their problems. In the end they did indeed destroy themselves and Minerva along with them . . . at least, they destroyed their civilization, if that is the correct term for it. They should have destroyed themselves totally, but, by a million-to-one chance, it did not quite happen. . . ." Danchekker looked up and left Hunt to fill in the rest.

But Hunt just sat and stared, overwhelmed. After the nuclear holocaust between the opposing forces of the two remaining Lunarian superstates had altered permanently the face of Minerva's moon and Minerva had disintegrated, the moon fell inward toward the sun to be captured by Earth. The tiny band of survivors carried with it had possessed the resources to set off one last, desperate journey—to the surface of the new world that now hung in the sky above their heads.

For forty thousand years the descendants of those survivors had merged into the survival struggle of Earth, but eventually they had spread all over the planet and emerged as an adversary as formidable as their ancestors had been on Minerva.

At last, Danchekker resumed quietly. "We have speculated for some time now that the Lunarians, and hence Man, originated from an unprecedented mutation that must have occurred somewhere along the primate line that was isolated on Minerva. Also, we have noted that somewhere along his line of ancestry, Man has somehow abandoned the self-immunization process that other animals have in common. Now we see not only proof that these things were true, but also how they came about. In fact many species went along that same path, but all bar one were destroyed when Minerva was destroyed. Only one—Man in the form of the Lunarians—came back again." Danchekker paused and took a long breath. "An unprecedented mutation did indeed occur on Minerva, but it was not a natural mutation. Modern Man exhibits fewer of the extremes that drove the Lunarians to their doom, thankfully, but all the same the legacy of our ancestry is written through the pages of our history. *Homo sapiens is the end-product of an unsuccessful series of Ganymean genetic experiments!*

"The Ganymeans believe that Man is slowly but surely recovering from the instability and compulsive violence that destroyed the Lunarians. Let us hope they are right."

Neither man said anything more for a long time. It was ironic, Hunt thought, that after all the Ganymeans had said, their own kind should turn out to be the prime cause of all the things that had come to pass over the last twenty-five million years. And throughout all that time, while primates evolved into sapient beings on Minerva, and the Lunarian civilization came and went, and fifty thousand years of human history were being acted out on Earth, the *Shapieron* had been out there in the void, preserved by the mysterious workings of the laws that distort time and space.

"An unsuccessful series of Ganymean genetic experiments," Hunt echoed Danchekker. "They started the whole thing. They came back to find us flying spaceships and building fusion plants, and they thought our rate of progress was miraculous. And all the time they'd started the whole thing off in their own labs, twenty-five million years ago . . . and given it up as a bad job! It's funny when you think about it, Chris. It's damned funny. And now they've gone for good. I wonder what they would have said if they'd only known what we know now."

Danchekker did not reply at once, but stared thoughtfully at the top of his desk for a while, as if weighing whether or not to say what was going through his head. In the end he stretched an arm forward and began toying idly with a pen. When he spoke he did not engage Hunt's eyes directly but continued to watch the pen tumbling over and over between his fingers.

"You know, Vic, in the last months before they went, the Ganymeans became very interested in all aspects of terrestrial biochemistry, including all our available data on Charlie, Man and the Oligocene animals from Pithead. For a long time they were bubbling over with curiosity and ZORAC couldn't find enough questions to ask about such matters. And then, about a month ago, they suddenly became very quiet about it all. They haven't even mentioned it since."

The professor looked up and confronted Hunt with a direct and candid stare.

"I think I know why," he said, very softly. "You see, Vic . . . they knew all right. They knew. They knew that they had brought a pathetically deformed creature into a hostile universe and left it to fend for itself against odds that were hopeless, and they returned and saw what that creature had become—a proud and triumphant conqueror that laughs its defiance at anything the universe cares to throw at it. That is why they are gone. They believe that they owe it to Man to leave him free to perfect the world that he has built for himself in whatever way he chooses. They know what we were and they see what we have made of ourselves since. They feel that we have suffered enough interference in the past and have shown ourselves to be the better managers of our own destiny."

Danchekker tossed the pen aside, gazed up and concluded:

"And somehow, Vic, I don't think that we will let them down. The worst is over now."

epilogue

The signal transmitted by the huge radio dish at the observatory on Lunar Farside streaked outward from the fringe of the Solar System and into the vast gulfs of empty space beyond. Its whisper brushed the sensors of a sentinel that had been maintaining an unbroken vigil for a long, long time. The circuits inside the robot understood and responded to the Ganymean code that had been used to assemble the signal.

Other equipment inside the robot transformed the signal into vibrations of forces and fields that obeyed laws of physics unknown to Man, and dispatched it into a realm of existence of which the universe of space and time were mere shadowy projections. In another part of the shadow universe, on a warm, bright planet that orbited a cheerful star, other machines received and interpreted the message.

The builders of the machines were informed and were at once filled with wonder at the things that were reported to them.

The sentinel extracted their reply from the superstructure of space, transformed it back into electromagnetic waves, and beamed it back toward the satellite of the third planet from the Sun.

The astronomers at the Lunar Farside observatory were completely at a loss to explain the information coming from the instruments connected to their receivers; there was nothing within light-years of them from which a reply could have been evoked, but a reply was coming in hours after they had commenced transmitting. The officials at UNSA were equally bemused and time went by while scientists used the information that had been transferred from ZORAC's data banks to translate the message from Ganymean communications code into the Ganymean language. But still it meant nothing to anybody.

Then somebody thought of involving Dr. Victor Hunt of Navcomms Division. Hunt immediately remembered Don Maddson's study of the Ganymean language and sent the text down to Linguistics to see what they could make of it. Forty-eight hours passed by while Maddson and his assistant worked. The task was not one that they had practiced and, without ZORAC on tap to guide them, not one that could be accomplished readily. But the message was concise and eventually a red-eyed but triumphant Maddson presented Hunt with a single sheet of paper on which was typed:

> *The story of those who went to Iscaris long ago has been told through the generations since our ancestors came from Minerva. However you got there and however you found us, come home. There is a new Minerva now. We, your sons and daughters, are waiting to welcome you.*

There were also some numbers and mathematical symbols that others in Navcomms had decoded, and which identified *The Giants' Star* as the source of the message by confirming its spectral type and its geometric position with respect to readily locatable pulsars in the neighboring regions of the Galaxy.

What physical processes might have been instrumental was something that Hunt could not even begin to guess at, but there was no time for academic speculation on such matters. The Ganymeans had to be told about what had happened and the *Shapieron* could not be contacted by ordinary means while it was in flight and under main drive. The only chance was to catch it at Ganymede.

The message from *The Giants' Star* was hastily transmitted to UNSA Operational Command Headquarters at Galveston, beamed up to an orbiting communications station and relayed out over the laser link to *Jupiter Five*. Hours passed while Hunt, Danchekker,

Maddson, Caldwell and everyone else at Houston waited anxiously for something to come in through the open channel to Galveston. At last the screen came to life. The message on it read:

> Shapieron *left here seventeen minutes before your transmission came in. Last seen accelerating flat-out for deep-space. All contact now broken. Sorry.*

There was nothing more that anybody could do.

"At least," Hunt said as he turned wearily from the screen toward the circle of dejected faces in Caldwell's office, "it's nice to know that it will all have been worth it when they get there. At least they won't have any nasty surprises waiting at the end of this voyage." He turned back and gazed wistfully at the screen once more, then added: "I suppose it would have been even nicer if they knew it too."

about the author

JAMES HOGAN was born in London in 1941 and educated at the Cardinal Vaughan Grammar School, Kensington. He studied general engineering at the Royal Aircraft Establishment, Farnborough, subsequently specializing in electronics and digital systems.

After spending a few years as a systems design engineer, he transferred into selling and later joined the computer industry as a salesman, working with ITT, Honeywell, and Digital Equipment Corporation. He also worked as a Life Insurance salesman for two years ". . . to have a 'break' from the world of machines and to learn something more about people."

Currently he is employed by DEC as a Senior Sales Training Consultant, concentrating on the applications of minicomputers in science and research. In mid-1977 he moved from England to the United States and now lives in Massachusetts.